TEKTIME

Guido Pagliarino

The Rage of the Reviled

A Story inspired by History

Translation by Barbara Maher

Guido Pagliarino
The Rage of the Reviled
A Story inspired by History
Tektime Distribution
Copyright © 2021 Guido Pagliarino - All rights belong to the author
Translation from Italian to English by Barbara Maher

Index

He had been detained by the officers of a Public Security patrol wagon in the late evening of September 26, 1943, suspected of killing a certain Rosa Demaggi, an attractive peroxide blonde in her thirties, a wealthy prostitute and a retail blackmarketer: the man, strong Neapolitan accent, square face, robust build but not fat, looked to be about forty. He was five feet eight tall, an above average stature in those times of widespread malnutrition, going bald at the forehead and temples and the top of his head, and across the nape of his neck had a semicircle of brown hair kept very short and shaved high. He was wearing overalls and a flannel shirt, both deep blue in color, and light greenish-gray wool gloves.

It was well-known at the *Vice Squad* in Naples that Rosa Demaggi turned tricks for wealthy men in her home, in Piazzetta del Nilo. Until July 25, she had also conceded her favors to fascist leaders and, after the armistice, when the city fell under the German heel, she had granted herself to officers of the Wehrmacht and the Gestapo. From previous investigations carried out jointly, it was common knowledge in the *Vice Squad* and *Commercial Offenses* departments, the latter created after the start of the conflict to combat the black market, that since the summer of 1940 Demaggi had asked to be compensated, preferably, with groceries, cigarettes and liquor, so she could do low-level trafficking on the black market; and it was known that, very quickly, she had expanded the business with purchases from wholesalers linked to the camorra.

As a result, the patrol teams had been ordered to also keep an eye on her dwelling along with others; but discreetly, because of Demaggi's sexual contacts with occupying officers and considering that, after July 25, when the OVRA had been dissolved[1] and the secret archive had been opened, it had been discovered that the woman had been a bribed confidant and had reported political information which escaped customers berween the sheets, the heriarchy included. It was therefore assumed that, after the

---

[1] Fascist political office at Public Security, but that was in fact completely independent. The meaning of the abbreviation OVRA had not been clarified by the regime, perhaps deliberately.

armistice and the German occupation, she had started selling information to the Gestapo officers she went to bed with.

Shortly before the suspect was detained, about 8.30 pm with only half an hour to curfew, as the police wagon was passing through Piazzetta del Nilo, the corporal in command had seen that individual in shabby clothes enter the house where the woman lived, in the only apartment on the ground floor. He didn't ring and went in through the door which had been left ajar. Since he had his back to the vehicle, the man had not noticed the arrival of the patrol.

After entering, he had not closed the door completely behind himself, but had left it pulled to. The officer had assumed that he, like Demaggi, was involved in the clandestine market and had left it open for other colluders who were on the way. The door left unlocked made it unlikely that he was a sex customer, not counting his roustabout's clothing and the prostitute's notoriously high rates. The corporal had ordered the driver to pull over outside the house. The officers had got out, except for the driver, and had let themselves into the apartment.

The suspect had been surprised in the entrance, just beyond the door, standing next to Rosa Demaggi. She was moaning weakly semi-unconscious, and was lying on the ground with a bloody hematoma on the nape of the neck, obviously the consequence of having fallen against a console, to the left entering, which had a blood stain on it. Rosa Demaggi had died a few seconds after the officers had entered. Considering him guilty of assaulting the woman, the man in overalls had been handcuffed. The patrol chief had said to him: "You came in here with the intention of killing her and it took you just a few seconds to hit her on the head: she was in the entrance waiting for you, she trusted you because she had left the doot open. But you, unexpectedly, without giving her time to escape, slammed her head hard against the furniture to kill her. You were counting on getting away immediately afterwards, in fact you hadn't closed the door when you came in, so as not to waste time reopening it as you went out: you would have pulled it behind you as soon as you were outside and toodle-loo, who knows who and when the body would be found. You hadn't imagined that we would arrive: you wanted to make it look like an accident, but it went wrong."

The officer had assumed that the individual had killed with premeditation for reasons related to the black market, perhaps becauase of his own direct interest, perhaps on behalf of third parties. That it was voluntary murder was supported by the fact that the man was wearing wool gloves even though it was already warm: *so as not to leave prints*, it had been spontaneous to think. At the time the suspect, in full mental reshuffle because of the unexpected intervention of the police officer, had not known what to say.

Since up close you could see that not only was he wearing workman's clothes, but that they were worn and rather dirty, the corporal was convinced that he could not be one of the woman's sex clients, and besides, the man had no money on him as he had ascertained by frisking him. He did not even have an identity card, but he did have a driving license which showed he was born in Naples forty-two years earlier, lived in Vicolo Santa Luciella and was called Gennaro Esposito, name and surname, however, that were very common in Campania and especially in Naples, which could have been false, as too could the driving licence. It was in fact well-known in Police Headquarters that the delinquency, and in particular the camorra, availed themselves of printers who were very skilled in forgeries. The patrol leader had not given much weight to the document.

He had called the operations room of the Station with the truck's radio and reported the incident. The *Violent Crimes Section* had telephoned the switchboard of the morgue to alert them, asking them to send the anatomopathologist on duty to the victim's home, for the initial investigations. Dr. Giovampaolo Palombella was on duty, a sixty-year-old with long thick gray hair which was always disheveled, tall, wiry and a little stooped, perhaps due to bending over the corpses to be dissected for more than thirty years.

At the same time a warrant officer had been sent to the victim's home. It was Bruno Branduardi, a short, obese and quiet man close to retirement and he was to carry out an inspection, listen to the patrol officers and the doctor, write everything down in his notebook and report to the superior on duty upon his return,

The non-commissioned officer had arrived in Piazzetta del Nilo on his slow motorbike, *The Little Italian*[2] which, small as it

---

[2] 100 cc engine, with two-speed Train engine, manufactured under French license and sold from 1933 to 1939 by the Giuseppe Navone workshop in Turin.

was, looked as if it could barely support the heavy weight of that enormous man. First of all he had first listened to what the officers had to say, then the coroner who had arrived a little after him, in a van for the transport of the corpses, with two orderlies. The anatomopathologist had ruled out suicide, he had considered an accident possible, since at first glance the blow did not seem to him to have been very violent. He had not ruled out murder, however, reserving the right to be more precise after the autopsy. The warrant officer had taken note of it, adding a comment in his notebook that in his opinion it was not misfortune but murder and that the arrested man, in his view, was the murderer.

In reality, he had simply aligned himself with what the corporal had assumed and reported to him. The corpse had been removed and loaded onto the van to be taken to the morgue for the autopsy. Branduardi, on his part, after having quickly inspected the apartment and found that there was no one there, had ordered the officers to affix the seals on the front door, to take the arrested man to the Police Headquarters and put him in the holding cell, while waiting to be handed over to a commissioner for interrogation. At that time the law did not call for the intervention of a magistrate neither at the scene of the crime, nor during the police officer's investigative interview with the suspect, which took place without the presence of his lawyer. The investigating judge took over if the investigating commissioner, using the autopsy report and having questioned the suspect, had considered it to be murder and had sent a report to the Public Prosecutor's Office. In the event of misfortune, the dossier, endorsed by the Deputy Commissioner, was simply archived without judicial follow-up.

Branduardi had followed the truck, but lost ground because the motorbike's engine was now old and worn out. When he arrived, with the detained man already in the holding cell, the warrant officer had gone up to his office in the *Violent Crimes Section* on the second floor which he shared with a sergeant and a typist. He had calmly prepared himself a *war coffee*, a surrogate, with his own Neapolitan coffee maker that he kept in the closet along with an electric incandescent stove. He had sipped it boiling hot after sweetening it with saccharin, not because he was diabetic but because since the start of the war, sugar was unobtainable for *ordinary mortals*. He had then smoked a Serenissima Zara cigarette with equally heavenly calm, savoring it almost to the end of the butt that, for the last two puffs, he had held by skewering it with a pin. In those times of famine and filterless cigarettes, a lot of smokers used to do that. And finally, at a leisurely pace, he had taken the sheet of paper with the report no more than fifty feet away on the same floor, to one of the deputy commanders of the *Violent Crimes Section*, a certain chief commissioner Riccardo Calvo who was on duty that night until twenty-four hundred hours. At zero hours and a few seconds Branduardi had gone home to sleep and, shortly after, Calvo did the same after leaving the warrant officer's report on the desk of his incoming peer, Dr. Giuliano Boni.

The man in overalls had remain locked in the holding cell.

Finally, following the orders of chief commissioner Boni, the Rosa Demaggi case had been foisted onto an almost beardless Deputy Commissioner who had come on duty at midnight, Dr. Vittorio D'Aiazzo. He had been in Public Safety for just under a year and had been assigned to the difficut *Violent Crimes Section* from the very first day.

It was about 3 o'clock in the morning of September 27, 1943 and the insurrection that history remembers as The Four Days of Naples was about to begin: the cauldron of the oppressed city was bubbling and the temperature had now risen to such a degree that it would be impossible for the occupying German to prevent its fiery eruption.

Chapter 2

What the Partenope people were feeling had been unclear to the contemptuous Nazi invader and the fear that they had intentionally spread in the city had resulted in hearts at boiling point and in the mood for rebellion. *Facimmo 'a uèrra a chilli strunzi zellosi*[3] was now the feeling of many Neapolitans, under the impression that, *San Genna' ajutànno*[4]*!* they would free themselves and, at last, peace would become real, very real and no longer the stillborn illusion of a couple of months before:

On July 25, Italy had rejoiced at the fall of the regime during the night, seemingly definitive with Mussolini defenestrated by the Grand Council of Fascism and the king having him arrested, and with the new Badoglio government which was no longer fascist, even though not democratically elected; but above all it had been the mistaken idea that the conflict had ended that made the nation rejoice. In any case, there were soon laments throughout the entire nation which, in Naples, had presented picturesque overtones in the alleyways and the *bassi*[5], such as: *Chillo capucchióne d'o nuvièllo Càpo 'e Guviérno, 'o maresciallo d'Italia Badoglio Pietro, 'o gran generalone! ha fatto di' a 'a ràdio, tòmo, tòmo:* "The war continues": *strunz' e mmèrda!*[6] Then there had been those who had pointed out: *Nossignori, strunzi noi ati a penzà che 'nu maresciallone vulisse 'a pace! Ma va ' ffa 'n 'c...*[7]

With the armistice of Cassibile signed between Italy and the Anglo-Americans on September 3 and which should have remained secret until the Italian armed forces had been reorganized to hold back the vindictive former ally, but had been made known on September 8 by vainglorious victorious generals,

---

[3] Let's wage war on those mangy assholes.

[4] Helping. (t/n – San Gennaro is patron saint of Naples, thus "with the help of San Gennaro")

[5] (t/n – slums)

[6] That big boss, the new Head of Government, Marshal of Italy Pietro Badoglio, the grand general! said on the radio, cool as a cucumber "The war continues": asshole of shit!

[7] No sirs, we're the assholes to think that a grand marshal – *Marshal of Italy* – wanted peace! Well, go fuck yourself...!

a worse evil than before had landed on Italy, through the Brenner Pass[8] Many new, combative and vindictive Germanic divisions had joined the German units already present in Italy. "Why on earth," wondered the most prepared Italians, "hadn't our rulers and military leaders been able to prepare an emergency plan in time? When surrender to the enemy had been likely for a long time? With the forces of the relentless former ally already here?"

After September 8, the only thing the king and his ministers had done was flee to the south, to Brindisi, taking advantage of the fact that the 1st English Airborne Division was about to take that city which, unlike the others, was almost free of German troops, and counting on the fact that the Anglo-Americans, having conquered Sicily, were invading the rest of the southern regions of the Peninsula[9] Breathless, the Sovereign, his Secretaries of State and General Mario Roatta, failed defender of Rome which had been abandoned to the disorderly and useless initiative of the department commanders, had left the capital to set up throne, government and high commands in Brindisi, under the protection of the former enemies, leaving the Italian troops on various foreign fronts and in Italy without orders, at the mercy of the mighty German army.

On September 8, Italy announced the armistice officially, made personally by Badoglio on the radio at 1900 hours and 37 minutes. Thanks to the reinforcements which had arrived rapidly, Germany had remained undisputed master from the Alps to the city of Naples, while the province of Salerno had become a combat zone for the Anglo-American landing on September 9.

The anger of the Neapolitans, already hot because of the war they had already been through, had become scorcing. They had had to endure too much in the three years and more after the regime's traitorous and improvident entry into the conflict on June 10, 1940, behind Nazi Germany. Naples had been systematically bombed by the British and then also by the Americans, with as many as one hundred and five raids until the armistice, all of which had hit the mark turning buildings to rubble and leaving

---

[8] (t/n - Passo del Brennero is a mountain pass through the Alps which forms the border between Italy and Austria. Source: Wikipedia).

[9] The operation called Husky had led to the conquest of Sicily, the Baytown to the landing in Calabria and the Slapsticka operation to the one in Puglia; the last two actions had been aimed at preparing the Anglo-American landing – Operation Avalanche – in salernitano, judged decisive.

large numbers of people dead, injured and mutilated, and hordes of homeless families. Not a single district had been spared, also because the political and military leaders had been unable to prepare adequate anti-air defenses, which had been entrusted almost entirely, in an improvised way, to the warships at anchor in the port.

And then, the hunger! That grim and voiceless hunger that takes your legs from under you; and since the illusion of peace of July 25 has faded, more bombs hail down on the city, bringing absolute famine and diseases with more deaths from the lack of medicines. From September 9, Naples had suffered material damage from the Germans, including serious damage to the port, and had been subjected to roundups and executions not only of Italian soldiers on the loose but also civilians.

Even the fascists, albeit in a subordinate position, had taken possession of the city a couple of weeks after September 8, risen again from the political tombs to become the newly born *Stato Nazionale Repubblicano*[10] – soon to become the Italian Social Republic – formed on the 23rd of that month by Hitler himself, headed by an unwilling but resigned Mussolini who on the 12th had been freed by German paratroopers from house arrest in his refuge-hotel of Campo Imperatore on the Gran Sasso, where the King had relegated him.

The traditional Teutonic harshness of wartime had become, if possible, even more barbaric, incited by isolated attacks from citizens with the support of sailors from the moored ships of the Regia Marina[11]. It was a very early, sporadic and spontaneous resistance, not yet connected to the adversaries of Nazi fascism. The rebellion had started in Via Santa Brigida where, on the morning of the 9th, about thirty residents had attacked a Wehrmacht squad after one of those soldiers had shot at an unarmed twelve-year-old shop boy with his ordinance rifle, a Mauser Kar 98k, as if he was at the shooting range in an amusement park, while the boy was at the door of the shop getting some sun.

The person who had kick-started that group of humiliated Neapolitans was the young Deputy Commissioner that we have already met in passing, Dr. Vittorio D'Aiazzo, who was passing

---

[10] (t/n National Republican State)

[11] (t/n – Royal Navy)

nearby on foot when the German soldier had aimed and fired at the boy. Very indignant, the young Public Security officer had shot from around a corner without taking aim into the Teutonic bunch with his ordinance Beretta M34, emptying the magazine and killing two soldiers. He had then vanished down a side alley, not so much for fear of the enemy but afraid of trouble, or worse, from his superiors.

As he disappeared, those of the thirty exacerbated civilians present who had knives in their pockets, which was almost all of them, had pulled them out. The crowd, which had now become white hot with anger at the sight of the enemy corpses and the image *d'o sbenturàto guaglio'* [12] who had been hit in the femoral artery and was dying fast, had thrown itself on the rest of the German squadron, screaming like savages. The soldier who had fired was the first to be slaughtered, emasculated by three outraged men, and a soldier had been punched on the nose by an assailant without a blade. Then someone behind him had attacked him with a large knife wounding him horizontally on the buttocks. Almost all the assailants had suffered bruising and lacerations to the arms and face, and one, worse, had lost his nose.

No German had managed to fire a single shot at the feral horde and, with the sergeant in the lead, the squad had fled quickly abandoning its arrogance on the cobblestones. The rifles and hand grenades of the slain and the rifles left on the ground by the most seriously wounded had been collected and hidden in the houses. Very soon they would serve to free the city. The three corpses had been taken to the slums and were dissected there. The shreds of flesh had been wrapped in rags and buried in various places in the area. It would be whispered later, true or false? that some nice piece of buttock though had ended up in undernourished bellies roasted. The street had been washed very energetically by the women of the fearless rebels, and never again would it be so clean.

At the same time in another area of Naples, completely independently, a group of improvised militants had attacked a handful of German sabateurs trying to occupy the headquarters of the telephone company, and had scared them off. The German platoon had avenged itself further on, capturing and shooting two carabinieri on patrol duty. Not long after, an entire German company of stormtroopers had arrived in front of the telephone

------

[12] Of the unfortunate little boy.

building and had quickly overcome the insurgents who were guarding it.

Yet, contrary to the intentions of the Nazis, the anger of the humiliated Neapolitans had grown even stronger and the following day, at the foot of the hill of Pizzofalcone between Piazza del Plebiscito and the gardens below, there had been a real battle, ignited by some sailors with their '91 muskets and hand grenades, and stoked by numerous civilians armed with MP80 machine guns and model 24 grenades, stolen from the occupiers the previous day, and improvised Molotov cocktails. The rebels had prevented the passage of an entire column of German trucks and jeeps. Six people had died, three Italian sailors who had fought in the front line and as many German soldiers, with many wounded on both sides.

Heavy measures and serious reprisals by the Germans followed, ordered by the new commander of the city Colonel Walter Scholl who, on the 12th, had officially assumed absolute power. One of his proclamations had dictated that weapons were to be turned in, except for public security forces, a 9.00 pm curfew and a state of siege for the entire city, while not only had the soldiers and civilians taken prisoner been shot, but also several citizens deliberately rounded up.

After the 12th the Germans had gone completely wild, looting, destroying and burning. The university was the first to be set on fire, after shooting a defenseless Italian sailor in front of it, forcing the citizens present not only to assist at the execution, but to applaud it. Up until September 25, even though the city had no longer acted openly against the occupiers after the first few days, the German patrols had apprehended anyone not a policeman, who had been caught in the street in Italian uniform or, if in civilian dress, simply seemed suspicious.

Naples had kept quiet but was sizzling and preparing for the insurgence. In particular, soldiers who had deserted had been picked up one by one by members of the anti-nazifascist parties and hidden and trained in guerrilla warfare, many inside the underground rooms of the Sannazaro high school, the main headquarters of the newborn Neapolitan resistance.

On September 25, the same day on which Italy had been subjected to two very serious bombings on Bologna and Florence by the Americans, an ordinance had been issued in Naples which stipulated that all citizens of working age were obliged to perform tasks of hard labor for the Germans. It was the fuse for the insurgency that would take place a few days later, in perfect antithesis to the intimidating intentions of the Germans. The posters of the decree had already been affixed to the walls in the early morning of Sunday 26, the day before the one that would see the first flashes of the rebellion.

If the substantial order of recruitment had come from Colonel Scholl, the formal one had been signed for Italy by the prefect Domenico Soprano who in August, appointed by the Badoglio Government, had taken the place of the *dismissed* fascist prefect Vaccari. Soprano was a man of order, anti-communist and anti-socialist and opponent of conceivable violent actions by the population, even if he was not fascist but liberal: certainly not a demoliberal Gobetti-style, but an old-fashioned aristocrat. More because of his hatred towards the popular masses than because he was in awe of the Germans, he had signed the decree of conscription to work: playing for time had been his immediate goal to maintain calm.

A few days before that September 26, after there had been contacts between US Army intelligence and the leaders of the Neapolitan anti-fascist parties, precisely in view of a hoped-for uprising in Naples, the prefect Soprano had been approached by representatives of the newborn National Liberation Front – later the National Liberation Committee – which had recently been founded with headquarters in Rome. It was composed of the Action Party, the Liberal Party, the Christian Democratic Centre, Labor Democracy, the Socialist Party of Proletarian Unity and the Communist Party. They had put pressure on him to cooperate with the nascent opposition through the police forces he directed, offering him all possible support. The prefect, however, had preferred the path of prudence because, as always, he opposed social communism and feared any revolutionary movement; thus he had limited himself to converse politically, in secret, with the moderate liberal leaders Enrico De Nicola and Benedetto Croce: without exposing himself.

Both Domenico Soprano and Walter Scholl had miscalculated. Since only one hundred and fifty people had presented themselves to the Germans before the date indicated in the notice, during the afternoon of Sunday September 26 and the early hours of the evening the Germans had started brutally combing Naples and had rounded up 8000 helpless citizens, including elderly men and thirteen-year-old boys. The Germans had fanned the flame of the rebellion igniting the souls of family members and relatives of those rounded up, who were eager to release them. In the early morning of Monday, September 27, there had been the first clashes, started not only by Italian soldiers who had remained in hiding until then in the basement of the Sannazaro high school and in private homes, but also by a number of civilians, although the real popular uprising in Naples would explode the following day, as droves of armed Neapolitans of all social classes spread through the streets and squares, from ultra-commoners to intellectuals, as well as twelve-year-old boys and young women.

Chapter 3

The young Deputy Commissioner, executioner of Germans and in charge of investigating the man in overalls, was a twenty-four-year-old Neapolitan by birth and maternal descent. He had thick, naturally curly black hair, kept short in military fashion according to the regulations of those years. He was not tall, five feet four, but well proportioned and robust. He had graduated in law at the Federico II of Naples with honors and recommended for pubblication and, if he was brilliant in mind, in spirit he was clean, forged in the family and in college on the basis of classic ethical principles, in essence the precepts of the ten Judeo-Christian commandments.

But because of his young age, however, which had made him suffer a few disillusions for the moment, Vittorio D'Aiazzo was a little immodest. He lived with his father, Amilcare D'Aiazzo lieutenant colonel of the Regi Carabinieri, and with his mother, Mrs Luigia-Antonia a graduated primary school teacher but housewife, in the apartment they owned. It was not located in a prestigious area as the family would have liked, not in Via Caracciolo or on the Riviera di Chiaia, for example, but in the popular Sanità district, in Via San Gregorio Armeno where there were lodgings within the reach of the not generous salaries, at that time, and the meagre savings of a high-ranking officer of the Carabinieri. Vittorio lived alone in the accommodation at the time, apart from a part-time cleaning lady, because his mother had been evacuated to the countryside at the beginning of the war. His father, had crossed the lines at night a couple of weeks earlier, even though he was sixty-one, fifteen years older than his wife, and he had done this because, in reality, he did not want to answer to the occupying Germans and to join his sovereign.

Until then he had served in the 7th Provincial Carabinieri Group of Naples, as head of the *Provincial Investigative Coordination Section*. The D'Aiazzo couple had two sons. While they were proud of Vittorio, they did not think highly of the other, Emanuele, who had been a lazy person since he was a child. After several failures, he had received the elementary school diploma at fourteen and with the lowest of grades. He had then abandoned his not hard-earned studies at the beginning of the first year of complementary school for introduction to the work-force. His father had resigned himself to enrolling him because, unlike high school[13], it did not require an entrance examination. At sixteen years old, he had run away from home, and could not be traced. He sent news of himself only years later, once he came of age[14], with a single postcard addressed to the mother, sent from Switzerland in May 1940, with a few words of greeting. Since Emanule had not presented himself for the call-up visit, he had been considered a draft dodger and sentenced *in absentia* to prison by the Military Court of Naples; and when war broke out, he had been considered a deserter.

That son had damaged the image of Lieutenant Colonel D'Aiazzo and he feared that, because of him, he would nor rise through the ranks, despite his many personal merits. Vittorio what's more, because of his brother, had not been able to follow in his father's footsteps and enter the Carabinieri, as he and his parents would have liked. In those days, in fact, not only those who were personally dishonest, but also those who had ancestors or relatives not absolutely unblemished, could not apply for the Benemerita[15]. Disappointed but not completely resigned, Vittorio had graduated and had participated in the public contest for Deputy Commissioner in the Public Security Guards Corps, an entity that required only the personal integrity of the aspirant and not his relatives as well. He had passed the test brilliantly and, at the end of the vocational graduate school which followed, he was the first in the standings with every hope, therefore, of being granted the chosen destination, his Naples, and had been assigned precisely to his home city.

After reading warrant officer Branduardi's brief report, Deputy Commissioner D'Aiazzo had headed to the holding cells on the ground floor to take a look at the self-styled Gennaro Esposito. He had then gone down into the damp underground archive and had checked if anyone with those personal details had a police record and if his photos, from the front and in profile, corresponded to the physiognomy of the prisoner. He had found

---

[13] Like the current 1ˢᵗ grade middle school in Italy, but a classic five-year course.
[14] 21 years in those days.
[15] (t/n – the Meritorious, as the Carabinieri were also known)

several criminal records with the same name and surname, but all of them concerned people who did not look like the alleged murderer. Back in his office, he had the arrested man brought to him.

He had interrogated him with the help of his assistant brigadier Marino Bordin who, sitting at his table, had typed his superior's questions and the answers from the man being questioned on the office typewriter, an obsolete black Olivetti M1, 1911 model.

Bordin was a sturdy blond Venetian, five feet nine tall. He was forty-five years old, had served in Public Security for a quarter of a century, and had a wife and two children that he had evacuated to a farmhouse in the Neapolitan countryside, sacrificing two thirds of his salary to the farmer hosting them and resigning himself to eat and sleep in the barracks with what was left.

For hours the suspect, without giving in, had said and repeated, in a correct idiom that made one think he had at least attended primary school classes, very strict at that time, that he was an unemployed cook, that he lived as was written on his license, in Vicolo Santa Luciella and that he was on his way home when he had seen the door of the dead woman's house ajar and had heard moans coming from inside. Out of mere altruism he had gone in, asking for permission, had seen the woman on the ground in the entry still moaning. Having noticed a telephone on a wall, he had decided to call an ambulance; but at that very moment the Public Security patrol had entered and had handcuffed him.

The Deputy Commissioner had kept at it and shortly after 7 am he had finally obtained a new detail, that the man visited the prostitute regularly and that he had gone into her house, because he was expected, to have some quick sex so he could leave early and get to his own house before the curfew. When asked, he had specified that he had made the appointment by phone from a bar, as he had done many other times. When asked to recite Demaggi's telephone number, he had said that he no longer remembered it and, when D'Aiazzo showed his skeptiscism, he had justified the amnesia because he was in a state of mental turmoil due to the situation. Otherwise he had not changed his version reiterating that, once he went in the door left ajar especially for him following the phone call, he had seen the woman on the ground and had immediately decided to call for help from the telephone in the apartment, but then the patrol had arrived and had detained him.

Just like the the patrol officers, the Deputy Commissioner could not believe that the man was a client of the pricey hooker, taking into account his cheap shabby clothing and no money in his pockets. Considering that the door had ostensibly been left open for him, he had conjectured that he was an accomplice in the black market. He had therefore accused him of killng her because of some argument: "Confess and I'll let you go to sleep!"

"It isn't true, it was definitely an accident that took place before I went inside," the other had denied.

"If you weren't an accomplice at loggerheads, then you were sent to kill her by a competitor," the officer had pressed.

"Commissioner I'm telling you again that it is not true!" the man had become angry, abandoning the docile attitude he had kept until then.

Without being asked, Brigadier Bordin had snapped: "*Busòn!*[16] Be respectful to the commissioner or I'll kick you where you like to get it!"

The Deputy Commissioner did not allow bad manners and had reprimanded him: "Marino, keep the kicks and the insults to yourself." He had resumed: "Gennaro, provided that Gennaro Esposito is really your name, and you can be sure that we'll check at the Registry Office tomorrow ... no, this morning, seeing the time, listen up: I too, like you, would like to finish this, so I'll make you a proposal," – the man had visibly raised his attention threshold, half-opening his mouth as his pupils dilated a little – "if you confess guilty to homicide, which means that you killed going beyond the intention you had ..."

"... I know."

"Then listen: you could tell me for example that you had no money and that the victim didn't want to concede herself on credit, so in an irrepressible impulse of anger you pushed her, without wanting to kill her but, unfortunately, she fell and was fatally injured; well, you know what I mean: in this way you don't end up in front of the firing squad[17], you just get a little jail time. Instead, if I write in my report for the investigating judge that I suspect you're the hitman for some camorra blackmarketer who wanted to

___

[16] Dialect term used with contempt towards the passive homosexual.

[17] In those years the penal code required the death penalty, by shooting.

eliminate her, or a direct competitor of the woman on the black market who wanted to take her out once and for all, you are already good and shot."

Even though he was more tired than the Deputy Commissioner, the man had not confessed: "Not only will I repeat yet again that I am not a murderer and, as far as I know, the woman died from an accident which took place before I entered her apartment, but now I'm also telling you that I am a sergeant major gunner and that I crossed the lines and arrived in Naples yesterday evening."

"Hmm... tell me more."

"I am also a cook, I was serving as kitchen manager in the officers' club of the 3rd battalion, 1st Coastal Artillery Regiment, stationed five miles north of Paestum, in the province of Salerno."

"I know where Paestum is... okay, assuming that you've told me the truth now, it's in your own interest that we check your military identity, so tell me about the school for cadet non-commissioned officers you come from and which course." In reality, that verification would probably have been impossible in the chaos following the armistice and D'Aiazzo knew it, but he had counted on the fact that if the other lied to him, he would give himself away.

The man had not turned a hair: "My career started with an apprenticeship: at twenty-eight, after I lost my job of assistant cook in a trattoria ..."

"... what did you do?"

"...nothing wrong! The restaurant had closed because, as the owners said, the final consequences of the crisis of '29 had arrived."

"Okay, go on."

"I had looked for work elsewhere but found nothing: no one was hiring, if anything they were firing. Then, so as not to weigh on my mother who had been widowed and worked hard doing the cleaning in shops and sewing and embroidering at home for strangers, I enlisted as a volunteer in the end, hoping to work my way up and become a non-commissioned office. I had been discharged from the service six years earlier, with honor, with the rank of corporal, which was recognized at the reaffirmation. And since I had already been in kitchens during the draft, after a refresher course on certain regulations, they had sent me in front of the pots again, apart from the periodic shooting exercises with the artillery, rifle and pistol. That's how it was right through my military career, first as a corporal, then as a sergeant and, finally, as a non-commissioned officer[18]: sergeant major manager of the kitchen of the officers' club.

After the armistice and the landing of our former enemies[19] on our coasts, I was left in the lurch with my fellow soldiers in the hope of not running into Anglo-Americans or Germans. I hid, eating fruit and vegetables I took from vegetable gardens and, the few times someone put me up in a farmhouse, bread, milk and eggs as well. But farmers, or at least the ones I met, are not generous people, and they all asked me for compensation, first in money, and little by little I gave them what I had left of the last salary, then when the money ran out I had to leave my watch: it was steel, but a good brand; and to the last *purucchio*[20] I gave my medal of *San Genna'* on a little chain, both in 18 carat gold, a gift from my parents for my First Communion, in exchange for the old shirt and the work overalls I'm still wearing. I got myself into plain clothes and threw away the military dog-tag and the military documents too, because they are not only another color for us career people but they say that we are in fact military and our rank as well..."

"... I know"

"Yes, it's like that for you too. I threw away my identity card and military license and only kept my civilian license. Then, no longer in uniform, I headed to my Naples and managed to cross the front line and last night I arrived in the city. I moved cautiously even though I was in civilian clothes and had a document with me, and I got to Piazzetta del Nilo, which is not far from the little house where mamma and I live in Vicolo Santa Luciella; and, because of my good heart, after what I had already been through, I still had the impulse to help that woman who was groaning and ... here I am, just when I was very close to home."

"How come your domicile in the area of Paestum is not indicated on your driving permit?"

"I had a room in the barracks, with another sergeant major who was a bachelor as well, I didn't have any place outside: I never considered the barracks my home and I never thought of

---

[18] At that time the sergeant was still considered part of the troops, as were corporals, and not a non-commissioned officer.

[19] This was Operation Avalanche that began on 9 September.

[20] louse.

having the address in Naples removed. I just had it changed on the identity card and the military driving permit because it was mandatory, apart from the fact that on the civil license I would often have to have the Department of Motor Vehicles change my address, since they moved me every few years. Whereas the military card and license were done again directly in the new department; and then, after all, I came back to Naples to see mamma every time I went on leave."

"You should know that we'll go to Vicolo Santa Maria to check if your mother really lives there and if other people know you."

"... and I thank you, Commissioner, because that is exactly where mamma lives and you will have confirmation about me from her and the neighbours as well. But please, I beg you with all my heart: don't frighten mamma. Tell her, please, that I have asked you to say hello to her since I couldn't come in person because of service reasons."

"If we find your mother, we won't scare her and we'll talk to her as you wish." At this point, however, the Deputy Commissioner had started on him again: "Earlier you tried to make me believe that you had an appointment with Demaggi and then you admitted that it was not true. So tell me: if that was the first time you saw her, how did you know that the woman was a prostitute?"

Unperturbed he replied: "I heard your patrol chief talking about it with his colleagues when they were with the deceased."

"I'll check. Now tell me one more thing" – D'Aiazzo had left the question for last, to fire it when the man was very tired – "Why were you wearing wool gloves at this time of year? So as not to leave prints, right?"

"... no, Mr. Commissioner," the other wasn't worried, "the reason is simple, I've been wearing them for some time now, I also had them when I was in service, with the captain's permission. I suffer from pain in my fingers and also in my left palm."

"Hm..."

"... yes I do, because of the humidity in the kitchens over many years, what with steam from pots and water where we washed the cauldrons, as the lieutenant doctor explained to me, and he was the one who told me to wear gloves."

The man was exhausted and the two policemen were physical wrecks; the Deputy Commissioner had ordered Brigadier Bordin to escort the alleged sergeant major Gennaro Esposito to the holding cell.

Vittorio D'Aiazzo had not been able to form a concrete idea with just the information he had collected: to his mind it could possibly be both an accident and a murder must, the latter not necessarily perpetrated by the man arrested; however, if he were guilty, the motive could be competition between black marketers if the self-styled Esposito's identity and in particular his position in the Army were not confirmed, otherwise a different motive would come into play.

Moreover, if the anatomopathologist established that it was an assassination, and even though he had not confessed, he would be transferred to the Prison of Poggioreale as a suspect. As well as that, the Deputy Commissioner would have to write a report containing both the medical examiner's conclusions and the details that D'Aiazzo himself had collected during the interrogation, and send it to the Office of the Public Prosecutor. Based on his report, the investigating judge would decide whether to open proceedings against the suspect or release him for lack of evidence.

It was almost eight in the morning and the young officer was about to finish his shift; but just the same, before going home he still intended to order the warrant officer to go to Vicolo Santa Luciella to check if the suspect's mother really lived there and, in this case, if she recognized her son in the photo on the license and confirmed that he really was a sergeant major in the artillery. But the Deputy Commissioner did not plan to wait for the man to return and he would hear the report the following day. At any rate, it would be two or three days at least before the anatomopathologist's report arrived in his office, during which time the detained man would remain in the holding cell.

After having taken the suspect back to the cell, Bordin had gone back to D'Aiazzo. As he entered the office he had said to him: "Mr. Commissioner, in my opinion that Esposito, or so he claims, was sent by the camorra to kill Demaggi for two possible reasons: either because of competition on the black market, or because that filthy whore no longer wanted to pay the kickback ..."

"... Marino, the woman is dead and you don't insult the deceased," the young superior had reprimanded him, "and in any case I'm not convinced that the suspect is a murderer."

"Forgive me if I take the liberty, but I think... well, that you are always too good: if we gave him a few blows in the stomach with sandbags ..."

"... that don't leave a mark?"

"Just to be prudent; and be sure that that delinquent sayts he is guilty and a *camorrista* to boot, and who knows what else. But like this..."

"... instead like this I didn't risk making an innocent person confess, apart from the fact that if I saw you hitting someone with a sack ... do you understand me, Marino?"

"Yeah...."

"If anything, it will be the investigating judge who makes him admit that he is guilty, provided the doctor doesn't tell us that it was an accident, and then I can archive the case and free that man."

"Yes, maybe, but speaking in general terms you, Mr Commissioner, are perhaps the only one here who doesn't give people being interrogated a few slaps. The late Dr. Perati I served with before you made everyone confess."

With the fervor of age, and not without that pinch of presumption that he always had, the Deputy Commissioner had instinctively let slip in the Neapolitan dialect that he used at home: "*Tu si' 'nu fésso.*[21]"

"What?!" The non-commissioned officer had turned red with rage.

His superior had partially corrected himself: "All right, Marino, I take back the *idiot*, but you are wrong to speak disrespectfully to me just because I am half your age. Be careful, because if it happens again I will punish you."

Bordin had thought it wise to apologize, albeit through gritted teeth: "Forgive me, Mr. Commissioner, I was just saying, I didn't want to criticize you."

If, over time, Vittorio D'Aiazzo would fully acquire humility thanks to the metaphorical slaps of life, at the time he still wanted to have the last word: "Alright, but from now on think about what you say, before saying what you think."

---

[21] (t/n – Your're an idiot!)

The man had thought it wise to stand stiffly to attention: "Signorsì."

"At ease, and don't be mortified," his superior had softened the tone, with compassion finally prevailing. He had continued: "You said that Perati made everyone confess: of course, I know that very well, they'd told me that when I arrived here; but do you remember who killed him?"

"Yes sir, the mother of a habitual thief..."

"... thief that Perati had accused of stabbing a baker in the hand, to rob him, and that he had indeed made him confess, but how? Tying him belly up on a table and whipping him with his belt; and two days later, do you remember? the suspect died of internal bleeding."

"Excuse me, may I speak to you freely but with all due respect?"

"You can."

"I believed that Dr. Perati had been right because he had not been reproached by superiors."

"Then you don't know that the matter had been buried by order of the federal of Naples[22], because Perati was extremely fascist and a bootlicker; and yet, in the mind of the dead man's mother the thing had not been buried at all, and what's more, a couple of weeks after her son's death, she had learned that he was innocent of both the wounding and the theft, and you knew this, didn't you?"

"I knew that the baker had recognized the real culprit in the street and had reported it to one of our patrols, who had stopped him and brought him here."

"Yes, and the dead man's mother had been made aware of it by a friend of her son's, who heard the truth going around, and you know what? It had not been too unjust, after all, that the woman had come to us asking to speak to Perati, with the excuse of having revelations to make to him, and once she was in front of him she had pulled out a small meat knife from her breast and let go a slash that had gone into his heart; and I'm almost sorry that she was blocked immediately afterwards and that she is now awaiting trial, because I fear she will be sentenced to death for premeditated murder."

____

[22] Local secretary of the fascist party.

"Let's hope they grant her mental semi-infermity," Bordin had agreed.

"Let's hope so; but apart from that, you can go to the vehicles depot for me now with this service sheet... here: it's my authorization to pick up a car with driver. Then go and check is Esposito is known in Vicolo Santa Lucia." He had also given him the suspect's license: "Show this photo to the mother, that's if she exists, and to the neighbors as well, and gather as much as you can on him."

"Yes, sir! On the way back though, Commissioner, maybe I could go to my room to sleep because I've already completed my hours of service for today."

"Duty and sacrifice is our motto," he had responded smiling.

Since Police Headquarters knew that the social temperature in the city was climbing and an uprising was quite likely, the brigadier had decided to go by the radio room to get some news on the situation outside before going to the garage. As soon as he had heard it, he had returned to his direct superior and told him that patrol trucks had communicated that isolated gun battles had begun. He concluded asking: "Sir, do I really have to go there today, or can I wait for tomorrow, when maybe things will have calmed down?"

Before D'Aiazzo had decided, the rumble of the diesel engines of vehicles had started to come up along Via Medina where Naples Police Headquarters were located, and still are, and were going past the main entrance of the building in column, as they had done every day for two weeks. It was a motorized platoon of German grenadiers going to relieve another one, of the same battalion, sent to guard a corridor on the top floor of Castel Sant'Elmo, a mighty bulwark that stands on the Vomero hill at 820 feet above sea level overlooking the Gulf and the city. Two non-communicating rooms opened onto that corridor and, at that time, were used as the armory of the fortress. One of them was a large room with conventional weapons and ammunition stored there and in the other, a smaller space, the secret armaments of Italian design and production were guarded.

The weapons were kept under surveillance around the clock in two shifts, from 8.30 am to 8.30 pm and 8.30 pm to 8.30 am. The Germans had occupied Castel Sant'Elmo since September 9, and had seized the armaments, with particular interest in the special ones. The castle itself was a primary target for the Allies in those days precisely because of these unconventional weapons, and for some time their own secret services had been interested in it.

Vittorio D'Aiazzo was about to tell his subordinate to ignore his previous order and to go and get some rest, when there were gunshots from Via Medina, first from rifles and a light machine gun, then, in rapid succession, an assault rifle and a machine gun.

Deputy Commissioner and assistant had instinctively ducked then, with their legs bent, had moved to the window and peeked out to look below, showing themselves as little as possible.

At the same time, several other policemen had looked down from their respective offices, both the staff coming off duty and those coming on, as it was chngeover time, 8.00 am on the dot. Having just arrived, the deputy Head of Police Remigio Bollati had also glanced surreptitiously out his window; his office opened off the same corridor as Vittorio's and the two rooms were next to each other.

Depending on the position of his window and as he looked down, he had seen or glimpsed the German platoon standing still in the middle of the road about fifty yards past the front door and the neighboring driveway. From the shelter of their vehicles, lined up transversely, they were engaged in a gun battle with people who had to be further down the street that couldn't be seen from the Police Headquarters building, but the gunshots coule be heard very clearly. It could be assumed that they were taking cover behind the walls in ruin and the piles of rubble of two nearby buildings facing each other, bombed a few days before September 8 by American fast-response fortifications.

Chapter 4

To better understand, let's go back a little:

With the Neapolitan Revolutionary Single Front having been formed, and given the reluctance of the Prefect Soprano to take charge of it, the seventy-year-old laborer Antonio Taraia had been elected to head it. On September 24, considering the situation now ripe for the insurgence, he had called a meeting for the following morning in the Sannazaro high school, so as to put the decision about it to the vote. He had arrived at the conviction that it was now time to act, not only because of the news that the Anglo-Americans were now almost at the gates of Naples which he had received in advance from the philosopher Benedetto Croce who had heard it confidentially from Dr. Soprano, but also because, following coded agreements made by radio with the Americans, weapons and two-way radios of the US Army intended for the partisans had just been parachuted in at night, near Naples.

They had been hidden immediately afterwards in seven cellars in as many different areas of the city; the operation had taken place with the essential contribution of a group of bribed *camorristi*, ready to run serious risks in view of the very high earnings promised to them by the Americans. We should not be surprised by this alliance, the United States had already availed themelves of, and continued to use the mafia's help in occupied Sicily where, among other things, numerous new notoriously mafia mayors had been installed by the conquerors. The camorra, as well as the Mafia, was organized in an almost military fashion and, in particular, had many large trucks available in Naples.

The arms operation had been meticulously organized by the Americans; among other things, instruction leaflets on the use of the parachuted weapons, written in correct Italian, had been taken to the Sannazaro high school by some American agents who had crossed the lines at night. In this way the Neapolitan patriots could be theoretically instructed on their operation by the agents themselves, which would make the practical instruction faster and easier. For logistical reasons, this would take place just a little before the uprising, at the moment the weapons were recovered from the seven storage places.

At the meeting of September 25, the decision to rebel was unanimous. Around noon, messengers had been sent to tell the custodians of the American war material.

The following day, Sunday, seven leaders of patriot groups who had already assisted at the storage of the weapons in the secret places, had presented themselves not long before curfew time, one at each storage room, to prepare the weapons to be collected the same night by their men, who would arrive at the hiding places around 5.00 am on Monday, September 27.

So, after 6 am on that same day of September 27, having collected their weapons, the groups of freedom fighters had headed to their targets. While the platoons trained in the Sannazaro High School by the American agents were carrying U.S. weapons, namely M1 Garand semi-automatic rifles and BAR M1918 Browning machine guns that used the same 7.62 caliber projectiles, Mk2 pineapple hand grenades and M1 bazooka portable anti-tank rocket launchers, the other groups of insurgents had weapons captured from the Germans in the clashes during the early days, namely Mauser Kar 98k rifles, MP80 assault rifles, 24 hand grenades and Panzerwurfmine grenades with their Panzerfaust anti-tank bomb launchers; there were also personal knives or taken from domestic kitchens and some double-barrelled shotguns previously secreted in cellars or attics by their fond hunter owners after the German occupation,.

That morning, however, the first gunshot had not been preordained. On the contrary it had ignited spontaneously at the Vomero by relatives of people that had been rounded up. They had stopped an off-road Kübelwagen Typ 82 of the Wehrmacht, killing the marshal who was driving it and putting the other soldiers to flight; other non-organized actions had taken place around Naples soon after and, here and there, carabinieri on patrol and officers of Public Security and the Guardia di Finanza had spontaneously joined the rebel groups.

Shortly before the start of school lessons, ten unarmed high school students had thrown themselves, on the spur of the moment, at three Germans who were on patrol in their Kübelwagen, proceding at walking pace. They had forced them to get out, disarmed them and set fire to their off-road vehicle, while the Alemannic threesome had fled. Those Germans, however, had raised the alarm with their department, and two German platoons had arrived with the support of a powerful sdKfz 231 Schwere Panzerspähwagaen 6 rad armoured car. The ten young people had taken refuge and barricaded themselves in the nearby San Martino Museum and the armored vehicle had begun to strafe the windows, as news of the students' action and the danger they were in was spreading through Naples, echo after echo.

Among the actions which, instead, the Resistance had prepared, were first of all the well-known attack on the column of German grenadiers in Via Medina and the action of a platoon of carabinieri who, with their colonel commander's approval had headed to the San Martino Museum aboard a Lancia CM truck[23] to fight the Germans were besieging the rebellious students with their short 91muskets and SRCM 35[24] hand grenades. Some civilians in the area had spontaneously placed themselves at the side of the Benemerita military.

That same morning, still in response to the democratic leaders' previous order, one hundred freedom fighters had attacked Castel Sant'Elmo. Inside, among the Germans barricaded there, was the tired platoon of grenadiers who had remained on guard at the armory the whole night, without being relieved because, as we know, the fresh platoon coming on duty had been engaged in combat in Via Medina.

As the pressure of events increased, the post commander, Colonel Scholl, had moved his powerful Tiger- and Panther-class panzers, but a number of them had been blocked and set on fire by rioters, thanks to a few *panzerfaust*[25] stolen from the enemy, American bazookas and Molotov cocktails.

---

[23] CM is a military abbreviation for medium-size truck (or wagon), a shorter truck with fewer seats in the caisson than the largest truck called CL. The CM and CL were of various brands of vehicles, but with the same characteristics.
[24] Assault bomb, commonly called "balilla" in the years of fascism.
[25] (t/n - shoulder-type German antitank weapon)

Chapter 5

As the gun fight in Via Medina continued, the head of Police Headquarters, Dr. Carmelo Pelluso, having moved away from the window of his office on the first floor, from which he had cautiously watched the German platoon engaged in combat, was about to call his Deputy Commissioners by intercom to give orders regarding it, when the phone on his desk had started ringing.

At the other end of the line was his direct superior Dr. Soprano. The Prefect had reported to the Chief Commissioner that armed conflict had begun in several areas of Naples and had told him the news that the American armed 5th and the 6th Corps as well as the British 10th were attacking the Germans in the direction of Naples and Avellino and the German units in the field were beginning to fall back, bypassing the Neapolitan city, to consolidate their lines further north. He had concluded by leaving the Commissioner in Chief free to decide which concrete orders to give his men, but with the constraint of not forcing them to fight the Germans.

Dr. Pelluso had not obeyed completely: after saying goodbye to the Prefect, he had indeed commanded his deputies to give their subordinates the simple invitation, not the order, to join the population against the Germans, but he had added decisively: "Tell everyone that I personally am on the insurgents' side; however anyone, for mere hypothesis, who does not want to follow me will not be in any trouble; he will though have to hand over his gun and remain clonsigned to Police Headquarters in the holding cells."

Carmelo Pelluso was not an anti-fascist of the first hour: like many others, including Deputy Commissioner Vittorio D'Aiazzo, he had carried the Fascist Party card until July 25, mandatory in reality for public officials. He had, however, already joined the Action Party at the end of that month and had not changed sides after the German occupation and the very recent return of Mussolini to the Government of the part of Italy not occupied by the Allied armies. On the contrary, he was now actively collaborating with the leaders of the anti-fascist parties of the Single Revolutionary Front and, first and foremost, with one of its leading exponents, who was also his personal friend, the *azionista*[26] Professor Adolfo Omodeo. On September 1, the latter had been appointed as rector of the University of Naples Federico II by the Badoglio Government. From there he fueled the rebellion against Nazi-fascism among the intellectuals, together with the liberal Benedetto Croce.

The policemen loyal to Mussolini, a commissioner and a dozen agents, graduates and non-commissioned officers had been disarmed and, under the direct control of the chief commissioner, had been locked up, respectfully but under armed escort, in the holding cells. Pelluso had inquired if there were already other prisoners in those rooms and had been told that the only one in a holding cell was a certain, real or presumed, Gennaro Esposito, suspected of the murder of a prostitute named Rosa Demaggi. The commissioner in chief had looked very disappointed.

In those same minutes, Vittorio D'Aiazzo was leaving the barracks from the driveway, at the command of an old, obsolete armored vehicle belonging to Police Headquarters. He considered himself a Christian demoliberal *in pectore* even though, after tossing away the Fascist card on July 25, he had not joined either the Catholic party or the Liberal party and, unlike the chief commissioner Pelluso, had not made contact with men of the newborn Resistance. On the other hand, that was how it was for the great majority of those Italians who would then fight Nazi-fascism, for over a year and a half, until the end of the war.

Brigadier Marino Bordin had climbed aboard the armored car with Vittorio D'Aiazzo even though, like him, he was tired out from the sleepless night. He was a courageous but rough man and, despite not having political ideas, he harbored deep animosity for the Germans because of their contemptuous arrogance towards the Italians. Two police officers had also boarded the armored vehicle, Tertini and Pontiani, and the ordinary marshal Aroldo Bennato, head mechanic of the police headquarters repair shop, who had placed himself at the wheel. All three were fresh after a night of rest, and had just come on duty.

The armored car, or to be precise the machine gun armoured car as it was catalogued, was a tool from the First World War, an Ansaldo Lancia IZ equipped with three 7.92 mm heavy Maxim machine guns. Only this armored car and two similar to it

---

[26] Member of the Action Party.

had not been confiscated from Police Headquarters by the occupants, having been judged no longer of any use because obsolete, unlike the most modern armored cars 611 FIAT 1934/35 and AB FIAT 1940/43 that the Teutonic tank drivers had willingly added to their armored vehicles. The Ansaldo Lancia IZ was a model which was slow and hard to maneuver. But it had considerable firepower, and in fact, when it came into service at the end of the First World War, it had made immediate destruction among the Austrians; moreover, contrary to what the Germans must have thought, the three twin armored cars had been kept in perfect efficiency thanks to periodic reviews by the workshop manager and his mechanics and, for the machine guns, by the gunsmiths.

With the five policemen on board, the armored vehicle had noisily entered Via Medina, emitting smoke, about seventy yards behind the Germans who were still intent on firing Garand rifles on the rioters, while the patriots' BAR machine gun was now silent with its operator slumped face-down over it, dead. The number of attackers still alive had been reduced to less than half, since the Germans had a so-called *Hitler's saw*, a tremendous 7.92 mm MG 42 machine gun, the best in the world for performance and lightness. In fact, even today in the 2000s, the model is supplied to NATO[27]; and for every ten bullets inserted into the tapes by the Teutonic machine gunners, one was an armor-piercing type, capable of breaching the crumbling walls and piles of rubble of the two bombed houses, from the cover of which the patriots were firing. Some Germans too were dead on the ground, a small part of their platoon.

Vittorio D'Aiazzo had ordered the warrant officer to stop the vehicle and the police officers to get behind the two machine guns, as he himself got behind the third. The trio had armed, aimed at the enemy grenadiers and, at their superior's order, had opened fire non-stop despite the risk of jamming the weapons. The three improvised machine gunners had eliminated the enemy platoon, whose men had not had been in time to turn their armor-piercing bullets against the Italian armored MG, though they could have had the better against the slender coverage of the Italian vehicle. Above all, they had not been able to launch an anti-tank bomb with a Panzerfaust, with which they were equipped.

---

[27] But with the caliber 7.62 "Nato".

After the massacre of Teutonics, the armored car had slowly resumed its passage, winding its way past the dead and the enemy vehicles; due to insufficient space it had pushed a small truck out of the way. About forty yards away the surviving patriots, only six people, none of whom had been hit, had emerged from the rubble and had come out into the open to meet the armored vehicle. There were five men and a small slender woman who looked no more than eighteen, on her face an expression of contempt.

When the armored arrived about ten paces from the small group, Vittorio had given the order to stop. He got out with three of his men, leaving the wrrant officerl on board at the radio. The policemen and partisans had taken care of the Italians on the ground, sixtcen of them, none of whom gave signs of life. Six of them were in appalling condition, four almost sawn in half by bullets from the MG, the fifth was missing the face, replaced by a bloody cavity, the sixth deprived of the skull cap so that you could see his brain and cerebral matter which had come out of his nose had set on his mouth and chin.

The girl had been beside the latter during the fight, and had told D'Aiazzo that the man's brain had pulsed for a while after suffering those devastating blows; impassive, she had concluded the gruesome report saying: "I don't know if he was still conscious, because he was immobile, but I think so."

"I really hope not!" the Deputy Commissioner had replied rudely, annoyed not so much by the macabre description, but by the coldness that the young woman had shown.

One of the Italians killed had a small bag made of jute slung across his chest which held a US Motorola Handie-Talkie SCR536 one-way radio, light but not powerful; still showing no feeling, the girl had taken it from the deceased and had put it on her shoulder. She had then examined the corpses of the Germans one by one, very carefully, and when she had finished the inspection, her face had darkened.

Vittorio had ordered the removal of the deadly MG machine gun from the tripod with its ribbons of bullets, and had explained that once it had been taken off the support, that weapon could perform very well as a submachine gun, because it was not very heavy, just a few dozen pounds, and the bipod folded under the barrel could be lifted up. The girl had appropriated it, putting down her Garand rifle, saying that she knew how to use it. She had put two ribbons of MG bullets across her body bandolier-style and the machine gun on her right shoulder, her hand on the barrel to keep it balanced.

D'Aiazzo had grabbed the dangerous Panzerfaust and asked: "Do any of you know how to use this thing?" He had had a yes from one of the six who, although he was in civilian clothes, had declared that he was a grenadier and had explained that he had been "caught by surprise here in Naples by the armistice."

A moment later the warrant officer had leaned out the door of the armored vehicle and told his superior that he had picked up the news from the radio room of Police Headquarters, that a female voice had telephoned their switchboard reporting that Germans were machine-gunning the houses in Piazza Carità.

Vittorio had decided to intervene. Since the armoured car could accommodate up to six people, he had asked the young woman if she wanted to get in. She had refused and, given the urgency, he had not repeated the invitation, and ordered his men to get on board. He was the last to get inside and had commanded the warrant officer to head to the target.

Meanwhile, many other policemen were leaving Police Headquarters to confront Germans: some left on foot through the front door or a secondary door, some via the driveway on trucks, jeeps, three-wheeled motorbikes or on board the two remaining armored cars. Most of them had nineteenth-century '91muskets, some had a modern MAB submachine gun[28] slung over their shoulders, many were carrying SRCM bombs or tear gas grenades in their pockets. Those cops were going to the most diverse destinations. In particular, upon chief commissioner Pelluso's specific order, a platoon with several men in civilian clothes and the majority in uniform, had boarded an OM brand flatbed truck and headed towards Piazzetta del Nilo, only a kilometer away from Via Medina: also on that truck, in the cabin next to the driver, was the alleged sergeant major Gennaro Esposito.

The armored car under the command of D'Aiazzo had set off again, clanking and sputtering, with the six patriots walking behind it. Warrant Officer Bennato drove it slowly, not only because of the vehicle's age, but so the partisans on foot who were using it as a kind of bulwark, could keep up with it without tiring

---

[28] Beretta Automatic Musket.

themselves. After the first hundred yards or so one of the six, looking at the minute build of the young woman, had offered to exchange the heavy MG with his own rifle, but she had refused annoyed and snarling "Naah" which, to all intents and purposes, must have meant no.

As they approached Piazza Carità, the eleven patriots had heard volleys of machine gun fire. Two minutes later, the echoes of assault rifles had reached their ears followed by a detonation. After another couple of minutes, more volleys of machine gun fire were heard and little by little as the armored car approached, the crackle had become louder. They had almost arrived at the square, and it was now beyond doubt that the shooting was taking place right there.

Vittorio had ordered Bordin and the two police officers to go to the machine guns and arm them, and to be ready to shoot at his command. He had gone behind a forward embrasure to watch what was happening outside, ready to order them to open fire.

Chapter 6

The armored car had emerged at walking pace from Via Cesare Battisti into Piazza Carità.

The German dragoon loomed through the forward embrasure, standing still about forty yards away at 45 degrees to the right of the Italian vehicle: it was a Panther tank with a formidable 110 millimeters armor, armed with a 75 mil cannon and two MG machine guns, one in the turret and one in the body of the hull forward, which until a short time before had been spewing fire. It almost seemed as if the beast was resting after a gigantic effort. And it was evident where its effort had been directed, because on the ground lay the bloody bodies of civilians of both sexes. The windows of the buildings all around the square were shattered, and there were deep rents in the walls. A semi-destroyed off-road Kübelwagen that was still smoking and four charred corpses, one inside and three on the ground, wearing Wehrmacht helmets which were now black, made it clear that the retaliation of the German tank had followed an attack on the truck with a Molotov cocktail:

At the moment of the assault on the Kübelwagen, the Panther was patroling the nearby Strada del Formale. The crew had heard two explosions a couple of seconds apart, and the tank leader, a career marshal named Konrad Müller, had realized which direction they had come from. He had ordered the vehicle to head towards Piazza Carità. When they arrived, the tankers had found the remains of their four comrades and the truck, but there was no one in sight because, after throwing two incendiary bottles, one of which had hit the mark, the bombers had fled, and the residents had taken refuge in the houses and shops, closing the doors and shutters.

Without hesitation, the non-commissioned officer had given the order to machine-gun the facades of all nearby buildings at eye level and, while his MGs crackled, he had radioed the Command for instructions. They had ordered him to take revenge by rounding up civilians, ten for every German killed, and to shoot them on the spot. The corporal deputy commander of the Panther and two tankers had got out armed with MP80 assault rifles and model 24 hand grenades and had thrown the grenades at shutters and gates, killing or injuring those who had sheltered inside.

With a loudspeaker, Marshal Mülle in a stunted Italian had ordered everyone to come out the houses, otherwise all the buildings would be blassted with the cannon, with the residents inside them; he had promised that if they presented themselves to the German sub-team in an orderly manner, they would just be questioned and then let go. Forty-two people had thus been rounded up, two more than ten times the dead Germans. All the same, even though the corporal had communicated to the tank chief who had appeared from the turret, that there was an excess of the people rounded up, his superior had considered the measure appropriate. He was a convinced Nazi even if he was not SS, and he had given the order to "execute" them all. Those unarmed civilians had been shot down by bursts of assault-rifle fire.

When the butchers had climbed back aboard their panzer, the marshal had commanded the gunners to start shooting again all around, this time aiming at the upper floors. The terrorist barrages continued for many minutes while that racist Konrad Müller, expressing himself in his Bavarian dialect, had pronounced hateful expressions that in Italian would have sounded like this: "Italians pieces of shit! Traitorous bastards! Breed of pigs!"

The steel dragon was about to resume its patrol through the streets when the armored vehicle with more *Italian pieces of shit* on board had arrived. It was much inferior to the Panther in both armor and firepower. Warrant Officer Bennato could do nothing but attempt to backtrack quickly, in the very faint hope that the enemy had other orders to carry out immediately and would not launch themselves in pursuit. He had braked suddenly, without needing to receive the command, engaged reverse gear and stepped on the gas, while the six patriots on foot, seeing the armored car starting to reverse, had stopped and were preceding it in the retreat. Only part of the vehicle had managed to slip into Via Battisti, however, because the engine had flooded and turned off because of the sloppy maneuver, and had stopped with the muzzle still exposed to the enemy.

Contrary to the Italian's faint hope, instead of resuming the patrol around Naples the commander of the Panther had decided to destroy the rebel vehicle and had ordered the gunner to aim straight at the enemy bow.

Through the embrasure Vittorio had glimpsed the turret of the tank start to rotate directing fire at the armored vehicle, and had shouted at his men to get out and lose themselves in the meanders of Via Battisti. As he gave the order, he himself had headed to the door, and was the first to touch the ground. He would later have reasoned that, after all, lingering would not have helped to get the others out faster; in reality the instinct of self-preservation had simply prevailed in him. Marshal

The cannon shot had rumbled an instant after Bennato, for last, had jumped out. The projectile had exploded precisely on the exposed part of the vehicle at which the gunner had aimed. In explosive sympathy, the Panzerwurfmine anti-tank bomb had also exploded inside the grenadier's Panzerfaust, the weapon which until a moment before had been on his shoulder but which he had thrown away to give himself a better chance of escape. The Italian armored vehicle had been hurled backwards and set on fire, hitting and crushing the four patriots nearest to it, as thick large splinters spread like the spokes of a wheel, wreaking havoc.

Warrant Officer Bennato had been killed, hit in the neck by a red-hot piece of sheet metal, and had died instantly with his head cut sliced from his body. The grenadier had been torn apart by the Panzerwurfmine bomb and shrapnel from the Panzerfaust, to which he had still been too close. The officers Tertini and Pontiani, hit in the back by a hail of fragments, had died minutes later, face down on the pavement. Only the Deputy Commissioner, the brigadier and the young woman had managed to get away, just a moment before the blast, into the nearest entrance hall. At the same time, because of the violent displacement of air, the decrepit exterior walls of two old buildings standing next to the armored car, had collapsed dragging the residents with them and burying them to death.

Vittorio and his two companions had rushed through the courtyard where they had taken refuge and then, passing under a transversal arch of a wall, they had entered the court of another building. Here the young woman, who had already thrown away the MG machine gun at the start of the hasty retreat, had got rid of the tapes of ammunition she was wearing across her body and was about to toss away the bag with the radio as well, but Vittorio had taken it from her and, without a word, he had put it crossbody on the brigadier: "It could come in useful," he had said. Going warily from court to courtyard, from courtyard to air shaft, from air shaft to courtyard, the trio had been able to arrive in Via del Chiostro, where there were no Germans, a street which ended and still does today in Via Monteoliveto, where the girl lived. She had intended to take refuge precisely in her own home. The two policemen instead planned to get to Via Medina, which followed Via Monteoliveto beyond the intersection with Corso Umberto I, and return to Police Headquarters.

Vittorio had peeked out into Via Monteoliveto glancing left and right. With dismay, not far away to his right where the street met Corso Umberto I, he had seen a checkpoint of a platoon of Waffen[29] SS equipped with trucks, motorbikes and a 47 mm Panzerjäger self-propelled tank-destroyer cannon. This was an antiquated model resulting from the adaptation of an even more ancient panzer and a not very effective weapon towards modern tanks, but was deadly against non-armored vehicles and buildings. The Germans had lined up the vehicles behind each other along Corso Umberto I, where it intersected Via Medina and Via Monteoliveto. The purpose was evidently to prevent vehicles from entering the Corso or crossing it. Since the tank-destroyer cannon was facing Via Medina, Vittorio had assumed, correctly, that the blockade was to stop vehicles and men from leaving Police Headquarters. He had also imagined that, to hinder the passage of vehicles in both directions, there would have to be another place further beyond Police Headquarters itself, approximately at the point where the patriots' battle with the German grenadiers had taken place.

So, crossing Corso Umberto I and joining his colleagues who were still in the office was not on the cards. It was now a matter of everyone sheltering in the girl's house. Since the brigadier was in uniform, D'Aiazzo had thought it best, before the trio arrived in sight on Via Monteoliveto and perhaps be noticed by the Germans, to give his employee the jacket of his own gray lanital suit[30]. In that way, he could slip it over his own jacket, hiding it as best it could and covering the bag with the radio that was hanging over the non-commissioned officer's abdomen. Which is what they did. Marino had also hidden his military cap on

---

[29] The combat departments of the SS.

[30] Home-produced fiber replacing wool, deriving from milk casein which in Italy, before the war, was produced in surplus.

his chest, over the uniform jacket and under the suit jacket before buttoning it.

The girl's house stood to the left of Via del Chiostro on the same side of Via Monteoliveto where the other exited. One at a time about thirty yards from each other, the threesome had moved, with the young woman in front, the brigadier behind her and the Deputy Commissioner last. As he had advised, they had walked slowly and, although the Nazis had seen them at the checkpoint, which was not safe, they had certainly aroused no suspicions since no German had left the intersection to come and check their documents.

It was a small building with only two apartments, one above each other, the most spacious of which was on the first floor with ceilings ten feet high, while the other, where the young woman lived with her parents, was a mezzanine with eight feet ceilings; it overlooked a warehouse on the ground floor that opened onto Via Monteoliveto through a small door to the left of the front door of the building as you entered, and even further left, a driveway which was closed at that moment by a shutter. The house was owned by a peddler of fruit and vegetables who lived on the first floor and used the warehouse for his business, while the mezzanine was rented to the young woman's family.

The girl had opened the front door and entered the small atrium of the building, which had a musty smell, leaving the door pulled to and waiting for her companions. Some fresh air had come in through the crack. One by one the two men had come inside. Vittorio had pulled the door shut behind him and with the young woman in the lead, the group had immediately gone up the half flight of stairs that led to the mezzanine.

According to the nameplate beside the door of the apartment, the family's name was Scognamiglio.

"You're called Scognamiglio and then ...?" Vittorio had asked the young woman.

"Mariapia."

"Nice to meet you, Mariapia," he had smiled, and the worried expression he'd had on his face since he left the Police Headquarters disappeared. "I'm Deputy Commissioner Vittorio D'Aiazzo."

"... and I'm brigadier Bordin Marino," his aide had echoed, unlike his superior remaining very serious, almost condescending, evidently proud of his rank.

Although Mariapia's face no longer looked worried, it was not happy: her dark expression had changed into sadness.

She had opened the front door with her own key, which she kept in a hemp purse inside the single deep pocket of the mouse gray skirt woven from a home-made yarn[31], held up by a belt in black matte cuoital leather[32], with a blue-colored blouse tucked into it. The young woman was wearing gray lanital socks on her feet inside two black coriacel boots[33] with black rubber soles which the craftsman had made from old car tires.

As the two policemen had observed, the apartment consisted of three rooms and a corridor about eight feet wide, which ran along the entire length of the accommodation and ended at a small window without shutters. The three rooms were all to the left as you entered, and at that moment the doors were closed but, as from the position, it would seem they overlooked Via Monteoliveto. On the right when you came in, there was a balcony that flanked the corridor and overlooked and area of vegetable gardens as wide as the building and three times as deep, with a few sparse apple trees and plum trees, dense vegetable seedlings and three short parallel rows of vines: the peddlar owned that piece of too. At one end of the balcony, to the left as you went outside through the single French door in the center of the corridor, there was a wooden hut that, as guests had guessed, housed the domestic toilet.

They coud hear the sound of someone moving around in the room next to the entrance, which would turn out to be a kitchen with dining room.

"Who's in there?" Vittorio had asked the young woman.

Without answering him, Mariapia had opened the door just a little and had slipped into the room, closing it behind her. Some incomprehensible discussion was heard, then the door had opened

---

[31] Autarkic fiber of the fascist period similar to cotton obtained from flakes of hemp and broom.

[32] The cuoital was an autarkic substitute for real leather, and was manufactured with a mixture of brittle and vulcanized leather waste.

[33] Autarkic competitor of the cuoital based on vegetable fibers, glues and leather waste.

again, completely this time, and the girl had come out followed by her parents.

The father, Antonio Scognamiglio, had come towards the guests frowing in apprehension, his eyes looking at Bordin's boots and his trousers with the obvious fuchsia-colored strip down the side. The manifest discomfort of the man of the house was accentuated when, a moment later, the brigadier had taken off D'Aiazzo's jacket to return it to the owner, thus displaying the rank sewn on the sleeves of his jacket. Nevertheless, Mariapia's father was essentially an honest man. His distrust had not been caused by having something to hide from the law, but by the fact that was rooted in him since he was a child, something usual with the Neapolitan common people, a sense of great prudence, not to say distrust, towards the authorities big and small, transmitted from generation to generation in the atavistic memory of being bullied by the *Birri*[34] and other public officials of the Bourbon kings.

The man was very small, a couple of inches shorter than Vittorio who was not tall. He had calloused hands, was thin like Mariapia and like her he had thick hair, once corvine like his daughter's but now white, despite being only forty-eight years old. His wrinkled face contributed to making him look older just as sailors and fishermen do after years at sea and the continuous exposure to the sun and salt air; and in fact he had performed the valued profession of head fisherman on ocean-going vessels, which was still indicated on his identity card. Fourteen months earlier, however, as he had confided almost immediately to his guests to justify his being at home, he had lost his job after more than three decades on the same fishing boat, first as an apprentice, then as a finished fisherman and, finally, as a fishing master.

He had told them that he had lost it dramatically, in July 1942, when the vessel sank after being hit by a bomb from an English navy fighter-bomber De Havilland Sea Mosquito. The stylized profile, seen from below, was very well known to Italian sailors because it was posted in the ports. Antonio had been the only survivor of the slaughter because, being a good swimmer, he had thrown himself into the water as soon as he had spotted the enemy silhouette descending on the fishing boat. He had been picked up by a destroyer of the Italian Regia Marina, en route to the port of Naples, which fortunately had been passing through the

---

[34] (t/n – guards)

area where the boat sank just ten hours later. It was still daytime, and with some more luck, the sharp eye of a first class[35] sailor was standing watch and had seen the fisherman clinging to a plank of the hull of the fishing boat blown up by the bomb.

Good too, in the bad situation, had been the fact that it was summer, with sea water at bearable temperatures, and that the sinking had occurred at dawn, so the ten hours in the water had all been in daylight. After that, Antonio had got by, like many of his countrymen, with work he picked up day by day usually in the port as a docker, but only until the port facilities, already damaged by the Anglo-American bombings, were destroyed by the occupying Germans and civilians had been banned from going any closer to the sea than than 300 yards.

Unlike her sullen husband, Mariapia's mother, Concetta, had welcomed the two guests with a smile, accustomed as she was to dealing with the public for thirty years as an employee of a Lotto botega. That Monday morning, however, when she had showed up at work, she had found the place locked and a sign on the door saying *Closed for bereavement*; so, whether it was a matter of real grief or prudence in anticipation of turmoil in the streets, which they had been expecting for a few days now, Concetta had returned home, which was not far from the Lotto bodega as it was on Corso Umberto I fifty yards to the right of Via Monteoliveto.

She had had no trouble either going or returning because, luckily for her, the Waffen SS had arrived to set up the checkpoint about ten minutes after she returned. Unlike her short husband and daughter, the woman was five feet six tall, a remarkable stature in those times compared to the average population of both sexes in Campania whose ancestors had endured hunger, as too quite a number of their great-grandchildren had suffered prior to the conflict and almost everyone after its outbreak. Concetta however, despite the starving war, was an obese woman. Going by her fine features and big eyes that stood out beautifully in her face which was deformed by fat, she must have been an attractive young woman; but now she looked older than her forty-four years and not only because of the flab, which wobbled under her chin even if she just moved, but because she had lost all the incisors and the two lower canines, as well as four not visible molars, teeth that she had

---

[35] Sailor chosen.

lost before reaching forty by dint of gorging on candy and chocolates, when sugar and sweets were not almost unobtainable as they were after the beginning of the conflict.

But since the ration book – not that it was much of a deprivation – concerned only sugar, pasta, bread, flour, milk, butter, lard, oil and meat, foodstuffs sold by law in very limited quantities at political prices, she made up for the lack of candy by eating fruit, especially grapes and figs when they were in season. She bought them from the greengrocer her landlord, and generously drank sweet wine thanks to the abundant viticultural production, and therefore oenological, not only in the area but in many other parts of Italy, a Mediterranean nation which, at that time, was mainly agricultural, and as a result the sale of fruit and wine had not been subjected to rationing.

Concetta Scognamiglio was born with the widespread surname Esposito, into the relatively well-off family of a pizza maker who owned a place frequented by sailors and fishermen, which camorristi had devastated and burned down some years later because their expecations for compensation for their so-called *protection* had not been met. Thus the father had been forced into becoming a pizza maker for others, the mother to sewing and ironing and cleaning other people's floors, the twelve-year-old son to work as a kitchen hand in trattorias. The eldest daughter, Concetta, who was then fourteen years old, had been lucky enough to find a job in the Lotto bodega, thanks to a relative of the owner who was a friend of her father's.

This kind of employment was highly regarded in the working-class environment, systematic players of the 90 numbers, because the person who was behind the cash register not only took the money, but had to know the *Scienza della Smorfia*[36] to be able to give advice on dreams and numbers. The *importance* of her work had provoked the ferocious defamation of two awkward spinster sisters towards the young girl. Uselessly lusting inside and elsewhere for a male, they had whispered between themselves, and had immediately spread to other ears, that *chilla pezzènte senza santi 'n Ciélo*[37] had only been hired because *without doubt!* she had agreed to do *'e schifezze c'o prencepàle*[38], an elderly widower

---

[36] (t/n – the science of numbers)

[37] (t/n – that wretch who had no saints in heaven)

[38] (t/n – dirty things with the owner)

reputed as a satyr. Those harpies were very sure of it, even if they had not personally seen copulations or any lascivious things between the old man and the young girl. It was definitely a slander, since the elderly owner had died just three months after hiring Concetta, and because the betting shop was being managed by a woman, the girl had continued to work there, appreciated by the new manager for her good work. And yet the rumor had not stopped, indeed it had been stoked by the adjunct that *o' vecchio puórco*[39] had died because he had been overexcited by *chilla purcellazza*[40].

Luckily the slanderous rumor had never reached either the person concerned or her vindictive father nor, later, her sanguine husband; and in fact the bitches in heat, if they had not been fools, should have realized it themselves, finally, after the marriage of Antonio and Concetta, because in those times the premarital virginity of the bride was still highly appreciated by all. Given that the new husband had not kicked up a ruckus on the wedding night, he must have found the bride just as her mother had brought her into the world.

Mariapia also contributed regularly to the household budget as a saleswoman, the only one, at the bazaar with tobacco shop belonging to a first cousin of her father, Giuseppe Scognamiglio known as Peppino and, by some, Don Peppino. Unlike Concetta, even though her daughter had quickly become employed, no malicious words had been said about her daughter, perhaps because she was a distant relative of the owner, but certainly for two other excellent reasons: because Mariapia had such a notoriously bad temper that no gossip would ever have dared to talk badly about her, afraid of being on the receiving end of multiple slaps in the face and a flurry of kicks in the butt; and above all, because the tobacconist was reputed to be linked to the camorra.

By now the parents considered Mariapia their only descendant, even though they'd had the joy of two other children, Gennaro, the eldest, and Giuseppe, one year younger than Mariapia. Both, however, had been killed in battle or, to be precise, it was certain for the older of the two, a sailor who died at sea in 1941 in the sinking of his ship, and almost certain for the younger,

---

[39] (t/n -the old pig)

[40] (t/n – that little whore).

because the Ministry of War had let the family know at the time that Giuseppe, a paratrooper fighting on the Libyan-Egyptian front, had gone missing in combat. Having received no news from the Red Cross that he had been taken prisoner, parents and sister were convinced that he had been killed, and since the body had not been found, they had assumed that their poor loved one had been torn to pieces and rendered unrecognizable by the explosion of a projectile.

The names of the two sons were usual in the Esposito and Scognamiglio families, handed down from ascendant to descendant: Gennaro had come from a maternal ancestor, Giuseppe from a paternal one, and not by chance the father's cousin also had the name Giuseppe, like an ancestor of the Scognamiglio. Gennaro, two years older than his sister, had become a fisherman like his father at just twelve years old, on another ocean-going fishing boat but owned by the same person, He had attended school only until the third grade and had repeated it a second time without passing the test for admission into the fourth, as at that time the course was divided into a three-year and a two-year period with examination at the end of the first primary cycle.

In 1937 he was conscripted into the Regia Marina as a second-class ordinary[41] and, not long after his discharge, he had been recalled to arms at the beginning of hostilities. On March 28, 1941 he had ended up torn to pieces by a British broadside on the deck of the cruiser where he served as a gunman, during the naval battle at Cape Matapan between the Italian fleet and the *Mediterranean fleet*, Anglo-Australian, which was superior not only because of the thicker armor of the battleships, but because it was equipped with radar and a Navy airforce. Unlike Gennaro, young Giuseppe had been a good scholar and, being much more intelligent, he had managed to graduate as a surveyor thanks to his personal ambition, his own effort and the financial support of his father and mother who, having discovered his intelligence, had not sent him to work as a teenager.

In June 1940, when Italy had only just entered the war, he had graduated with a really great average in those times of very tight evaluations: all 7 and 8. Thanks to his surveyor's diploma, knowing that he was close to beiing drafted, the young man had applied for admission to a school for trainee reserve officers and

---

[41] Simple sailor.

had been accepted. Promoted to aspiring officer at the end of the course, after three months of service in a regiment of the Engineers he had been elevated to second lieutenant, as per regulations, and had asked to attend the Parachute Training Center of Tarquinia with that rank, having considered the extra money paid to those specialists. After completing the second military school, he had been incorporated into the 185th Folgore Parachute Division, formed specifically for the occupation of the island of Malta but, as the events of war unfolded, it had been senselessly used from July 1942 as a simple infantry unit in North Africa. In the Libyan-Egyptian desert Giuseppe, who had risen to the rank of lieutenant, had been lost during the Second Battle of El Alamein fought between the Italian-German and British troops.

Concetta had transformed the bedroom shared by the two boys into a domestic chapel, filled with candles and statuettes of the Madonna, San Gennaro and other illustrious saints, and photos of the two *guaglio'* [42]. There were very few snapshots, but were printed in many copies put everywhere, even on the two beds. The mother kept the room locked and entered it only to dust every day and pray there early in the morning and after dinner, sometimes with her husband who, although not being a religious man, whispered something and grumbled something else in memory of the two, independentaly from her Hail Marys and the Eternal Rests. The daughter never went in there, she did pray for her brothers' eternal peace, but alone and mentally when it came spontaneously to her.

Mariapia, not ugly, not beautiful, despite being of petite build overflowed with goodwill and vigor and had been – but no longer for the reason that will be discovered – a cheerful and satisfied girl. As an independent spirit, it had not been unusual for her to be absent from home without telling her parents, at the beginning of the war only on holidays and during the day. Until the conflict, she would be away until the first hours of darkness when there were festivals, first the one in Piedigrotta, the night between September 7 and 8 and for San Gennaro on the 19th of the same month. Those freedoms of hers had been fostered by her amazement at the beauty of the world and by the spirit of discovery that filled the young woman's soul. In essence, they consisted of

---

[42] (t/n – young men)

wandering around Naples alone discovering fresh things and meeting new people.

She had never stayed out for reprehensible reasons and not only from the point of view of the law but, considering the narrow mentality of those years for which even a kiss on the mouth was a sin, not for amorous reasons either; on the contrary, she had not had a single romantic relationship, feeling in her heart that only the *right man* would make her fall in love and take her to the altar. She was certain that when she had met *her man* she would have had no doubts and it would have been love forever: since adolescence, she had been immersed, in substance, in that feeling that is improperly called romantic, common to the young girls of yesteryear.

Mariapia's parents had not hidden from Vittorio and Marino that their daughter had not returned home at the usual time, around 7.00 pm, on the evening of September 26, Sunday, when the tobacconist had been open for the biweekly festive shift to which the State monopoly shops were obliged, and not even after the curfew of 9.00 pm, with her bed intact in the dining room kitchen where she still slept despite the fact that her brothers were no longer there. In the beginning Antonio and Concetta had thought that her failure to return at the usual time was due to working longer and had not worried about it too much. They had started worry only around 8.30 pm. At the curfew, later, they had begun to seriously fear some tragedy.

Being officially a fisherman, her father was among the people authorized to circulate during curfew hours, given that the night trawlers went out and returned before dawn. Since after September 8 it had been forbidden for anyone to go near the shore, not only inside the port but anywhere in the city, the owners had pulled up their boats on the beaches outside Naples. From there they could still legally go to sea. It was their fish that arrived in the city's markets.

On the evening of September 26 therefore, shortly after 9.00 pm, Antonio had decided to go out and go to his cousin's nearby tobacconist shop, hoping to find his daughter there or, if not, to at least have news of her from his relative who lived behind the shop. With the identity card that still declared him a fisherman in his pocket, the parent had gone to the store and had knocked on the middle shutter, the front door, of the three in front of the large outlet covering the windows. Nothing, silence and no light at all in the store. Back home, he had continued to wait with his wife, in the hope that his daughter would arrive at any moment.

At about 10.00 pm the couple had gone to bed with the intention of staying awake, but around midnight, first the husband and then the wife had unwillingly succumbed to sleep. She was the first to wake around 7.30 in the morning and when she saw that her daughter had not returned at all, she had shaken Antonio very agitated. Just to put something hot in the stomach, they had thrown down *'a schifezza*, as Naples called the broth of chicory which was a substitute *d'o café*, which Concetta prepared with the Neapolitan coffee machine. They had immediately started discussing whether to go out and look for their daughter and ask around with acquaintances, starting with the relative Peppino, or whether, apart from the cousin that they still had to ask, to let it go, knowing full well that it would be the classic search for the needle in the haystack. Moreover, feeling that they would risk their lives going around Naples, not only because of the rumor of impending disorders that had been circulating in the streets and alleys for days, but above all because, around 8.00 am that morning, they had heard rifle shots and volleys of assault rifles and machine gun coming from not far away.

The couple could not know that it was the clash on Via Medina in which Mariapia was taking part. Although the shots had continued to echo, at a certain point Concetta had decided to go out to work afraid that, otherwise, she would lose her job; but she intended, as she had told her husband to reassure him, to move *cuòncio cuòncio assaje*[43]; and since she had to go past the cousin's tobacco shop, she would ask him herself for news of Mariapia. She had found the shop locked, as indeed were many others that morning. She had knocked hard on the shutter of the entry for a long time and then on the one over the two windows, calling out so he could recognize her voice. But no one had opened up to her or, at least, no one had answered her. She had then asked the elderly owner of the place next door, a bicycle repair workshop, Gennarino Appalle who was the only other resident of the low building where the two businesses were located. The technician had opened the door a little when he heard the knock, and when Concetta asked about Mariapia he had reminded the woman that it was a Monday and that, therefore, the day before was a Sunday,

---

[43] Very cautiously.

sissignora, and he had been closed *you understand*. Worried, the mother had gone on towards the Lotto bodega feeling sorely disappointed and when she found it locked had returned home.

When the couple had finished reporting this to the two policemen reliving all the past hours of anguish, which had been evident from their agitated gestures, the valves of emotion had finally opened and they had begun to reproach their daughter harshly:

Antonio had started dramatically: "*Mariapi', tu si' sèmpe 'a dannazione nuósta a fa' sèmpe senza cunzìglio quanto vvuoi tu! Uuuh! Ooh! uh!*"[44]

The mother had followed in a heated tragic tone: "*Uhe', Mariapi', tu accidi 'a màmma tua 'e crepaccore!*" [45] and with such a sorrowful expression on her face that, in comparison, the classic mask of tragedy was all merriment. Unfortunately for the good effect the woman had wanted, her mournful grimace had been rather spoiled by the notable flaccid double chin she had, which had trembled like a pudding, that calorie bomb with cream that she would have so willingly prepared and eaten for breakfast, if only she could find plenty of sugar, cream and eggs somewhere.

Mariapia was not as young as she appeared because of her still almost childish features, her five feet two and a skinny little body: she was the same age as Vittorio, and had turned twentyfour on February 12. So she didn't take it in the least, her cheeks had gone red and she had replied sharply: "Mammà, papà, I have been an adult for a long time! I am a woman and you have to respect me!" She had spoken in Italian so her two companions in ams would understand too. Vittorio would actually have understood anyway, as he knew Neapolitan which, at that time, even the bourgeoisie used to speak at home and, when necessary, with strangers. Not Marino Bordin though, despite having been stationed in Naples for a couple of years, because his father was Venetian and his mother had grown up in Venice.

The young woman, however, expressed herself preferably in Italian even outside the home, and did so correctly: she was more educated than her parents and intelligent like her younger brother. After elementary school she had successfully attended a

---

[44] (t/n - Mariapia, you are always our damnation always doing whatever you like without asking pout advice. Uuuh!Uuh! Uh!)

[45] (t/n – Oh Mariapia, you'll make your mother die of a broken heart)

three-year complementary school for introduction to commercial work, and had obtained her diploma with honors. It had also been because of that small qualification that she had been taken on in the tobacconist shop belonging to her father's relative.

Chapter 7

Opening a parenthesis, let's get to know the person and the environment of the cousin Peppino Scognamiglio, not so much because he is related to Antonio and Mariapia, but because before long he will prove to be one of the fundamental characters of our story.

Giuseppe Scognamiglio, known as Peppino, was a very ugly fifty-year-old bachelor. He had been wearing a black mustache since he was a boy, which he tended to daily in front of the mirror with scissors and a greasy pomade, and in his opinion it was a real beauty. To his great regret he had been completely devoid of hair from a young age. He had big flat feet that made his gait rather clumsy, even though they served to avoid military service for him. Right in the center of his ugly mug, below piggy bleary eyes[46] and above a mouth with almost non-existent lips and overlapping caffelatte-colored teeth, was an oversize flattened nose, not from nature but from the numerous punches he had received as a teenager in local brawls, in response to just as many beatings that he had given and usually won, muscular as he was.

At the front of his still robust figure, a disproportionate fat gut had been evident for years, the result of a lot of eating and above all drinking an excessive amount of alcohol, which was all the more obvious because he was small in stature, almost the same as his thin cousin, just a little taller. It was whispered that Peppino was not only a camorra facilitator, but that for decades he had been an active member of the most influential and largest crime syndicate of all Naples and province. Because of the trouble that the Esposito family had been subjected to at the hands of those delinquent groups, there was no love lost between the tobacconist and his acquired cousin. Rumors about him had arrived in the Lotto bodega years before, leaked by two regular players who had talked about him in front of her, perhaps without knowing that she was related to Peppino by marriage, or perhaps precisely because they did know.

––––––––––––––––––

[46]A tear secretion that, drying out, stops at the corners of the eyes and on the eyelashes.

It was not, however – if it matters to the reader – the rumor mongers who had attacked Concetta's good name behind her back in the past. Then again, despite the deep-rooted dislike for her acquired cousin, Concetta pretended to respect him when she met him in the street by chance, less infrequently in the shop where she bought salt[47] She exercised that centuries-old practical sense of a certain populace, Neapolitan and not, who in exchange for bread and perhaps pottage, was able to pretend she had forgotten past abuses, but in reality still held the memory warm in her bosom.

What is certain is that the woman did not disdain the salary that her daughter received from her relative at the end of each week, which she handed to the family almost entirely. Unlike the past gossip about Concetta, popular opinion was right when it came to Peppino: he had made money at a younger age, serving in the most important of the camorra clans that divvied up Naples and its surroundings, sometimes fighting against each other to acquire more territories in those years when the old camorra was not yet organized. For those good people, and here by good we mean, of course, violent and overbearing according to the classic etymon, he had carried out activities contrary to the law, such as beating and scarring people, inducing beautiful poor girls to prostitution with flattery or beatings, in order to exploit their degradation, throwing rotten dog dung and old horse piss in vats and barrels of wine and oil manufacturers and merchants reluctant to pay *protection money*, setting fire to the shops of traders of other kinds equally reluctant to let money to be extorted from them.

Who knows, perhaps he was one of the young camorra workers who had set fire to Mariapia's maternal grandfather's pizzeria during the night; but if he hadn't been he was, in a certain way, responsible because he had burned others. Peppino had never killed, however, which would be rather strange nowadays but not for the old camorra, which has long since disappeared, almost something else compared to the current homonymous consortery, which is to say, yes, is involved in crimes of burning down, beating, scarring, raping, sex pimping, smuggling and, during the war, wholesale black marketer, but is exceptionally murderous, even if only out of caution and not for lightness of spirit.

---

[47] (t/n – The Italian state monopoly for tobacco also held the monopoly on salt which was sold by tobacconists)

At the end of 1936 the scoundrel had asked his boss if he could retire because of permanent damage to one hand which had happened during a fight between gangs, and prevented him from still handing out slaps and punches with his left, and also because of another illness, that he had been careful not to tell him about though: a now chronic diarrhoeal colitis, perhaps due to the tension of the continual violent lifesyle. It was semi-disabling disease because it caused him, between powerful stomach aches, to frequently need move his bowels. Who knows if it would have given him a bit of consolation to know that a scoundrel enormously greater than him, suffered from the same indisposition, albeit attenuated by medical luminaries with papaverine and various astringents, an international bloodspiller named Adolf Hitler.

Since it seems that you can only leave organized crime in a coffin, Peppino's boss had indeed given him the authorization to retire because of the injured hand, but only in a limited way, in the sense that he was to remain available for favors. With the money earned from crime for thirty years, systematically accumulated on a postal book with a spirit of social security that would have done honor to an honest family man, in 1937 Peppino Scognamiglio had purchased the tobacconist shop-emporium. Since then he had only provided services for his boss that did not involve the personal use of violence and physical risks, firstly by allowing the gang to hide illegally trafficked goods in his large basement. Peppino had bought not only the license but also the premises, becoming a co-resident with the bike repairer Gennarino Appalle, who had owned his own laboratory since the beginning of the '30s.

To better understand, further on, certain tragic developments in our story, it is good to know, even at this stage, some things about the low building and its appurtenances, in which they will manifest themselves:

The building had been built by a merchant in the early '900s to be used as an emporium-tobacconist, as it had remained, and a storage facility for wagons which its second owner, the artisan, had transformed into his cycle repairs workshop in 1931. It had a courtyard at the back and sat on top of a large cellar, the courtyard owned by both residents in proportion to their respective thousandths, the basement which spread out under the entire building, belonging only to Peppino. At the outbreak of the war he had built labyrinthine zigzag walls in reinforced concrete, like in the anti-aircraft shelters, which formed corridors that converged in the center like a kind of spiral so that, should a bomb explode nearby, the violent displacement of air would be broken by the elbows of the corridors and would not damage the dubious goods that the owner stored in the internal area. And, more importantly, so that he could use the heart of the cellar himself as an anti-aircraft shelter.

The basement was accessed by a solid wood door which had its base ten feet below the surface, at the end of a staircase that descended about twentyfive feet from the low-standing building starting in the courtyard, in front of the middle of Peppino's house. The courtyard was a square shape: on the sides at the bottom of it and to the right as you entered it was surrounded by a high corner fence kin wood, which had arrived after a wrought iron gate had ended among requisitions for wartime purposes. On the side to the left as you entered, the property abutted one of the perimeter walls of a four-storey residential building, in the fascist style of the 30s, where there was a small lodging facing onto the street, owned by Gennarino Appalle, who lived there with his wife.

The wall of the building that overlooked the courtyard of the two businesses, and also the one opposite on a piece of land kept as a vegetable garden, had no openings. Perhaps there had been a thought of constructing other buildings next to it in the future on the vegetable garden on one side and the area of the low building and its courtyard on the other, if the owners had wanted to sell. Keep in mind, for the purposes of our story, that it was therefore not possible to look out of the building onto the neighboring courtyard and see any movements of people and vehicles on it. A driveway entered the couryard from the street and ran along the length of the low building. The owners of the neighboring building did not have permission to access this passageway, as they did not have rights to the same courtyard, apart of course from Appalle who was the co-owner; and on the other hand, their building had its own courtyard at the back, used mostly to dry clothes, which was accessed by a rear door.

Looking at Via Monteoliveto from the two buildings, they were close to the intersection with Corso Umberto I on the left and to Mariapia's home on the right, on the same street but on the other side. Despite being a wealthy person, Peppino Scognamiglio had chosen to live at the back of the tobacconist shop, both for convenience and to save money. It was divided into three rooms: a kitchen that opened onto the courtyard through a glass door and was connected to the shop by a internal passage which, during working hours, was covered by a sliding curtain of reddish-purple velvet. To the side of the kitchen, on the left with your back to the courtyard, there were two rooms one behind the other, the closest a dining-sitting room, the other a bedroom. They received daylight from as many windows onto the courtyard. The three rooms were connected with two doors in the middle of the wall, with no need to access the corridor.

The latrine was outside the building: since in our story it will prove to be particularly important with accumulating disasters, let's explore it quickly holding our noses. It was a shed six foot square built with wooden planks. It had a simple hole on the floor, above a secondary sewerage connection under the courtyard that joined a major sewer that ran under via Monteoliveto. It stood six yards from the low building, between Peppino's apartment and Gennarino's workshop. It had no running water, unless a tap on the wall with a long rubber hose attached could be considered such, and was used to clean the inside of the small room after each use. Since Gennarino also used the service and the water came from the Peppino's water system, he charged the co-user a monthly sum for using it, which would have been correct if the amount had not been exorbitant, considering that the bicycle repairer used it modestly only on weekdays, and the abnormal use by the diarrhoeal tobacconist, seven days out of seven.

Even though he harbored a grudge against that local despot who treated him with arrogance and bad manners, Gennarino Appalle had resigned himself to paying it for the sake of a peaceful life. There was no electric lighting in the latrine, and a candle was a poor substitute. Without that it would be hard to see the dung hole at night. The candle was stuck in a white candlestick resting on the ground in a corner of the shed, to the left of the door entering, with a box of wax matches next to it. When the candle was lit, the light filtered between the poorly connected wooden planks of the toilet, meaning that anyone outside it at night would realize that the poky little room was occupied at that moment.

Even this apparently superfluous observation has not been peregrine, as will be perfectly clear later.

Gennarino Appalle's cycle repair workshop was a rectangular room just over twelve feet wide and about fifty feet long, which was the same depth as the low building. Before the new owner had purchased it, two carts and a buggy lined up one behind the other had been kept there. At the back, the workshop gave onto the courtyard through a large opening with a shutter, originally made for the vehicles to pass through and that the craftsman had not felt needed to be modified. At the front the workshop opened onto Via Monteoliveto with a double door in wood, each side with a transparent glass window of twentyfour inches square and fortyseven inches from the ground: even with the door closed from the inside, and this too will be important in our story, you could see to the opposite side. What's more, from April to early October, the owner kept the door wide open, except on rainy days .

Chapter 8

It was now almost 10.00 in the morning. Concetta, now calm at last, had asked her daughter, in tight dialect: "... and do you want to tell us now, mamma's heart, *che facisti da' seràta d'ajère* [48]?"

Dad Antonio had liked the question and had given a sign of that with a nod, but moderating his assent with a sort of dissatisfied grunt, because of that *mamma's heart* which had spontaneously come from his wife's lips; she had followed, some in Italian and a bit in jargon: "... and tell us also what *facisti (tn - what you were doing).*"

The young woman had become angry: "*Lu vulite capi'* " [49], had escaped her in dialect, but returning to Italian she continued, "that I am a woman and not a child?!"

Vittorio had thought it better not to remain silent: "Mariapia, your parents have the right to know, don't they?"

"Public Security order?" she had joked without smiling; then: "Okay, at this point the uprising is no longer a secret: our cousin was storing weapons to be used against the Germ ..."

"... that camorrista?!" the mother had interrupted her impulsively.

"Not for idealism: he had received a payment of 2000 lire."

"Ah!" was all the mother had said in comment.

"Last night Peppino sent a group of patriots to his cellar, to collect those weapons. I was there and I watched everything. Then I fought too, as the Commissioner knows very well."

"Yes," Vittorio had confirmed, "and we saved her life with one of our armored cars."

"Thank Heaven most holy!" had come from her mother; a moment later she had also comprehended the merit of the two human saviors: "... and thanks to you, very, very much!" Then, eager to understand better, she asked Mariapia: "*Addò stàn, mo', li cumpàgni tui*[50]?"

"All killed, mamma."

---

[48] What you've been doing since last night.

[49] (t/n – when will you understand)

[50] Where are your companions now?

"Aaah!" Concetta had exhaled, then remained for a good second with her mouth open.

The father, for his part, had said in an approximate Italian hoping to be understood by both policemen: "*Primma 'e tutto* I too thank the Commissioner and the Brigadier for saving you. But you, Mariapi', you must explain finally, well, well, well, why you were there being *'a garibaldina* instead of coming home."

"Yes, well you see... well, it went like this: last night it was about ten minutes before closing time at the shop when ..."

"... precisely?" Vittorio had stopped her.

"It was 7:20 pm, okay? there were still ten minutes left, right? and by law all shops must close at 7:30 pm, no?"

He had agreed: "Yes, apart from the pharmacies on duty ... okay, all right Mariapia, go on."

"Oh, good, because if you all start talking... I was about to say that, ten minutes earlier, the cousin went out on the street and lowered the shutters himself, but he closede the one at the entrance only halfway, then he came back and told me to take off my apron and go home passing under the shutter."

Her mother had tried to intervene "... *e avevi 'a veni' stantemènte, comme o' viento! e nun...*[51]"

"...Let her finish, *donna Conce'* ", the Deputy Commissioner had stopped her: "Mariapia, tell me if you're the one who usually closes."

"Yes, that's what the cousin wants."

"What do you do to be precise?"

"To be precise, when it's 7.30 pm and if there are no customers, I take off my apron, go out, pull down the shutters and lock them, go back via the driveway in the courtyard, the cousin opens the door of the house at the back, I give him the keys and at that point I leave through the driveway again: there is no need for a key from the inside, the gate opens with a handle, then I pull it behind me."

"Last night?"

"I was about to leave going under the shutter, when a young man came into the store and we almost banged our heads. I would find out later, from the man himself, that his name is Cesare Nemo. The cousin must have expected him because they greeted each other with a *ciao*. I think he had arrived before I'd left, by mistake,

---

[51] ... and you had to come instantly, like the wind! and not...

because I saw an annoyed look on my relative's face, even though he made no comment and just told the young man to go around the back. He more or less gave me an order: *Now close up, leave the keys on the ground at the back door in the courtyard, knock and leave, you don't need to wait for me to open.* Obviously I was curious..."

"... and obviously, instead of going to close up, you eavesdropped," Vittorio had insinuated slyly.

She must not have grasped the irony for she had replied seriously: "Yes. The two of them were talking in a low voice, but not low enough that I couldn't make out what they were saying, from behind a curtain across the passage between the shop and the back. The young man told the cousin that he would stay with him until 5.00 am, then he would go to the gate of the driveway, open it and leave it half-closed. Then he would stay there as a lookout, he would direct a group of patriots a few at a time and an American captain, a certain Jones, to the courtyard as they came to collect the military weapons hidden in the cellar. He said those men would arrive on foot one at a time, so they could hide from the patrols along the way more easily. For his part the cousin would send them down to the cellar a few at a time and they would arm themselves. Then the American would give him some gold for the camorra, and for me that was a confirmation of the rumors that are going around about out relative."

"*Cumme vulévasi dimustra' e cumme già era canósciuto, Peppi' è membro da' suggità*[52]" had come from dad Antonio,

"*'Mmiezo a chilla gente d'a camorra, Peppi' sta nninto bbuono, bbuono*[53]", Concetta had added.

Vittorio had ignored the comments and, intrigued by that relationship between the insurgents and the camorra, had asked Mariapia: "Did that Nemo say how the camorra had got involved with the weapons?"

"Yes, the American army had parachuted them onto a plain near Naples and some camorristi had taken them from there under the direct control of some anti-Nazis, as he called them yesterday. They had transported them on trucks and hidden them in seven different places in the city, including Peppino's cellar. All this had

---

[52] Just goes to show as we already knew, Peppino is a member of the society (Camorra).

[53] Among those people of the Camorra, Peppino fits in well, very well.

happened a couple of days earlier, folllowing a previous agreement made with the U.S. army."

"Did that Nemo also talk to Peppino about what was to follow? I mean what would happen after the patriots went down to the cellar?"

"Yes. They would wait until 6.00 am. A lorry would arrive to pick them up at that hour. The young man discovered me just after saying that, perhaps because the curtain moved: he pushed it aside and saw me, then pulled me by the arm into the kitchen and made me a sign to be silent, putting a finger straight in front of my nose staring straight at me, eye to eye, like a threat. The cousin went into the shop and I heard him pulling down the shutter at the entrance. Meanwhile, the man told me not to be afraid, because he was a king's officer, a lieutenant of the Folgore paratroopers[54] to be precise ..."

"... of the Folgore?!" Concetta had exclaimed getting excited, "but then maybe he knows something about your brother! You didn't ask him anything about Giuseppe?!"

"N... no, mamma."

"Mariapiaaa!"

The husband had called his wife to order, calmly: "*Méttete 'o core 'n pace, Cuncetti', Giuse' è muorto cumme Gennari'.*"[55]

A tear had appeared in her right eye, just one, which had run down her cheek and fallen on the floor and, a moment later, she had lowered her head staring at the floor, in reality looking beyond, far away, to Africa.

Overcoming pity, Vittorio had urged Mariapia: "Go on."

"As my cousin was returning from the courtyard, Lieutenant Nemo asked me what I intended to do, since there was no way I could go home until after 6.00 am; and without waiting for an answer he asked me whether I'd rather join him and his men, instead of being bound and gagged and locked in the cellar. I immediately said yes."

Vittorio had reflected for a few seconds, then: "I find it strange that they didn't wait until you'd left, before starting to talk freely about such delicate things: I feel it would have been more logical for your relative to tell you to leave and close the shop

---

[54] (t/n – the 'Thunderbolt' Paratroopers Division "Folgore" was a Parachute division of the Royal Italian Army during World War II)

[55] (t/n – Put your heart at peace Concetta, Giuseppe is dead like Gennaro)

himself after you'd gone, making the guest wait in the back; and it was only at that point that the two had started to chat."

Mamma Concetta had suggested: "They say that the cousin is not very intelligent and I think so too." So as to be understood by the Venetian Bordin as well, she had intentionally spoken in Italian, which she knew well enough, having learned it by working for decades in contact with the most heterogeneous public, including certain *dotto'* and *professo'* no less keen than the ordinary people to play the 90 numbers.

"This would explain things as far as your cousin was concerned, but it is unlikely that an officer would be so careless: he should have asked your relative immediately to be prudent! Strange, really strange. Alright, then what happened, Mariapia?"

"Cousin made some dinner and we ate, then the lieutenant ordered us to go down to the cellar. It was the first time I had been down there. Peppino was very protective of it, and during the air raids I had to run to the shelter in Corso Umberto, while he went to shelter comfortably downstairs. When we went in, he took four candles from a box full of them lying on the ground next to the entrance, he kept two of them and handed the other two to that Nemo. They lit them, then the cousin went ahead and took us towards the central area where there were stacks of wide low boxes. He poured the melted wax from the candles onto the floor, then fixed them at a good distance from the boxes though because, as the officer said, it was not wise to put the flame too close, because of the gunpowder.

When he opened the packaging, and despite the poor light, I saw that there were bullets, rifles, hand grenades and other weapons, as well as radio transmitters. The lieutenant checked each piece and then told the cousin that everything was ready to be handed over to the patriots. He asked me if I had ever fired a weapon, and I said yes, in the Young Italians cadets with the model '91 short musket. Then he showed me a rifle called Garand and taught me its use practically, telling me that the sight is American style, not European like muskets are: he showed me how to take aim, then explained how to put on and remove the safety pin and also how to insert the packet of bullets, and told me that it is automatically expelled when its eight shots have been fired, and he told me that you have to pick it up and put it in your pocket so you can fill it again, and he showed me how to fill it..."

"... okay, but then?"

"Nothing, we went back into the house and the cousin set the alarm clock that he keeps in the kitchen for ten to five, then gave it to the lieutenant and went to the bedroom to rest. Nemo and I sat on a couple of armchairs in the dining room with the alarm clock beside us, but we didn't sleep. He stayed awake perhaps to watch me, and I simply because I couldn't get to sleep even though I kept my eyes closed. At one point I looked at the time and I saw that it was half past three and seeing me awake, he started talking to me in a low voice."

"What about?"

"A lot of things, for example he told me that we would have the chance to take weapons off the dead Germans and, above all, we would have to set our sights on the MG machine guns. He explained how they work in theory, then he pulled a sheet of paper out of his pocket that showed me the design of the whole weapon and its parts: and that was why this morning I put it on my shoulder, the MG."

"I see. Anything else?"

"He told me about the missions."

"More than one?"

"Yes, the unit that was about to arrive had been split up days before, by himself and the American, into two platoons with similar objectives; and last night Nemo assigned me to the group that was to operate on Via Medina, telling me that our mission would be the first in order of time. The other platoon had a much more important objective and was much more dangerous, taking the armory of Castel Sant'Elmo, thus it would be directly under the orders of Captain Jones and himself, whereas a non-commissioned officer would lead us."

"Did he tell you other things?"

"No, I finally fell asleep but only for a short time, he soon woke me up. At six a truck picked us all up..."

"... Peppino too?"

"No, he had nothing to do with it, he stayed. The truck crossed Corso Umberto I, slipped into your Via Medina, passed the Police Headquarters building, continued for a hundred yards and stopped. Our platoon got out. The truck continued on again with the other group which was composed of soldiers, unlike ours who were almost entirely civilians apart from two soldiers, a sergeant of the *bersaglieri*[56], who was in command, and the grenadier, the one you, Vittorio, later entrusted with the German grenade launcher."

"I see, and...?"

"... and we walked back, silently, for about eighty yards. We hid among the ruins of the two bombed houses that you know, and we would later shoot at the German column from there. Our aim was to prevent those soldiers from relieving their comrades on guard at the armory of Castel Sant'Elmo. And since they would be tired and sleepy, they would put up little resistance to the platoon led by Jones and Nemo. We stayed there lying in wait in the rubble for over an hour and a half, before the German column arrived around eight: a truly nerve-wracking wait, also because we had been ordered not to be seen by anyone, not even your cars or motorcycles leaving or returning to the barracks. Nemo had explained that precisely that position, even though it very close to you, was the best place to engage the enemy platoon along the way, thanks to the two bombed houses there and because the street narrowed because of rubble which had not been cleared, meaning that the German column would have to slow down."

"Do you know anything more about the other group's mission?"

"They had to take over the armory for a specific purpose: to appropriate certain chemical and biological weapons, as the two officers called them when they were talking about them on the truck before our group got off. I understood that they're of Italian manufacture but that the Germans took possession of them a couple of weeks ago, occupying Castel Sant'Elmo. The American said that studies in the chemical and biological field in our country had reached advanced levels already at the beginning of the last decade, and that Italian scientists had created weapons of that type, completely in step with similar American armaments and other major nations and, moreover, at a lower cost[57].

---

[56] (t/n – military unit of riflemen)

[57] For example, a poisonous gas had been extracted from the castor-oil plant based on ricin, an energetic natural cytotoxin of the seeds of the plant capable of causing the cell death of an organism, as had been proven on sheep and cattle: a deadly weapon almost as much as the more expensive German nerve gas Tabun, chemically *di-methyl-cyano-phosphate-di-ethyl/mono-ethyl-di-methyl-amino-cyano–phosphate*, also called Agent GA or Trilon 34, which had been, in order of time, the first nerve gas in the world, synthesized in 1934 by Hitler's scientists.

"He also said that despite massive uses before that[58], Italy had entered the war with one of the largest chemical and biological paraphernalia in the world and that those weapons were ammassed in various places in the country including here in Naples, precisely at Castel Sant'Elmo. The Anglo-Americans fear that they are being used by the Germans to contain their advance towards the city, and that's why their secret services have organized the mission to the castle. Just before I got out, I also heard that the platoon of Jones and Nemo must get inside Sant'Elmo from some underground streets, and maybe they're already inside now, then go up to the top floor where the corridor of the armory is and try to take out the guard: a very difficult undertaking, Jones stresed, even if our platoon in via Medina should be successful."

"Success achieved above all thanks to us and our armored car!" Brigadier Bordin who, until that moment, had only listened attentively, had hastened to brag.

"Uff," Vittorio had snorted not approving that remark.

---

[58] mamong the Italian bacteriological weapons had never been used, the gases yes, using them in the war of Abyssinia, not only on the battlefield but, ultra criminally, against the civilian population, including children and women of the villages. The gases had also been used in anti-guerrilla operations in Libya and finally in Spain in support of the troops of Generalissimo Franco.

Chapter 9

The Scognamiglio apartment had no telephone, as was common in social housing at that time, so it wasn't possible to call the Police Headquarters. To attempt a contact Vittorio had decided to use the small Handie-Talkie radio he had entrusted to Bordin. He asked him for it and tuned in to the standard wavelength of the Police patrol cars. That portable FM radio, made for the open field, had a range of action in the city of a few hundred yards at best, but the proximity of the Scognamiglio residence to the Public Security building and the semi-continuity of Via Medina with Via Monteoliveto meant it was quite likely that the waves reached the head office.

For about five minutes meanwhile, Chief Commissioner Pelluso, who had personally collected information for two hours and given orders over the air to those of his men who had gone out to fight, had left chair, headphone and microphone to a Deputy Commissioner, Attilio Badalamenti head of the *Thefts and Robberies section*, and had gone to stand in the middle of the radio room. He had taken a flat cardboard box of beloved Macedonia cigarettes from the right pocket of his trousers, opened it and lit one of them, filling the room with the sweetish fumes of those oval cigarettes.

Satisfied by the good dose of smoke of the tumorous red-hot dry herb, he had smoked almost all of it and was now crushing the butt that he had dropped on the floor, under his right foot, with additional *mantegazziana*[59] satisfaction, when Vittorio's radio call had arrived.

Fearing German or fascist interceptions, the Deputy Commissioner had considered it best not to provide his surname, nor to provide rank and qualification. He had only said: "Vittorio

---

[59] Paolo Mantegazza (1831 - 1910) had been a famous Darwinist anthropologist and physiologist whose name was and would remain known to the public, throughout the first half of the '900, especially for his popular treatise "The physiology of pleasure" related, in fact, to pleasures of all kinds, such as the pleasure, in his opinion, of planting a nail in the wood. From a more strictly scientific point of view he was interested in the most diverse types of drugs by publishing the treatise "Pictures of human nature. Parties and intoxications", in which he collected what was known in his time about psychoactive drugs.

with assistant calling Police Headquarters Command, Vittorio with assistant calling Police Headquarters Command, over."

The voice of deputy commission Badalementi had arrived clearly to him, although not very strongly even if D'Aiazzo had gone to stand at the open window of the kitchen-dining room of the Scognamiglio house: "Head office here, Vittorio we hear you loud and clear, over": the large modern Allocchio Bacchini[60] radio-transmitters of the signals room of Police Headquarters were all two-way, but by returning that "over" the deputy commissionr had wanted to facilitate the interlocutor.

Commissioner Pelluso, who had listened in from the speaker on the wall connected in parallel to the operator's headphones, had ordered Badalamenti: "Tell him to identify himself exactly, we are at war now and either we win, or they hang us all; and then tell him I want a report."

"Vittorio, order of Mr. Chief Commissionr: we are at war now and therefore you and your assistant identify yourselves then give us a report."

"We are Deputy Commissioner D'Aiazzo and Brigadier Bordin, of the *Violent Crimes Section*"; and then he had presented a brief report on what had happened since they had gone out on board the armored car. He had concluded: "Out of five, the two of us are still alive and, as for the group of patriots, only one woman was saved. Now we are at her home, not far from you. We would like to get to you on foot, but there is a problem: a motorized enemy squad which, if I'm not wrong, is equipped with a mobile cannon, is blocking the crossing of Corso Umberto I. I request instructions."

Pelluso had gone to the microphone: "Chief Commissioner here. We are aware of the checkpoint and the cannon and you need to know that there is another barrier, complete with tank, which prevents us from going along the other side of Via Medina. Those Nazis don't want to let the people who have remained in Police Headquarters get out or let the ones who are outside to return. But there is a but: on my orders, about forty of our men who were

---

[60] The company Allocchio Bacchini was originally created for the production of instruments for underwater measurements, but in 1924 it had begun the production of excellent radio receivers and amplification systems made 100% with components of its own design and construction. Not long before the war he had largely transformed his own production by designing and constructing radio-transceiver material for military and law enforcement use.

operating outside the area should attack the checkpoint on Corso Umberto I very soon. What's more, as the Carabinieri Command has informed us, one of its platoons has arrived on the other side of Via Medina, with an armored vehicle and a pair of grenade launchers ... ah, yes, right now we can hear the carabinieri starting to shoot: can you hear the shots too, from where are you?"

"Yes, Mr. Chief Commissioner, in the distance."

"Our men who are on the way are well armed too, above all they have two American mobile rocket launchers that are fine for that self-propelled cannon in the middle of the Corso. They would have already attacked if their lorry hadn't been blocked by some fascists in Via Candelora: they informed me that they are still fighting but that at this point they are definitely getting the upper hand. You listen in for now, I'll get back with more, over."

"Received, I'll listen in, over."

After less than a minute, the voice of the Commissioner was heard again: "Head office to Vittorio, over."

"Vittorio D'Aiazzo here, over."

"Listen, Vittorio: our men have told us that they have sorted out those fascists and that they're about to reach the intersection with Corso Umberto. You and your assistant go down into the foyer of the building and let me know as soon as you are there."

"Yes sir!"

Deputy Commissioner and brigadier had gone downstairs and, once in the atrium of the building, Vittorio had called: "Vittorio to head office, we're at street level, over."

"Vittorio, don't go out for now: when our men attack, you should hear the shots since you are very close, and then you will go out to give support. I have already announced your presence to them. You have weapons, don't you?"

"Well, only the two ordinance Berettas in our belt."

"They're no good: listen, our men told me that they'd taken MABs from the dead fascists ... oh, wait, they tell us that they're arrving at the intersection right now."

The noise of a moving truck had reached Vittorio and Marino from the street and, peeking from the door that was ajar, the Deputy Commissioner had glimpsed a CL Public Security lorry passing by. There were several armed men on board. A few others in the cabin.

The Chief Commissioner had continued: "Yes, they've told me that they've arrived now and that they will give you some weapons. Go outside, and go to them and... good luck."

Vittorio had opened the door of the building and, sticking his head out, had looked everywhere, right and left, checking that the road was deserted as far as the point where the Italian lorry had stopped.

Shots had come from it, exchanged by the enemy.

The two policemen had gone out and had started running towards the lorry. They had not realized that Mariapia was quickly coming down the stairs, after grabbing an empty hemp shopping bag in the kitchen and putting it over her shoulder.

Concetta's screams, inaudible from the outside, followed the young woman: "Disgraziataaa, what do you want to do again to mammàaa?! Come back uuup."

Not a sound came from dad Scognamiglio: despite being, most certainly, a tough man used to the sea, this time, because of the enormous amount of tension accumulated since the evening before, he had fainted and ended up slumped on the floor, fortunately without major damage.

Vittorio, the brigadier and, about twenty yards behind, Mariapia with her shopping bag had not been able to run far: the bullets which where whistling around and above the three, as the Germans fired at the men in the truck had not hit people or things and had continued uselessly into nowhere. Bitterly disappointed, the trio had had to throw themselves on the ground and had stayed there until the end of the battle.

The Italian division was commanded by a chief marshal of Public Security, Gustavo Piombini, who served in the *Vice Squad*. According to a preordained plan, as soon as the CL had arrived at shooting distance from the enemy he had given orders to the officer who was driving to steer sharply left and stop. The lorry had become stuck sideways with its nose towards Peppino Scognamiglio's tobacconist shop. The men in the cargo bed had quickly taken their position at the sideboards facing the enemy, and had started firing with BAR machine guns, MAB assault rifles, Garand rifles and '91 muskets. There were four men in charge of the bazookas, two lackeys and two markers, all Public Security officers; the lackeys had inserted the two rockets and the others had taken aim and, a moment later, at the "go!" from the highest ranked lackey, a corporal, the rocket launchers had ejected their explosive carriers against the German self-propelled cannon. Meanwhile Piombini, the driver and Esposito had quickly climbed down from the cabin of the CL, on the opposite side to the enemy, had hidden behind the vehicle's large wheels, the first two at the rear left, the others to the corresponding front wheels, and had opened fire with MAB machine guns stolen from the fascists.

The Waffen SS, however, had two issue MGs and, before their artillerymen managed to turn the cannon against the lorry, the gunners and their assistants had already turned those machine guns against the Italians and had begun firing deadly volleys: the tapes had one armor-piercing projectile every ten ordinary ones, according to a combat procedure which had been used for some time, and those shots in particular had gone through the side of the lorry's cargo bed killing several men needlessly sheltering behind them.

In contrast, one of the policemen's bazookas had hit the anti-tank cannon full on before it began to fire a single projectile against the CL.

Ultimately the very bloody clash had been won by the Italians, who had left a dozen dead on the ground and about fifteen wounded, but had completely annihilated the SS of the checkpoint, who were not very numerous, but were very well armed.

On the other side of the Police Headquarters on Via Medina, minutes later, the carabinieri had also prevailed, they too with a great loss of blood. Among the dead and wounded, a good half of that platoon had been left on the ground.

The Neapolitan headquarters of Public Security had finally been liberated in both directions. Officers had come outside and had joined the carabinieri, helping them to rescue the wounded and to arrange the dead of both sides, including those from the previous clash that Vittorio and the six surviving partisans had had to leave provisionally on the field.

Marshal Piombini's men were carrying out similar operations on the other barricade and in the meantime had asked Police Headquarters by radio to ensure that ambulances be sent for the wounded and, hopefully, some reinforcements, if possible in sufficient numbers to replace the wounded and dead.

Chapter 10

When the hissing of the bullets had ceased Vittorio, Marino and Mariapia, defrauded of glory this time but with their skins intact, had been able to get up from the pavement and join the group of surviving patriots. Being the highest in rank, the Deputy Commissioner had assumed command of it. He had asked warrant officer Piombini to update him on what had happened before the clash and tell him of any other orders from the Chief Commissioner. He had learned, with surprise, that Pelluso had ordered the non-commissioned officer to send his men to the home of the deceased Rosa Demaggi, to get the American weapons hidden in the cellar which was evidently, like Peppino's, one of the hiding places which Mariapia had mentioned.

Piombini's men had also found foodstuffs in the basement: goods that Demaggi traded on the black market that the warrant officer knew about for some time, having investigated it with men of the *Vice Squad*, in collaboration with the *Commercial Offenses section*. Piombini had told D'Aiazzo that he had received the order by radio to attack the Germans on the trivium between Via Monteoliveto, Via Medina and Corso Umberto I, only after they had seized the weapons and also that, according to orders they had received when they had left, there was now a further mission to be carried out: to attack the walls of Castel Sant'Elmo, where several groups of patriots were already fighting, while others were converging on it to launch a more massive attack on the German occupants. He had added that, in any case, before giving the order it might be good to wait for the arrival of the reinforcements he had requested from Police Headquarters.

While Vittorio listened to the report, some of the survivors were providing first aid to the injured while waiting for the ambulances requested by radio or, at least, lorries or pickup trucks to transport them to hospital. Other patriots were scrounging enemy weapons and still others were opening a passage through the Corso, removing the remains of enemy motorcycles and *motocarrozzette* by hand. It was clear though that there would be sufficient space for the movement of large vehicles only when, subsequently, the CL lorry had moved. With not too much difficulty thanks to its weight, they had moved the Kübelwagen off-road vehicles away by pushing them, but had not moved the far too weighty carcass of the cannon that would in fact remain on the Corso until the evening of October 1st.

Brigadier Bordin was at work among the weapon collectors.

Mariapia on the other hand had reviewed the dead Germans, one by one, not only with very hard eyes, but with a very tight sneer on her lips that seemed, ambiguously, as much of pleasure as of dissatisfaction: if someone had observed her closely, her malevolence towards the Germans would have been not only evident, but much greater than the normal aversion of the Neapolitan population, and the time has come to explain the reson for that.

Much animosity had arisen only a few days earlier, on Friday, September 24, at the end of a sunny afternoon. The air was still, clouds of midges were buzzing in front of the windows and the entrance of Peppino's tobacconist shop, now close to evening closing time as it was 7.28 pm. Mariapia had taken off her apron and was about to go out to pull down the shutters when two Germans of the Wehrmacht arrived in Via Monteoliveto on a motorbike with sidecar. Having seen the shop still open, they had stopped in front of it with the intention of stealing cartons of cigarettes. They had entered and the higher ranked, a certain corporal Bieler, had seen the young woman and had been attracted to her, even though she was not a beauty. Perhaps it had been for the almost childish face and the petite figure that contrasted with the gorilla face of the graduate, in civilian life a muscular butcher's apprentice over six feet tall with everything else in proportion.

Without any hesitation, before starting to raid cigarettes, the excited beast had thrown himself on the young woman, had thrown her prone onto the floor, raised her skirt and petticoat, pulled down her underpants and had deflowered her in the animal position with extreme violence and, like an animal, in a few seconds had vented himself and pulled out. She had fainted. In a kind of deviated spirit of comraderie and pulling his still dribbling thing into his breeches, the corporal had invited his side-kick, a certain private first class Ganzen who as a civilian was a salaried farmhand, to possess the still unconscious girl. No less vile and filthy, he had of course settled himself in Mariapia, but not being affected by *ejaculatio praecox* and unlike his comrade, he had martyred her for quite a while before pulling himself out of her satisfied, amidst her screams as, unfortunately, she had come back to her senses.

Her cousin Peppino had been present at the disgraceful scene and taken care not to intervene in defense of the young woman. He had remained motionless behind the counter, watching it happen. Mariapia had returned home in devastated psychic conditions: the girl who, according to the spirit of the time wanted to go to the altar intact for her imaginary *Prince Charming*, had remained not only physically but psychologically torn apart by the brutality of the rape, the same bestiality that inspires every carnal violence where the victim is treated as a worthless object. She had said nothing to her parents and that evening had almost not spoken a word at table, limiting herself, in response to their usual banal words, to a "yes" or a "no" or short phrases such as: "I'm very tired today". When she returned home, the fear of being pregnant flashed through her mind accompanied by an irrational feeling of shame, as if it the sexual abuse was her fault: the scientists of the psyche say that is a very common feeling among the raped. Almost none of them can see the male figure as they did before, felt more or less consciously to be treacherous and threatening after the affront, and when they are not assisted by an able neurologist, the violated can remain in post traumatic shock – but this term was unknown in Italy at that time.

Some experts in psychology say that, after a short time, with the unjustified shame still present, the trauma normally gives rise to anger and desire for revenge by the raped person, and that in particular cases it can backfire on the victim herself, even leading her to suicide. There are abused women, however, who just as exceptionally, if they already know or have traced the rapist, kill him when the favorable occasion presents itself. The latter was indeed the impulse born in poor Mariapia; and when the opportunity arrived to fight and kill Germans, she had grabbed it immediately, in the faint hope that by a stroke of funereal luck, her rapists were in the pile of adversaries "to be removed".

The poor young woman had stopped inspecting the enemy corpses, among whom she had not recognized her torturers, nor could they have been since her rapists were soldiers of the

Wehrmacht and not the Waffen SS, but she could not tell the difference between the German flashes.

Dissatisfied, she had started towards the lorry that the driver had just removed from its sideways position in the street and had put it back in line in the direction of Corso Umberto I. When she arrived behind the cargo floor, she had seen a Garand rifle, which probably belonged to a police officer lying nearby, dead. The weapon had fired all eight rounds of the magazine, as was evident from the shutter that was still open after ejecting the empty packet. Climbing onto the cargo floor and grabbing the Garand, Mariapia had inserted the safety lock, then had searched for full magazines in the pockets of its probable last owner. She had found only one that the miserable slain man had not been able to take out and insert in time before being hit. She had inserted it by pushing it down with her thumb and almost at the same time had closed the shutter over it, thus arming the rifle, making sure not to leave her finger inside because, as Lieutenant Nemo had explained to her when he was teaching her how to use the weapon, "Garand eats lazybones' meat." The young woman had also searched the pockets of other dead lying near a rifle of the same model and had recovered four full packets. She had put them in the shopping bag that she had put on her shoulder when leaving the house, in the hope of filling it with ammunition. Putting the strap of the Garand cross-ways on her chest, across the belt of the bag. When she got down from the lorry, she had started to help those who were beginning to collect their dead friends, starting with the remains of the man who had had her rifle. The bodies were positioned along the sidewalk in front of Peppino's tobacconist shop.

Having fulfilled her distressing duty, Mariapia had taken a pause and had sat down on the ground. Very soon, however, a sort of wailing had caught her attention and made her get up again: "What are you doing here, you delinquent?!"

It was the voice of Marino Bordin that had shaken her: the brigadier had just seen Gennaro Esposito busy transporting the corpse of a German towards the sidewalk in front of the tobacconist, along which the assortment of dead enemies was arranged.

The man, who was very strong, was holding an automatic musket in his right hand at the narrowest part of the butt, and with the other was holding a dead SS over his left shoulder, balanced there belly down, head and arms forward and legs at the back.

"Mr. Commissioner, Mr. Commissioner," the brigadier had called with all the breath he had, not looking around for his superior so as not to take his eyes off the suspect: "That murderer is here! The one we interrogated last night!"

It took just a moment and Mariapia, although she was not very close, had recognized the beefy man that was carrying the enemy body: it was her mother's brother, her uncle Gennaro Esposito.

The relative had meanwhile laid the corpse on the ground and, making a half turn, he had headed towards the brigadier, who was still holding his own MAB.

Seeing him coming towards him, Bordin had pulled out of the holster the only weapon he had at his disposal at the time, the ordinance Beretta, without realizing that, if the other had wanted to, he could very well have flattened him before he could point the gun at him, not to mention the two pineapple hand grenades that were sticking out of the chest pockets of the man's bluish-green overalls.

"It's my uncle Gennaro!" Mariapia had shouted to the brigadier, but neither he nor her relative had heard her, as they were quite far apart and, above all, too busy scrutinizing each other and avoiding rash gestures.

Vittorio, who was closer to the young woman, had heard her clearly and so had warrant officer Piombini.

Esposito had tried to explain to Bordin: "I fight the Nazis too, don't shoot me! I'm putting the musket on the ground and then I'll explain."

With an expression that could not have been more arrogant, Marino had intimated to him: "Put it down slowly, your MAB, and show me some respect or I'll shoot you": a squabble which was involuntarily laughable, as it was not clear if the threat to fire was also related to the injunction to respect his rank.

"*...ma va' a fa' 'n cùlo, piezz'e mmèrda!*" [61] Gennaro had yelled at Marino, having now run out of patience, which was not proverbial moreover, as his cooks in the barracks had known very well. He had not laid down the MAB and, continuing towards the brigadier, had increased the dose, this time in perfect Italian: "I am

____

[61] (t/n – go get fucked you piece of shit)

Sergeant Major Esposito, of equal rank to you, and I'll talk to you just like you talk to me, you piece of dry shit!"

At the persistent insult the brigadier had turned red with rage and, who knows, perhaps he would have made a real ass of himself if, bless him, Vittorio's voice had not come from behind him: "Back off the pair of you!"

"Yes sir," they had both replied.

The Deputy Commissioner had gone quickly towards the squabblers and Mariapia and the marshal had followed him. Having noticed from the corner of his eye that the young woman was following him, Vittorio had asked her, without stopping or turning towards her: "Is it really your uncle?"

"Yes, it's my uncle Gennaro."

The three had joined brigadier and sergeant major who had arrived, meanwhile, in front of Bordin. Esposito had said to Vittorio: "Doctor, sir, ask warrant officer Piombini about me... indeed, better still, call Chief Commissioner Pelluso by radio, because he's the one who let me out of my cell this morning and he knows very well who I am: he has been aware of my mission since the other day, because the political leaders like him and we group leaders had met in assembly with Commander Taraia...oh, but you...you're Mariapia!" He had recognized his niece only in that moment.

She had kissed the relative on one cheek, in silence and without a smile, but certainly with enthusiasm.

Uncle Gennaro had asked her sternly and worried: "What are you doing here?" He was unmarried and very fond of her, just as the girl was of him.

"I fought the Germans alongside the commissioner and the brigadier," she explained to him.

Before the relative asked her anything else, it was Vittorio who asked her: "What does your uncle do for work?"

"He is a non-commissioned artillery officer and manages the kitchens at his barracks."

"Just as I told you last night," the sergeant major had commented with a tone of reproach, the same one he often used with his military cooks.

"Okay, but your identity has been ascertained just now," D'Aiazzo had responded; then, addressed to Bordin: "See, huh?

You who would like to make people confess using certain methods?"

The brigadier had no reason to oppose him, but he had not wanted to come out of it as a total loser and had quickly remarked to Esposito: "Okay, but you could have told us something more to convince us, couldn't you?"

"Maybe talk about my mission, right?" said the sergeant major, and without waiting for the other to speak, had added: "You could have been fascists, no? How would I know? If I talked, you could have handed me over to the Gestapo and sent the Nazis to confiscate the weapons and ambush my men last night."

"I understand your reasons Gennaro," Vittorio had recognized, "but now tell me more about your mission."

"I had been assigned the command of a platoon of civilians and I had to wait for them at Demaggi's house. The weapons that we would use to fight the men occupying Castel Sant'Elmo were hidden in her cellar. Once I arrived at that woman's place, yesterday evening, I was supposed to wait for my people who were to join me around five this morning, and in the meantime I was to personally open the boxes, check and prepare the rifles and the rest. You know how it went instead. The Chief Commissioner saw me locked in the security cell and let me out, I told him we had not been able to collect the weapons and he had me join warrant officer Piombini's group, giving us the order to go first to Piazzetta del Nilo to arm ourselves and then go on to Sant'Elmo to fight." He had turned to the swarrant officer: "Isn't that right?"

"It's right."

Vittorio had nodded and said Esposito: "I know that a certain Lieutenant Nemo had the same task as you, which by chance was to be carried out in the cellar of the tobacconist's shop here next door where your niece works."

"Hmm..." Esposito had muttered.

Vittorio became suspicious: "Is there a problem?"

Mariapia had replied for him: "No, it's simply that my uncle is hesitating to say that Cesare Nemo is a code name and that it's my younger brother Giuseppe: Lieutenant Giuseppe Scognamiglio."

"Ah well! But when your mother asked you if you had asked that Nemo about your brother, you..."

"... I know, I didn't tell her anything, because Giuseppe himself had asked me to keep quiet about it even with dad and mom."

He had remarked: "Yes, but since the insurrection began this morning, it was no longer a secret: you could have safely told your parents that your brother is alive."

"W...well, yes, agreed," she had admitted; "and so, while we're at it, I can tell you something else that I learned tonight from Giuseppe, which is that some days ago he was the one who had made arrangements with the camorra for the American weapons."

"Explain yourself better."

"I can be more precise," the sergeant major had said, "because I know about it first-hand."

"Let's hear it."

"My nephew had made contact with Peppino, a first time days ago. Giving him a compensation of 2000 lire he had convinced Peppino to introduce him and an American secret service agent, a certain Captain Joseph Jones that I know too, to a camorra boss that Peppino deals with. In the meeting those two and the boss had agreed that, on a certain night, men of his gang would pick up the weapons on our behalf, that would be parachuted by the American air force onto a clearing near Naples. The same men would transport them into the city with their trucks and, just before five in the morning of that same night, they would pick up seven group leaders, including myself, in front of the Sannazaro high school, one for each truck, to check the storage operations of the weapons in the seven secret depots, including Demaggi's and Peppino's cellars.

According to the agreement, the Americans would pay a large sum to the cosca chief, all in gold bars, in three equal instalments, the first at the time of the agreement, directly to him, the others later, through Peppino who is one of the trusted debt collectors for those people: and more precisely, the second instalment on the night they were stored in the hiding places, the third the night the weapons were collected, that is, this morning between five and six. I know that the second payment was made two days ago; the payment of the balance should have taken place last night."

His niece had confirmed: "Yes, I was there: the last instalment was delivered to Peppino in the courtyard of the shop, shortly after five this morning."

In the policeman Vittorio's mind a doubt had suddenly arisen: that the storage of weapons in the protitute's cellar and her violent death could be related. He had asked Esposito: "How come one of the hiding places for the guns was actually at Demaggi's place? Did the woman have ties with the camorra?"

"She was one of their victims, Mr. Commissioner, she had told me that when I met her last Saturday: after the weapons were stored in her cellar, and while I was waiting to leave on foot at the end of the curfew, she had confided to me that for some time she had to pay a percentage on the proceeds of her activities to the cosca chief, that she also knew intimately because, when he felt like it, he took advantage of her sexual services free of charge; and days ago, between the sheets, that good-for-nothing had ordered her to hide and guard those weapons, threatening her that if she didn't accept, not only would he not let her work anymore, but he would send someone to hurt her; he had not promised her any compensation for the favor, he had just demanded it and that's it, as a sort of extra payment. The woman had been forced to accept and was very unhappy about it."

"Do you have any idea why Demaggi had opened up with you?"

"Yes, Commissioner, I do: essentially because she had the hope that she would get some money from us at least. She expressly asked me to ask my superiors for it. I told her that neither they nor I had power over things like that. She had been very disappointed, but she hadn't insisted, she just made me promise not to talk to anyone that she had asked for money, nor anything else she had confided to me, so that these things would not reach the ears of the camorra. I promised and I kept it, but she died all the same."

Bordin had suggested to his superior: "The camorra will have known in any case, in some other way."

Vittorio had ignored the intervention; in the faint hope of obtaining something that would lead him to Demaggi's murderer, provided of course that it was murder and not an accident, he had asked Esposito: "Tell me more precisely about the night you unloaded the weapons at Demaggi's place."

"Yes sir. As I had been ordered, a little before 5.00 am I left the Sannazaro high school and waited for a truck was to come by and pick me up and it arrived shortly after. It is owned by two young itinerant greengrocers, husband and wife, who have authorization from the Prefecture to circulate, despite the curfew, from 4.00 am onwards to go to the market and set up their stall before selling commences at 6.00 am. The couple hid the weapons in the truck's caisson under the fruit and vegetables. After Demaggi opened up to us, we piled the boxes with the weapons in the atrium of the apartment as quickly as possible. Even though Piazzetta del Nilo was still dark at that time and the truck was parked with the lights off, there had been some very tense moments because a German patrol could pass by and want to know why that vehicle was parked there. Then the greengrocers left for the market and I..."

"... how had those two behaved towards Demaggi?"

"I'd say well, Mr Commissioner, except that you could see that they were nervous about the danger they were running, in fact they kept glancing around the square while they carried the boxes into the house with me and it really seemed that they couldn't wait to get away from there."

"They had not shown any hostile feeling towards the lady of the house: is that correct?"

"Yes sir, it seemed like they had performed the task only out of duty, they didn't even seem to know her, that woman. I don't think they went back last night to kill her, if that's what you were thinking, Commissioner; but if, let's say, they had done so, it would not have been on their initiative anyway, but to obey an order."

"All right, go ahead and tell me about that night."

"Immediately after those two had left, I took the boxes of weapons down into the cellar, which is accessed by a spiral staircase that descends from a large trapdoor in a corner of the kitchen: last night, evidently, your policemen did not notice that trapdoor, they only inspected the rooms before putting the seals on the house, if not they would have discovered the boxes of weapons in the cellar. But to go back to that first night, after I took the boxes downstairs, as I had already said, I remained at Demaggi's until the end of the curfew and, not long before I left, the woman had confided in me and had asked me to tell my superiors that, because of the risk she was taking, she wanted a reward. At six o'clock I walked back to the high school where I told Commander Taraia about the success of the operation, but I didn't say anything about the compensation the woman had asked me for."

"Anything else?"

"According to the plans, the weapons would have been picked up by our seven groups in the same number of hiding places in Naples, during last night around five in the morning. So my men too, if everything had gone as planned, were to go into Demaggi's house at that time, in the hour or so before six, the time when we would be going out to fight. I would have trained them in the practical use of the rifles and the rest of the weapons. I had already given them theoretical lessons at the high school, based on some drawings the Americans had given me and that I brought with me when I passed the lines, but concrete teaching was necessary too. Instead..."

"... instead we arrested you the evening before, I know, needless to tell me again: *nostra culpa, nostra maxima culpa*", Vittorio had jokingly beaten his chest twice.

"... and instead that is not what I was going to say, Mr Commissioner, because I do not repeat things a thousand times," the non-commissioned officer was a little annoyed: "I wanted to say instead that this morning I had to quickly explain the use of the American weapons to the Piombini group and that, despite the improvisation, the men have been able to use them well."

"I see. As for the men in your platoon, I imagine they will have been disoriented, finding the seals on the door when they arrived."

"Yes indeed sir, exactly, I don't imagine it, I know it for sure. When we arrived in Piazzetta del Nilo this morning, those of them who had remained in the area told me: when the group saw your seals at the entrance and because I wasn't there, they didn't know what to do at first. Then five of my men, the ones who would tell me how things went down, decided to hide in the dark and wait to see if I arrived, while their companions had preferred to return to the high school to receive new orders. The former had been very lucky that Germans or fascists did not pass through the area until the end of the curfew, and after that they were able to rest easy, as they were all Neapolitans and didn't have weapons on them. They joined us in the end and unfortunately two died in the earlier clash with the fascists and another here."

Vittorio had nodded, then his mind had returned to another violent death, Demaggi's, a death not related to the revolt, at least apparently. Addressing Bordin and Piombini, he had said: "One can wonder whether the camorra boss had considered himself offended by Rosa Demaggi. He may really have heard that she wanted compensation from the Resistance, and we know that the camorristi don't want people to go looking for earnings behind their backs."

"Information though that did not come from me, let's be clear," the sergeant major had wanted to point out.

"I don't doubt it. However, some other type of *sgarro*[62] is possible, for example Demaggi may have talked to someone else about the weapons operation, which should instead have remained very secret. If there had been any affront, whether it was that or who knows what else, the camorra might have wanted to give her a lesson as is their style, although not necessarily wanting to kill her, since the woman gave them money: perhaps just beat her, and in that case the murder would have been preterintenzionale. Be that as it may, we could find the perpertrator of the crime by investigating inside the gang Peppino belongs to, maybe just interrogating him for a start: provided that it was murder and not an accident, and we must always keep this in mind."

Warrant officer Piombini had remarked: "Nevertheless, last night the murderer had to act like lightning to go inside, hit her and get out in the short time since the woman had left the door ajar waiting for Gennaro, certainly not long before the time he was scheduled to arrive, and when he did arrive."

"Unless," the Deputy Commissioner had suggested, "the victim had let the murderer into the house beforehand, because it was someone she knew, perhaps following an appointment, and after he hit her it was the delinquent himself, for some reason we do not know, who left the door open as he left, instead of closing it behind him. Perhaps the autopsy will be able to establish in particular whether the woman was hit shortly before Gennaro's arrival or earlier."

Brigadier Bordin had intervened: "I'm sorry, Mr Commissioner, but apart from the autopsy, in my opinion the murderer would have been careful to close the door when he was leaving, so passers-by would not be suspicious."

---

[62] (t/n – affront)

Before Vittorio could reflect on the observation, Mariapia's uncle had interrupted: "Mr Commissioner, I don't know if that woman was killed yesterday or if she died by accident, and I don't have the professional preparation that all of you do, but I think it as simply an accident. Like the brigadier, I think, that a murderer would have closed the door behind him, so as not to attract suspicion from outside, and I also think, sorry everyone, that he would have first made sure the woman was dead, but instead, when I arrived she was still alive."

Vittorio had pointed out: "Yes, but only if the cosca boss had wanted to have her killed and not simply have her beaten up to give her a lesson."

"Yes, that's very true; and yet I suppose that the camorristi would have waited for the weapons operation to be conclude before they acted, so as not to make things difficult for us, or worse. As we know, according to their code of honor, let's call it that, when they make a commitment, they keep it fully."

Warrant officer Piombini had agreed with Esposito: "A misfortune seems more likely to me too, for the same reasons and also for another reason: we in *Vice* know that Demaggi was addicted to alcohol and, from time to time, she also smoked opium, a drug that we suspect the camorra procured for her. So it is possible that yesterday afternoon she had taken that filthy stuff, I imagine because she was worried about the nerve-wracking situation of having the weapons in the house and so on, and as a result she had a dizzy spell at a certain moment, or maybe even fainted, and fell down banging her head on the furniture."

"This is very important information: bravo Piombini!" his superior had praised him though in his heart nevertheless he was feeling a little mortified: more than ever now, he wanted to solve the case to prove to himself first of all, that he was be up to it, since even someone like Gennaro Esposito who was not a policeman seemed to have reasoned better than he had. He had continued: "We'll see whether the coroner confirms a state of intoxication from alcohol or was dazed from drugs, and in that case I think I'll archive the case as an accident; and what Gennaro said is certainly to be taken into account, meaning that those delinquents would hardly have put the weapons operation at risk before hitting Demaggi. No, in retrospect, it could have been a sexual client who killed her during a quarrel, even though that was not his intentions. But it wouldn't have been an evil-minded man," he had noted; and was happy when he saw on everyone's face that they wanted to know more.

The brigadier had asked: "Mr. Commissioner, what makes you think that it wouldn't be an evil-minded person?"

"Because of the front door left ajar as he went out. One could suppose that yesterday evening when the man saw with relief that Demaggi was not dead, he did indeed take off, let's say so as not to pay what he owed, but he left the door of the house slightly open on purpose, to catch the attention of the men in a patrol car, ours or someone else's, to induce them to enter and call an ambulance; that's why it wouldn't be someone wicked at heart, even though he was a coward, yes."

The sergeant major, however, had not thought that the idea of a violent sexual client was plausible. He had said: "Excuse me, Mr. Commissioner, but apart from the door left ajar, I doubt very much that Demaggi would have taken a customer to bed just before my arrival."

The brigadier though had supposed: "... but what if it was not a sex client, but someone buying black market goods?"

Vittorio had regretted not having thought of that alternative himself and, mentally noting Bordin's plausible idea, he had half-admitted with him: "I can't exclude that you're right," and subordinate had smiled smugly. Perhaps just to get rid of his discontent, the Deputy Commissioner had momentarily changed the subject, and addressed Gennaro: "It goes without saying that the story you told us tonight, that you went into hiding after September 8 and the farmers who sold you civilian clothes and so on, as well as your statement that you arrived in the city only last night were all lies."

"Yes sir, but always and only because I could not know whether I could trust you. I had arrived days ago actually, with a certain John Cappuoni, an Italian-American captain who lilke Jones was a member of the OSS[63]."

"Of the oss... what?"

____

[63] Office of Strategic Services, the U.S. intelligence that forerunners the CIA, an office created in December 1941 a few days after the Japanese attack on Pearl Harbor and directed by Colonel and then General of Division William J. Donovan and, for the Italian area of operations, by Major and then Colonel Peter Tompkings who had landed first in Sicily and then in Salerno with American troops.

"It's the acronym of the American military secret service, and their commander in Italy trained us all personally: he is a very young major who speaks Italian perfectly, called Peter Tompkins. On his orders, Captain Cappuoni and I passed the German lines at night in civilian clothes and with a false civil identity card in our pocket. My name was Annibale Cuomo with the profession of nurse, and he had his surname Cappuoni and his English name John turned into Giovanni in our language, and he too was a nurse. When we had passed the lines, we found someone called Dr. Crivelli waiting for us on the outskirts of the city, in a place that had been agreed beforehand by radio in code.

Dr. Crivelli is a doctor who has been an adversary of fascism and the like for twenty years. He was there with his car, a 500 Topolino, and he had brought two white coats that he asked us to put on, to pretend to be his nurses. Then he took us to Sannazaro high school. I had hardly any room in back seat, which is only intended for a child or a couple of suitcases, and besides that I was drowned in the stench of burning charcoal[64] that back there was particularly strong because the system was in the trunk and under the seat as well: it was a very unconfortable ride. But never mind, the important thing is that we got away with it at a German checkpoint: the two of us showed our false cards, the doctor his real one, and everything went well.

"The fact is, though, that immediately afterwards, I automatically put my false identity card in a pocket of the shirt and, when I reached my destination, I gave it back to the doctor forgetting, like a fool, to get back my own document: it will still be in that pocket, I imagine. I realized it only the next day and told commander Taraia abut it, but he told me that the doctor had gone out of Naples on a mission. He reassured me, however, by adding that an aides's identity card in the pocket of a gown in a doctor's

---

[64] Due to the scarcity of gasoline and other petroleum products after the economic crisis known as '29, but that lasted a long time, into the 30s and later, even more so during the war this alternative source of energy was used to move vehicles; the engines were powered by a gas-fired system placed wherever possible, on the roof of the car, on its sides or inside the car; was able to draw gas from wood and lignite – the young Sardinian coal of Sulcis. The device did not burn these basic fuels completely and produced a smelly mixture of methane, carbon monoxide, hydrogen and other gases in smaller quantities, andn had a caloric value adequate to run the engine, even if not very much power.

office should not have created problems. So, to make a long story short, I was left without the document."

"Did you tell me this because of the license you later showed us?"

"Yes sir: since I had brought my license with me, hidden in one of the many inner pockets of the *special* underpants and the singlet *kindly* provided by the OSS, I used that afterwards to move around Naples, and it's what I showed your patrol. If I'd still had the false card, I would have presented myself instead as the nurse Annibale Cuomo assistant to Dr. Crivelli."

"Muddling things worse; but go ahead."

"Yes sir. Days later, since I was a career non-commissioned officer, Commander Taraia put me at the head of the group of civilian patriots that you know. As I have already said, once we had the weapons the final objective was Castel Sant'Elmo, which we would attack alongside other groupings to carry out a strike attack, all together."

"Gennaro, you can be sure that we will join those others, as soon as the ambulances arrive for the wounded and the reinforcements they promised us via radio. But I'm a little curious: how is it that a cook was enlisted as an agent?"

"Through my nephew. The Americans had taken me prisoner with my battalion on day 10. They had concentrated us in a prison camp that they had quickly created in and around our own barracks: shacks on the parade ground in two separate enclosures for the officers and for we non-commissioned officers, other barracks for the troops, with barbed wire fences around the barracks.

"The Americans set themselves up in our rooms and dormitories and our clubs and mess rooms. Two days later, several Italian officers and non-commissioned officers enlisted by the OSS arrived, and among them was my nephew, who as you know went by the false name of Cesare Nemo. They were to train under the direction of Tompkins. Most of them would have to penetrate among the German troops to spy, disguised as Waffen SS, while my nephew's mission would take place here in Naples and would concern the weapons you know about: all things that Giuseppe himself told me after he had recognized me as he was going past the non-commissioned officers' enclosure.

"I hadn't noticed him from a distance, though, because he was wearing an American-style uniform. He had asked me if I wanted to collaborate in an action in Naples and, since he was involved in it, I said yes. He introduced me to Major Tompkins telling him that I too was of pure Neapolitan blood as well as his relative and that like him I knew the camorrista who was to be the contact with his boss: I had actually only met Peppino once in my life, during a short furlough when I had stopped by in a hurry to say hello to Mariapia in the tobacconist shop. My mother and I and my sister Concetta as well detest those people, because they had damaged us badly in the past. Apart from that, Giuseppe had convinced the Americans that I would be very useful so I had been accepted as an auxiliary in the OSS.

"As for the fact that I was a chief cook in the army, my nephew had not even mentioned it. They put an American uniform on me too, then just before the mission they gave me the civilian clothes that I'm still wearing."

Chapter 11

"*Guàrdie, guàrdie, ajùto! Aggio truva' 'nu muórto... acciso*!" [65] These words had arrived very loudly from the sidewalk in front of the low building that housed the tobacconist and the bicycle workshop. The repairman Gennarino Appalle had shouted, calling Warrantm Officer Piombini and Brigadier Bordin who, unlike their superior, were in uniform.

"Just one murdered dead person? Where did all the others disappear to?" Marino had joked impulsively and unintentionally releasing the tension that had built up inside him.

Vittorio had not appreciated that and had glared coldly at his subordinate. Then he went to meet Appalle who was coming towards the group, and had said to him: "Talk to me, I'm Deputy Commissioner D'Aiazzo."

They had stopped a couple of yards awaay from each other, and in short gasping breaths, Gennarino had managed to say: "*'O tabbaccàro Peppi' Scognamiglio... è dinto a' o' cammarìno, muòrto… ncòppa a' mmèrda sua... cazòne e mutànda acalàti... uuh! Tene 'a cànna recisa e tene... o' pisce* e *'and ppalle appusà azzìcco a o' cuorpo.*[66]"

In addition to Vittorio, Mariapia, Bordin, Esposito and Piombini, who had followed him, had heard what he said too but not everyone had been able to understand. The Deputy Commissioner had translated into Italian, for the benefit of the Venetian brigadier and the warrant officer, originally from Livorno: "He said that the tobacconist Peppino is inside the toilet lying dead on his feces, with his trousers and underpants lowered, and that his throat has been cut and his penis and testicles amputated and lying next to the body." He had asked Mariapia: "When did you see Peppino alive for the last time?"

"Last night, when I went down to the cellar to get a weapon. I don't know if he was still alive when we came back up, but I didn't see him again."

---

[65] (t/n – Guards, guards, help! I've found a dead body... murdered)

[66] The tobacconist Peppino Scognamiglio... he's inside the toilet, dead... on his shit... trousers and underpants pulled down ... Ooh! His throat is cut and... his penis and balls are laid alongside the body.

Vittorio had turned to the repairman: "Tell me who you are, but speak in Italian, if you are able to, so that everyone understands."

"Yes sir I know how talk in Italian; and 'n Italiano I say that I am, modestly! the repairer 'o bikes and various cycles who has putèca (t/n bottega or shop) there" and had pointed to his workshop.

D'Aiazzo had started to search him.

"Why?" had escaped the craftsman.

The Bordin had stopped him: "Because you are a suspect."

"Me?! Me who *vi vuttài*[67] '?!"

The non-commissioned officer had insisted, condescendingly: "Many murderers have the habit of calling us thinking they will divert suspicions."

The man had opened his mouth wide, frightened, as the brigadier had received a sharp "Uff!" from his superior who had wanted to quickly reassure the artisan: "Being a suspect does not mean being a culprit: this is a simple formality, don't worry, because if you are innocent you have nothing to fear."

"... and let's hope so," the other had not been convinced.

After completing the personal search and not finding anything compromising, Vittorio had asked the man for his identity card. He had checked his name, address and profession, then had confirmed with him: "I see that you live in the building next door."

"Yes sir."

He had noted the details in his diary then, after returning the document, he had said to the repairman: "I didn't see you earlier: where were you?"

"I was hiding because of *d'a uèrra de poco fa dinanzi a' pputèca mia.*[68]"

"When did you discover the corpse?"

"Just before *'a uèrra*, but I was hiding out of prudence *fino a mo*[69]; and then when the gunfire stopped a little while ago, I called you."

The officer had ordered him: "Tell me everything in exact order."

---

[67] Who called you.

[68] Of the war (combat) of a little while ago in front of my shop.

[69] Until now.

"Yes sir. *'Sta matina priésto sun ascìto e sun venìto puntualmente a fatica'*[70]. Not long after *c'avevo aprito* [71] I heard gunshots coming *da 'a stràta d'a Questura*[72] and I locked the door from the inside, prudently."

"Were you closed until a short time ago?"

"No sir, I opened *'a* door *'nu* little before *d'e* 9, but only *pe' nu muimènto, pe' parla' cu' donna Conce*[73] that I know and who is the mother of the here present *Mariapi'*... by the way, hello Mariapi'*!*" – and the young woman had replied: *Bòna jurnàta, Gennari'* – "and her mother wanted news of her *criatùra*[74] who is... I mean to say was *Peppi's* shop assistant and that, as Donna *Conce'* had told me, had not returned from work *'a* night before."

"Yes, I already knew these things; tell me the rest in detail."

"Signorsì, in detail. First of all, as soon as I opened *'a pputèca* I repaired a tricycle whose chain had *carùta*[75] for the owner of the wine and oil warehouse nearby, who had asked me to do it as fast as possible because he uses it for deliveries; then I *accuncia*[76] a punctured tire *de 'na bicicletta 'e fémmena co' portapaccòtti*[77] belonging to Donna Maria Cammarata the florist, then I repaired the handlebar *de n'ata*[78] bike, which is a racing bike and belongs to Luigi Torrano *'o* delicatessen owner, the handlebars had come loose..."

"... okay, but when I said *detailed* I didn't mean these things: apart from the work, what happened?"

"What happened was that, just before *'a uèrra* started outside, as I was about to check the gears on Luigi Torrano's bike as he had asked me, I got *'na* great need ... you know what I mean, don't you?"

"No."

"I said I felt *'na* great need... eeh... *inzómma* to make water: you know what it's like. So I went to *'o cammarìno*[79] in the courtyard, going out from the back of *a' pputèca* under the shutter,

---

[70] Early this morning I went out and came on time to work.

[71] I had opened.

[72] From the street of the Police Headquarters.

[73] For a moment, to talk to Donna Concetta.

[74] Young daughter, *creature* even if now adult.

[75] fallen off.

[76] fixed.

[77] A women's bicycle with a luggage rack.

[78] Of another.

[79] Small room, toilet.

pulled up *mmity surtànto*[80], and I realized after I tried to turn the key in the lock, that the door of the john was not locked at all, not even from the inside *cu ancìno*[81] because *girànno*[82] the key the door opened a bit towards me as I moved it.

"I pushed it wide open and made the very ugly discovery of Peppino *co' cazóne e mutànda* down to his ankles and slumped *co' panàro*[83] contact with the hole in the floor directly above *'a chiàveca*[84]; the corpse was on top of a soft shit, because Peppi' notoriously suffered from diarrhoea, as anyone outside the little room could realize because of the noises his ass made, and also because he was always running to poop; and his crap, speaking with respect, was *spannuta*[85] around the hole: clearly Peppi' had had one *de' li sciuglimiénti sòleti de' sùi, tremendissimi*[86]. He always had to throw lots of water after he had taken a crap, much more than me who, I assure you, Commissioner, consumed very little..."

"... and okay, but what does that have to do with it?! And apart from that?"

"Apart from that, meaning that I drank very little water and Peppino made me *'mmece pava*[87] much more than was right, unfairly..."

"Ah!"

"What?"

"No, nothing, go on."

"No, because you said: *ah!* and then I was thinking who knows what."

"Come on, come on, there's nothing!" D'Aiazzo had snapped at him, only apparently annoyed though in reality he had made a mental note of that exhorbitant request that displeased Appalle: *Revenge?* he had wondered.

"I was saying: There was a cut all the way across Peppi's throat and, always speaking with respect *'o pèsce e 'e ppalle*[88] were

---

[80] Only half-way.

[81] With hook.

[82] Turning.

[83] With deretano in contact with the hole in the floor.

[84] Sewer

[85] Spread.

[86] One of those usual loose ones, tremendous.

[87] Instead made me pay.

[88] (t/n – his cock and his balls)

cut off in one piece slapped down next to the body, but I have already told you this, Commissioner."

"That his male organ and testicles had been cut off in one piece, no. Anyway, what happened then?"

"Before I had recovered from the terrible shock, I heard noise and gunshots coming from Via Monteoliveto, much worse than the grand finale of the fireworks at Piedigrotta. Stay hidden in the little room, no way, because of the dead body and because the little room is made of wood and does not give any shelter, not to mention the stench that was terribly strong. Going back to my shop would have been very risky because bullets could come through the door that opens to the street, which is made of wood and glass as well. So I ran against the wall, right between my shutter and the nearest window at the back of *don Peppi's* tobacconist shop hoping that no bullets would arrive behind that wall and, always speaking with respect, since I really couldn't hold on any longer I peed on the wall.

"Right after that, I saw that the back door of the tobacconist shop was only half-closed and then I thought I'd go in and protect myself *là dìnto*[89], but I realized immediately that I would protect myself better if I went down those steps that lead right to the door below, *annànze*[90] *don Peppi's* cellar. So, crawling on the ground like a snake I slid head down and feet up and, *scènnenno accussì*[91], I saw that *Don Peppi'* had left the door of that cellar ajar as well and not just the door of the house, so *son sciuglia'*[92] into the cellar, and *age*[93] that it is a kind of refuge with many walls *zigghete zagghete*. When *'a uèrra* ceased, after a *d'àti*[94] minutes for holy prudence I went upstairs and went into my *bodega, mena' 'n uúcchio*[95] out on Via Monteoliveto through the glass in the door and when I saw your uniforms, I opened and *dimanna'*[96] for help; and that's all, yes sir."

Victor had wondered: *If what Appalle has reported is exact, and I'll check that immediately, how come the cellar and back*

---

[89] Inside there.
[90] In front of.
[91] Descending like this.
[92] I slipped.
[93] I saw
[94] A few more.
[95] Looked outside.
[96] Asked.

doors are ajar? It would seem like an analogy with the door of Demaggi's house. Or maybe it's just a coincidence? Perhaps someone rummaged through his premises in search of the gold, , before they found and killed the tobacconist, without worrying about pulling the door closed behind him? Is the last instalment of the gold still on that Peppino's corpse? Or has it been taken from him? I have to check these things too immediately. But... is the gold really the motive for the crime? What if instead they killed him because he knew something about Demaggi's death? If, in some way, the two murders are linked? Perhaps it is no mere coincidence that both victims, whether they liked it or not, had offered their cellars as deposits and that both have been killed.

Since the driveway was closed, Gennarino Appalle had taken Vittorio into the courtyard through his workshop. Warrant officer Piombini and Brigadier Bordin had followed them and after a moment of hesitation, at some distance, Mariapia and her uncle, not sure if Vittorio would like that; but when he saw them in the courtyard he had not reproached them.

The Deputy Commissioner had glanced first at the corpse in the lavatory, then had ordereed Piombini and Bordin not to let anyone in and had gone to see the back door of the tobacconist shop, then the door of the cellar, and had verified that, in fact, both had been left just pulled to. He had also noticed that the door of the basement did not have a deadbolt and a key was needed to lock it. Back in the courtyard, remembering that Mariapia had told him that a key wasn't needed from inside the sliding gate on the driveway and it was enough to use the handle, he had invited the young woman herself to open it. She had done this while he had gone to the lavatory to examine the corpse more carefully. Appalle had remained at a distance, and before anything else Vittorio had made the warrant officer and brigadier take a quick look at the cruel spectacle from outside. He had not allowed Mariapia's uncle to do so, nor would he have allowed the young woman when she returned.

He had then gone into the small room, leaving the door wide open to let out the stench, and had Piombini and Bordin stand in front of the door as a screen. Finally he had analyzed the crime scene, noting that the repairman had been conscientious in his description. He had told his subordinates: "I have to check if there is gold on the corpse"; and overcoming his disgust, had rummaged in the pockets and under the clothes of the dead man. He hadn't found anything. Being likely that the tobacconist had not left the precious metal in the house or in the shop but had kept it on his own person, Vittorio had assumed that the murderer had taken it off the corpse. He had been unable to avoid getting dung and clotted blood on his hands, and after closing the door of the small room, he had gone quickly to the tap in the courtyard to wash them under the hose. Then he had then dried them on one of the two handkerchiefs that he usually carried with him.

Meanwhile, he was reasoning: *This is what could have happened: the group of patriots leaves at the end of the curfew, the tobacconist is in the house and is about to go down to close the door of the cellar, when a very urgent bodily need takes him and it is so urgent that he does not even close the back door in the courtyard and just runs to the lavatory. Perhaps he thinks that, in any case, there is no one still there, or so he believes; but no, his murderer is there, but who would take advantage of that moment to go after him to the latrine, kill him and rob him? Someone from the camorra? Perhaps from his own gang, because the boss had known that he, hypothesis, wanted to keep the third instalment of the gold for himself and escape? Or a competing camorra group? Or a thief who had nothig to do with the camorra? Perhaps... Gennarino Appalle? That man seems like a simpleton, but what if he was pretending? After all, he knew that the tobacconist was subject to regular diarrhoea and that he used the toilet very frequently. Yes, but had to have been aware of the weapons and gold in advance, and this seems implausible to me. Oh, yes, dear Vittorio, you're in the marshes for now.*

Since he was at the beginning of his career, despite wanting to do well and make a good impression on his superiors, the young man was still proceeding hesitantly. Only years later, when his professional knowledge had grownn, would he would operate more confidently and with faster results. On the other hand, it must be considered that the war was increasing the difficulties of judicial investigations, and not just for him, and that the fact that they were in the midst of the days of the uprising in Naples made things even more difficult. It should also be noted that the scientific wherewithall available to the police forces, at that time, were rudimentary compared to those of our years in the 2000s. For example there were no DNA tests on organic materials, only the blood group could be established, which was not a great thing because, although it is true that it narrowed the field of investigation, it did not allow the identification of a precise individual.

Vittorio had said to the brigadier in a low voice: "Marino, take Appalle with you now, you don't have to handcuff him but watch him, and without letting him move away call the radio room at Police Headquarters with the transceiver in the truck, tell them about the corpse and ask them in my name to inform the people in the morgue, requesting that they send us the medical examiner on duty ..."

"... yes, Commissioner."

"Wait: then go and inspect Appalle's shop and immediately afterwards go to inspect his apartment in the building next to it, and the cellar: among other things, check each time that there are no loose tiles on the walls or the floors and, if so, remove them and see if the gold is hidden there. Ah, and I'm telling you now to do the same in the premises of the dead tobacconist." He had addressed the repairman: "Appalle..."

"...command yes sir!"

"No, just tell us what floor you live on."

"Eh, a *o'* first. Inside the house there *should* be my *muglièra.*"

"You heard, Marino, his wife is in the house. As soon as you go in and before looking around, search the lady, but very delicately, to see whether she has the ingots on her: out of respect you will do it in front of her husband. The main goal is to find the gold, but if there are knives or razors in the shop, take them, and the same goes for all the razors and sharp knives you find at Appalle's home, in the bathroom and kitchen or even elsewhere, including the cellar. We'll give them all to the coroner when he arrives. Ah, after you've called the Police Headquarters, it's best if you choose one of our officers outside here to help you in the searches: tell him it's my order. Actually, better still, take a second officer and order him to come and stand guard here in the courtyard and that, if any stranger comes in, he will have to block him and bring him to me. You can go now."

"Sissignore," and Bordin had told the repairman: "Follow me and be careful what you do, because I'll be watching you."

"Eeh..." is all the other uttered with humiliated heart.

Vittorio had thought it was better to remind the brigadier: "Remember that every suspect is innocent until proven guilty."

"Yes sir", the employee had agreed.

Then, having plucked up some courage, the repairman had said to the Deputy Commissioner: Excuse me, your Excellency..."

"I'm not excellency," Vittorio had brushed aside, "I'm just doctor and also Deputy Commissioner."

"Sorry, Mr. Doctor and also Deputy Commissioner, I wanted say to you, very respectfully, please! let me go up home *pe' primmo* because, if not, my wife, *abbedénno i vuòsti pulizziòtti pe' prìmmi, se fa méttere appaùra: assapéte cómm'è*[97], Mr. Doctor and Deputy Commissioner..."

"... just doctor or commissioner."

"Yes sir. I was saying: sorry, Commissioner, *assapéte cómm'è*: even honest people are not very sure, let's say, that *'a* justice is always infallibly *'a* Justice with a capital letter. Sorry if I took the liberty, excellenc... no, I mean commissioner."

"Alright. After the inspection in your shop, you will go up before my men, you will open the door with the key and your wife will see you first. Once the inspection of your home has been done, assuming that the gold isn't found, you will not stay in the house but you will go out with my officers and come back here to me with them. You will have to remain at my disposal for a while longer. Of course, I repeat, only if my men do not find anything compromising for you; if not..."

"... and what on earth would they find, Commissioner?! No they won't find anything, apart from razors and knives, because *tutt'o munno*[98] has them at home."

"We'll have the blades analyzed anyway. You, Appalle, do as I said and, if you're innocent as you say you are and as I think unless proven otherwise, then you'll have no trouble. But I'm telling you right now that, even if nothing compromising is found and that you will be free as a result, you will be summoned to Police Headquarters as soon as possible for the official testimony and the relative report. So you are not to leave your home before you have been summoned: this is a police order."

"Yes sir."

-----

[97] If she sees your cops first, she'll be scared, you know what it's like.
[98] Everyone

The brigadier had again commanded Gennarino Appalle to follow him and the two of them had gone out into the street through the driveway.

Vittorio had said to Mariapia: "I will also have you officially testify in my office as soon as possible, to repeat what you told me this morning and confirm, officially as well, that this morning you left Peppino alive and well."

"Yes, I confirm that I saw him alive for the last time when I went down to the cellar and that I never met him again on the way out."

"It isn't necesssary now, you will tell me in an official way when the time comes. As for what you told me this morning about Nemo, alias your brother, obviously it wasn't entirely true and you'll correct yourself."

"I had invented a little bit to hide his identity from you, but it was essentially correct."

"You can correct yourself now, unofficially, before the deposition at Police Headquarters; and be aware that I will call your brother to testify with you."

"Yes, that's fine. It goes without saying that I recognized Giuseppe as soon as he came in under the shutter, and my heart almost stopped because of the emotion, as I believed he was missing in action, which almost always means dead. He told me that he had arrived in the store early on purpose knowing that I was working with the cousin, just to meet me before I went home from work. He always trusted my absolute confidentiality, as I had already told you. There was no threat to tie me up, of course, not only from him, but not even from Peppino, and when I realizied that it was about fighting those German pigs, I wanted to join Giuseppe and his men. The rest of my account this morning was essentially accurate."

Vittorio had nodded his head in agreement; then, personally curious, he had asked her: "During your meeting, did your brother explain to you why he was considered missing in action?"

"Yes, last year he was with his Folgore in the Libyan-Egyptian desert, in the army at a place called El Alamein. On November 2, just before 9.00 pm, during one of the breaks in battle, which had lasted for about ten days at that point, he had been thrown to the ground by the displacement of air from the sudden explosion of an enemy projectile a few yards away from him, the first cannonade of that last night of clashes[99]. Luckily he had not suffered serious physical damage, only a slight contusion to the head, perhaps hitting it against something in the tent; but he had been dazed by the noise of the sudden explosion and the British military doctors would say it was shell shock.

"The projectile had exploded while he was completely naked in his officer's tent and, with a sponge moistened with some of his own water, which he hadn't been drinking in that desert, he was trying to relieve the itching all over his body from parasitic insects. He told me last night that he can only try to imagine it, everything else, because he was no longer conscious. He thinks he was unconscious for the duration of the battle, perhaps considered dead by the soldiers of the platoon he commanded. He would learn of it only once he returned to the world, months later actually, that at the end of the battle, while his surviving comrades carried out the order to withdraw, he had been taken prisoner by the British with other wounded and transported to the military hospital of Alexandria in Egypt. The enemy stretcher bearers had picked him up as he was, naked, lying what was left of his pants and his completely tattered shirt on top of him because Giuseppe had placed them on a small table that, unlike him, must have received a shower of splinters.

"He was picked up without his ID plate and the chain as well, which he had taken off to pass the sponge over his neck. It had ended up in the sand from the displacement of air; and as if that wasn't enough, he had lost his wallet with his documents inside, which must have come out of the back pockets of his trousers ..."

"... if some cunning enemy had not taken it," Vittorio had commented.

"Maybe, but since the lining of the pocket was torn, he thinks the wallet had slipped into the sand. Anyway, since his identity had not been ascertained, the hospital had not been able to report a name to the International Red Cross until Giuseppe had returned to his senses and declared who he was. That is why our Ministry of War had believed he was missing. Once he was judged to have recovered, he had been transferred to an officers' concentration camp, and the International Red Cross had finally

---

[99] The Second Battle of El Alamein had taken place, in successive stages, from October 23 to November 3, 1942.

been notified; but Giuseppe presumes that the information that he was alive and prisoner had not arrived in Italy due to the succession of events from the landing in Sicily to the armistice."

Vittorio had suggested: "Or maybe the Red Cross had sent the information and maybe it had even arrived in Italy but because of the chaos that reigned here by then, the Ministry of War didn't bother to tell you. But tell me another thing: how come he was recruited by the Americans?"

"Giuseppe had been a convinced anti-Fascist since high school even though he had felt it was his duty to serve in the army when Italy entered the war. As he was leaving for officer's academy he said to me in English, which I know fairly well because I had studied the basics at the technical schools, whereas he knows it very well: *Bad Country, but my Country!* which means..."

"... Yes *A bad country, but it's my country!* Tell me the rest, Mariapia."

"Yes. My brother hadn't been interned in the concentration camp for long when the news of the fall of Mussolini was leaked at the end of July. So he tried to spread anti-fascist propaganda among his fellow prisoners, but since Italy had continued to fight the Anglo-Americans, his activity had not expanded in favor of the enemy. With the armistice, after certain agreements the Anglo-Americans made with circles close to the king, my brother had been released and, with him, all the other Italian prisoners who confirmed their oath to the sovereign and declared their anti-fascism ideals[100].

Giuseppe had volunteered to work against the Nazis wth the former enemies. As a result he had been subjected to an interview, something which they carried out among the other former Italian internees in his prison camp, and maybe in other camps, he doesn't know. They wanted to find out who was Neapolitan by birth and lived there, knew his city very well and also, an apparently unusual question but which, he said, was the only one which was really of interest to the interviewers in the end, whether the person being questioned personally knew any camorristi. There was already a plan, it seems, to contact those

---

[100] The kingdom would have officially declared war on Germany only on October 13, 1943, but had suddenly assumed, famously, a very clear anti-German position.

people. Since he had been the only one to respond that, yes, he actually knew a camorrista, although through no fault of his own because it was a distant relative, he had been chosen. He had been taken on as an auxiliary in the OSS and then, as my uncle told you, they had enlisted him as well. They had instructed them quickly, given the urgency of the operation. You know the rest, Vittorio."

"Thank you, Mariapia."

Chapter 12

D'Aiazzo had turned to Piombini, who had remained beside him until that moment, as had Mariapia and uncle Gennaro: "Warrant Officer, since I have not forgotten that I am a policeman, I am going to continue dealing with this dead body which is still without a solution, in the hope of more success. Take over the command of the unit and I'll join you at Sant'Elmo as soon as possible."

"Yes sir," and the non-commissioned officer had gone out onto the road through the driveway and joined his men.

Bordin had just returned via the same carriageway, followed by Appalle and two officers, one of whom, following the non-commissioned officer's previous command, had planted himself on guard in the center of the courtyard. Having overheard what D'Aiazzo had said, the brigadier had tried to seize what seemed like a good career opportunity, and going closer to him had suggested: "Excuse me, Mr Commissioner: look... couldn't I take over this investigation? I am familiar with the procedures, and that way you could go to Sant'Elmo to take command of the unit."

"No, Marino, I'll direct the investigation, not only because it is my duty, but because the case intrigues me since it is an incongruous death in a scenario of people being killed in combat. You will just work with me."

"Yes, Commissioner," he had resigned himself.

Mulling over the crime, Vittorio had gone out onto Via Monteoliveto with Mariapia and Gennaro at his heels. Piombini was there giving orders to his subordinates; and it had occurred to him all of a sudden that, from what he'd heard, the non-commissioned officer had had a varied and long experience of homocides in Milan, before being transferred a year earlier to Naples to the *Vice Squad*, a less stressful department. Officers in the *Violent Crimes* section who had been subjected to too much stress with killings and other atrocities, were quite often transferred there. The Deputy Commissioner had thought he could get some advice from the warrant officer, but he hadn't wanted to ask him a precise question, afraid that he might belittle himself, and had said to him: "The gold could have been stolen from the victim by camorristi, but I don't rule out the possibility that it could have been taken by someone else who may have castrated Peppino just to make us think it was the camorra. We'll know from the autopsy if they cut off his attributes when he was dead or alive. What's more, the theft of such an important amount of gold would certainly have been a major motive for an assassination. On the other hand, we must keep in mind that the victim could have already handed the gold over to his boss's courier before being attacked and killed by someone who was unaware that the delivery had taken place. We need to find out whether the tobacconist died while the patriots were still here or later: the time of death is important so we can determine who to suspect. In the first hypothesis, in fact, a crime committed by the camorra is unlikely as I think they would have waited for the group to depart before acting. The time can be established, approximately, by the coroner if and when he gets here and takes the external temperature of the corpse; but only the autopsy will give us a more precise confirmation of the time when the temperature of the liver will be measured."

Piombini, who had sensed from the uncertain look on his superior's face and his tone of voice that he would like some advice from him, even if he had not asked him for it, had suggested: "Excuse me Mr. Commissioner, what do you think of this other hypothesis? Couldn't a possible motive be the inheritance of the tobacconist shop and anything else that dead man owned? In Milan I had a lot of experience of people killed and I learned that sometimes it's the relatives who kill, out of interest: I think we should also investigate the heirs."

"Oh no, eh?" Mariapia had flared up impetuously.

"Why?" Vittorio had asked her.

"... what do you mean why?! Because the closest relative is my dad, no? Peppino had no closer relatives, so he is the heir; but apart from the fact that he is a gentleman, dad was in the house with mama waiting for me when we left with the truck at six o'clock this morning; and in the hours that folllowed, he and mama were worried about me, they certainly weren't thinking about going out and killing someone! What nonsense is this individual inventing?"

"No, you don't refer to me as an individual, understand?!" Piombini became angry, his cheeks, nose and forehead turning purple, while she went red in the face, but certainly not because she was mortified: it was out of anger.

Vittorio had quelled them: "Okay, calm down both of you. Listen Mariapia, theoretically the warrant officer was not talking nonsense, but in practice no one is accusing your parents and I agree that, at the very least, it would not have been an opportune time for your parents to go out and kill someone, worried as they were about you; and besides your cousin could also have been killed more recently, maybe while we were at your house with you and parents, or even during the gunfight here: the medical examiner will establish the precise time of death. Don't worry, because there are so many hypotheses to ponder."

"Meaning robbery or things like that, right?"

"Yes. Listen, stay here with me, because I may need more information from you. Leave your rifle with someone else... ah, good, I see that our reinforcements are coming ... hmm... very few though... well, if nothing else there are also ambulances behind them. So listen, Piombini, after they've taken away the injured, you should certainly leave for Castel Sant'Elmo with your group. I'll join you as soon as possible."

"Yes sir."

Mariapia had shouted at Vittorio: "I want to go and fight too, now!"

"No, you can fight later, we'll go to Castel Sant'Elmo together. We'll find a car or a motorcycle and I'll take you there, but now you're staying here: it's a police order, not an invitation." In reality not only did he not have a license, but he didn't know how to drive a car or a motorcycle at all, so he had made a false promise with the purpose of later convincing her to stay safely at home with her parents.

"Well I'll keep the rifle for later," she had responded.

"Hmm... alright, keep it, there is always the risk that Germans could swoop on us at any moment. Actually, I'll take a MAB now too," and had gone to get one assigned to him.

Warrant Officer Piombini's function as commander had been short-lived. Dr. Remigio Bollati had arrived at the head of the reinforcements and, as the highest in rank of those present, he had taken over the general management of operations. Before leaving Police Headquarters, the official had changed for the occasion and instead of his civilian suit he had taken his Public Security officer's uniform from the closet in the office which bore the rank of lieutenant colonel, corresponding to his position as deputy Chief Commissioner.

Vittorio had gone to meet him, with the MAB on his shoulder, to give him a quick verbal report on the clash, then he had told him about the dead man killed outside the field of combat, concluding: "I intend to stay here with my aide and two officers for the initial investigation into the death of that man, even though naturally I would prefer to continue fighting; but I consider it my duty."

"It is, Vittorio: we are still policemen, aren't we? Do your duty, because we'll start by attacking Castel Sant'Elmo. Oh! and has the anatomopathologist been called?"

"Yes sir, we informed the radio room of the Police Headquarters of the corpse and asked them to let the morgue know. But whether a medical examiner will come on a day of chaos like this, remains to be seen."

When the ambulances with the injured had departed leaving the dead friends and enemies on both sidewalks for the time being out of necessity, the few police vehicles which had arrived as back up and the truck with Piombini and his group had left for Castel Sant'Elmo. The deputy Chief Commissioner Bollati was at the head of the column in his own jeep, with seven officers. Behind them were two sidecar motorcycles with six people, and bringing up the rear was the flatbed truck. Driving the second motorbike of the short convoy was sergeant major Gennaro Esposito, with a policeman sitting on the back seat. The disobbedient Maria Pia, who had run after it like lightning with her Garand over her shoulder, had leapt into the sidecar a moment earlier. As she got in she had said excitedly to her uncle: "Go, quickly, if not that man there will stop me!" Her relative, complicit, had quickly done so as *that man there,* Vittorio, seeing what had happened had resigned himself to joining the young woman at Sant'Elmo when his official duties would finally allow him.

The column had traveled the first part of the route in the opposite direction to the route that Vittorio, Mariapia and Marino had made on foot as they escaped the Germans. From Via Monteoliveto it had turned into Via del Chiostro and had gone along Via Cesare Battisti and Piazza Carità; it had then continued along Via Roma[101] arriving at Via Pedamentina San Martino through subsequent streets and, finally, turning right, it had arrived in view of Castel Sant'Elmo. They had not encountered enemies along the way, because most of the Germans and fascists were now concentrated in areas where combat was taking place.

The patriots who had preceded them had been fighting for a long time. An enormous din came from the ramparts of the fortress and the surrounding area and there was smoke and the smell of gunpowder everywhere.

The unit under the command of Joseph Jones and Giuseppe Scognamiglio had been among the first to arrive, when the battle had not yet begun. It had penetrated the fort through sewers and waste water canals, which stretched under the area, and ancient underground passages, following the indications of maps that the captain and lieutenant had been given in the Sannazaro high school. A few days before an architect who was a member of the Resistance had taken those floorplans, and some maps of the rooms in Castel Sant'Elmo, from the Civil Engineers and the Neapolitan Historical Archive, after agreements with the OSS. Since Lieutenant Scognamiglio was a surveyor, he was able to interpret all those small floor plans.

Following a long and tortuous underground route, made more difficult by some errors of orientation that had forced them to turn back, the Italian raiders had finally emerged in the cellars of the castle, around 10.00 am. Very cautiously, they had started movonh to the upper levels of the fortress and, once they reached the corridor of the armory, they would try not just to overwhelm, but annihilate the grenadiers on guard. The two commanding officers were hoping that the sounds of the shots would be confused with shots coming from the German weapons on the battlements and those of the attacking Italians being fired from the plateau in front, and would therefore not attract the enemy.

---

[101] It became Via Toledo in 1980.

Chapter 13

Marino Bordin had presented himself to the Deputy Commissioner for a first report with the agent who had accompanied him on the inspections and the cyclist repairman: "Mr. Commissioner, no gold bars in Appalle's workshop or home or the cellar. Not on his wife either."

"Knives and razors?"

"Only in the house, not in the shop or in the cellar. As you ordered, I seized them and officer Rozzani has them in his waist bag."

"We'll give them to the coroner."

"Mr. Commissioner, I'd like to inspect the back of the tobacconist shop and the dead man's cellar."

"Yes, but wait a moment." He had turned to the repairman: "You, Appalle, can close the shop now and go home to your wife."

"Yes sir Mr. Commissioner," the other had replied, had turned around and taken a first step towards his shop.

Vittorio had continued with his brigadier: "Alright, go and inspect those premises and this time ask those two officers to help you. I'll stand at the gate of the driveway to make sure no one enters. Find the keys of the premises and their likely duplicates for me. Get the ones for the shutters on Via Monteoliveto and check whether the deceased had locked and closed the three of them properly. Don't bother looking in the clothes on the body, I've already checked that myself and there are no keys, so they should all be in the house, somewhere.

After you've finished the inspections, close everything and order your men to affix the seals to the doors and shutters: use sheets of paper, adhesive tapes and the office sponge[102] which you will certainly find on the shelves in the shop. When you've done that, come and report to me and give me all the keys. If the doctor doesn't arrive within a reasonable time, we'll leave, but in that case you'll put seals on the lavatory as well, with the dead man inside.

---

[102] Scotch-type adhesive tape did not yet exist in Italy, although it was invented as early as 1930 by Richard Drew, an American scientist. In Italy the tapes were made of paper with dry glue on one side that had to be softened by dampening it on a wet office sponge, before affixing the tape: the result was rather precarious.

Just in case, keep some masking tape and whatnot, so you don't have to reopen the shop to get it. Go."

In order not to attract the attention of any enemies who might go past on the street, Vittorio had closed the driveway gates which had been left open, leaving just a gap so they could keep an eye on the road. He had started watching what was happening outside, so he could quickly catch the attention of the driver if and when the van from the morgue arrived.

Not long after, Gennarino had passed in front of him on the sidewalk, going home.

Following orders, Marino and the two officers had carefully checked all the rooms in the victim's premises. They had not found the gold in the most likely place, the cash register in the store, nor anywhere else. On the other hand, they had found the keys and the copies hanging on a nail in the kitchen in two separate bunches. The brigadier had taken the material for affixing the seals to the doors from a secondary shelf in the store where stationery products were displayed. Following the orders from his superior, he had locked the cellar and the back of the tobacconist's shop and told the officers to seal the entry doors, apart from the lavatory door, and the shutters on the street as well. While they were doing that, the brigadier had presented himself to report to his superior.

The van from the morgue had arrived and Dr. Giovampaolo Palombella got out of it.

D'Aiazzo had indicated where he should go and the doctor, followed by the four policemen, had gone to the terrible lavatory and its human remains with a surgical mask tightly tied over his nose and mouth. He had come out a few minutes later and removing the mask had said to Vittorio: "Looking at the wounds and blood clotting, I would say that it looks like they cut his throat and then the male attributes, when he was already dead, but I'll know that exactly in the laboratory: if I verify that the blood between the legs and on the mutilated lower abdomen contains serum which has separated from the red blood cells, I will establish that the tobacconist was already dead during castration; if I see instead that it had not separated, I will conclude that he was alive. Second thing: they definitely used a knife, or something like that, with a wide blade that was not very sharp. It certainly wasn't a well sharpened weapon, much less a razor or a scalpel, in fact the cuts are frayed, and in fact the amputation of his sex is even in shreds. Anyway, give me the the razors all the same and not just the knives seized from ... what's his name?"

"Appalle," Bordin had told him.

"Appalle. Well, with a surname like that, at least he will still have them, the purported," he had jested. [103]

Bordin and the officers had smiled, but not Vittorio who, having been raised by a strict officer father and teacher mother, had found the joke in really bad taste.

Turning serious again, the anatomopathologist, had continued: "Under the microscope I'll be able to see whether or not there are traces of blood on the blades of Appalle's razors and kitchen knives and, if so, I'll check if they are the same group as the victim's. As for the time of death, from the surface body temperature, for the moment I can say that it is somewhere between five and six this morning, approximately, but the autopsy will allow me to be more precise; don't expect it today, though."

Palombella had explained that he was very tired, because he had been on duty since the previous day, well past his shift: "I'm still here working because that young slacker Dr. Giordano Bruno Amicale didn't turn up to take over from me. Anyway, I'll load the castrated corpse and his attributes into the van and take it to the morgue and I'll open it only to measure the temperature of the liver immediately and analyze the blood between his legs, then I'll simply put the corpse in the refrigerator and, finally,even if the whole world collapses and Naples with it, I'm going home and that's that. Someone else will do the rest of the autopsy, probably *that babbalùcco*[104] Dr. Giordano Bruno Amicale, if and when he deigns to resume his duties."

This had raised a doubt in Vittorio's mind and he had said to the doctor: "You don't think that Dr. Amicale could be taking part in the revolt?"

"Hm... well, maybe. He should have let me know, though! We have a telephone. But in any case, I'm going home to my wife. She's alone in the house and will certainly be worried about me, because with the salary they give me we don't have a phone, and I haven't been able to let her know, poor woman. Imagine how she must be feeling. Let's hope that some idiot doesn't decide to bomb

---

[103] (t/n – a play on words because 'palle' means balls and Appalle sounds like 'has balls'.)
[104] Good-for-nothing

the city, because with those Anglo-Americans who have destroyed us from above for years you never know, eh? Oh, while I'm here, one more thing, about something that happened yesterday. I'll tell you now, Commissioner, because my written report will be late arriving at Police Headquarters, given the circumstances. That way, perhaps, you can tell whoever is in charge. It concerns a prostitute..."

"... Rosa Demaggi?"

"Yes, Rosa Demaggi."

"I'm following the case."

"Ah, very good, then I can tell you that she died from a hemorrhage inside one of the cerebral hemispheres as a result of trauma, which caused a large deep subdural hematoma ..."

"... can you tell me if Demaggi had alcohol and drugs in her body?"

"So you knew that? You're already well ahead in the investigation, huh? Yes, going *ex ante* the fact, she died because she was under the influence of opium and also a very strong liquor. She'd had a lot to drink, in my humble opinion, and her state of dizziness was, *ex post*, due to heavy drinking and smoking an opiate which caused her to lose her balance and slam her head on the piece of furniture, which caused the trauma that led her to death. So in the report I'll be writing that it was accidental death. Don't expect the report for today, okay? Maybe the day after tomorrow, all being well."

"In any case, what you've told me is enough for me to consider that the case is solved and I can dedicate myself entirely to this other one."

"If the young *babbalùcco* doctor or, as you think, heroic patriot doesn't come to work, then maybe, and I emphasize *maybe*, when I resume service tomorrow afternoon I will dissect the castrated corpse completely and then, if the phones are still working, I'll call you at the Police Headquarters with the results before I write the report. You are..."

"... Deputy Commissioner Vittorio D'Aiazzo. If I'm not there leave a message with someone in my section."

"I'll do that," and the doctor made a note of his name; then he had added: "Now there would be a small problem ... very smelly: one of the two porters on duty refused to come because he is a rabbit and is afraid of the gunshots, and since I have only one stretcher bearer with me, the very brave Luigi Malagatti here present!" – huge smile from the praised one – "and strictly speaking, I personally do not want to mess around in the shit without being able to disinfect properly before and immediately after. Do me a great favor, Dr. D'Aiazzo, and order your two officers here to help this one brave stretcher bearer to get the body and its attributes onto the stretcher and then load it into the mortuary van."

The two policemen had looked at each other without saying a word but with an eloquent expression of dismay. D'Aiazzo had taken no notice and had ordered them to help the stretcher bearer in the awful necessity, recalling that he himself, after all, had soiled himself while inspecting the corpse earlier.

Once the dead man had been loaded, Vittorio had asked the doctor: "Can you take us to the police station, before you go home?"

"... well alright, Police Headquarters is close: it means that I'll arrive home three minutes later. Get in with the corpse and hold your nose."

The funeral van, driven by the stretcher-bearer, had left.

They had met no enemies along the way, nor would the doctor and the porter run into any later on their way to the morgue.

At Police Headquarters, D'Aiazzo let the two policemen go off duty, and had gone up to his office with Bordin. He needed to store the two bunches of the dead man's keys in a drawer of his desk, and having seen the deputy Chief Commissioner in uniform, he also wanted to put his on too, with the rank of lieutenant, corresponding to his position as Deputy Commissioner. He had pulled it out of his locker and, as he started to change, had said to the brigadier: "I am going to Sant' Elmo; what about you?"

"I will too because, as they say, I've done 30, so I'll do 31."

"... and maybe, when you can, play those two numbers at lotto: straight pair on Naples," his superior had smiled at him.

"Yes sir, and on all the wheels as well, just to be prudent."

Bordin had a driver's license. They had taken a motorcycle from the garage and left for Castel Sant'Elmo.

Unfortunately, unlike the morgue van and, earlier, the deputy Chief Commissioner's convoy, the bike had run into some enemies along the way. Alarmed, the two policemen had seen a fascist department composed of about forty men a hundred yards in front, all armed with MABs. Those soldiers were marching in a column on the side of the road the wrong way, with their commanding officer in the lead.

"Òstrega[105]!" the brigadier had blurted out in his Venetian dialect.

D'Aiazzo had not lost heart. Putting his mouth to his subordinate's right ear so as not to have to raise his voice but be understood just the same, he had said: "Keep going and don't accelerate and when we're about twenty yards from them, give them the fascist salute."

Of course their heartbeats had accelerated a lot as the bike arrived at the fateful twenty yards from the fascist division.

As well as greeting them like Bordin did with an outstretched arm, Vittorio had stood up planting his feet on the rear running boards of the bike, so that his gesture was more evident and, perhaps, they noticed his rank of officer.

When he saw the bike arriving the column leader had ordered: "Halt! On the alert!" but was reassured by that familiar salute and had responded by raising his arm too *Roman-style*[106].

The two policemen had continued on their way unperturbed and the fascist division had resumed its march.

---

[105] *oyster!* But it is masked blasphemy.

[106] As the fascists called it, but in reality the salute among the ancient Roman soldiers was completely different: it was forearm and right fist on the chest at the height of the heart.

Chapter 14

The platoon led by Captain Jones and Lieutenant Scognamiglio had annihilated the German guard, favored by surprise and the enemy's fatigue. The grenadiers lying wounded on the ground had been immediately slaughtered mercilessly, according to previous mandatory orders of the OSS. Not a single German guard at the armory was to be taken prisoner, so that he could not later shout a warning to his comrades. The raiders had not escaped without shedding some blood, on the contrary: at the end of the battle less than half of them remained. The American captain had been killed too, so Mariapia's brother had assumed the command of the survivors. As well as Scognamiglio there were eleven left, six of whom were unharmed including him, two were injured though not seriously, the last two had been mortally wounded and died shortly after.

The lieutenant had removed from the body of the same ranking German the keys to the doors of the two rooms where the weapons were kept. He had opened both rooms and given orders to hide the corpses of friends and enemies in the one where the containers of the gas and biological weapons were stored, then had commanded his eight survivors to barricade themselves with him in the same room, but had instead left the room with conventional weapons wide open.

When everyone was inside, he had locked the door behind him, telling them to keep absolutely silent. Obvious prudence, because if it is true that in the chaos of the battle, what with the roar of gunfire and explosions echoing around the castle, no enemy had been attracted by the shots that had exploded in the corridor of the armory, it was foreseeable that they would arrive very soon to back up their comrades in the battlements. Which had indeed happened. The fact that the corridor was deserted and the room with the conventional weapons had been left open had made them assume that the platoon on guard had moved to the battlements to assist their comrades. So after taking magazines and tapes of bullets, the munition carriers had left. The special weapons had to be defended by the small Italian group. It would not be at all advisable to destroy them on the spot with explosives, and then try to escape via the same route they had taken to arrive at the armory. In fact, the explosion could have caused the leakage of deadly material, with very serious consequences for Naples.

The OSS haad given peremptory orders for the containers to be delivered intact to a team of American specialists after the Americans entered Naples: following the surrender of the castle which he would have heard about from the portable transceiver he carried, the commander of the group, Captain Jones, now Lieutenant Scognamiglio, was to open the room where he had hidden with living and dead and order his men to leave it; then he was to close the room from the outside and organize surveillance in the corridor, as they waited for the Americans.

At the same time that the platoon of Jones and Scognamiglio were fighting and then taking over the armory, D'Aiazzo and Bordin had joined the deputy Chief Commissioner Bollati's unit in front of the fortress and had started to fight. They had seen Piombini and Esposito amongst the bedlam; but they had not seen Mariapia. At about 5.00 pm the young woman's uncle was hit in the liver and stomach by machine-gun fire, and had collapsed to the ground a few yards from the two policemen. They had crawled over to him. The wounded man was lucid and had said through the pain: "Keep fighting, don't worry about me and... protect... my niece." They assured him they would. They could not have known that Mariapia was no longer in that area but had moved from there some time before to join a unit of civilians who were fighting further away, out of sight, against fascists and other Germans who had arrived in the meantime and were engaging the patriots on the flank.

Deputy Chief Commissioner Bollati had been fatally shot after a lightning barrage of MGs that had rocketed from the ramparts. It was therefore up to D'Aiazzo to take command of the now smaller group of attackers. The clashes had been very harsh and had continued until dusk. Castel Sant'Elmo had been taken as the first shadows fell, when the patriots' fire had been able to concentrate entirely against the defenders of the ramparts, after the Nazi-Fascist reinforcements outside had been decimated and forced to flee. But they would still do damage elsewhere; in fact, sheltering at the Vomero inside the Littorio Sports Field, they would harass the population in that area.

When silence fell on the battlefield, Vittorio had said to his adjutant: "Marino, let's go back to Mariapia's uncle to see if he is still alive, then we'll look for her. But I want to thank you first with all my heart. You saved my life shooting at that German who was aiming at me from the battlements."

"*Eeh*," the brigadier had rejoiced.

"Listen, call me Vittorio from now on."

"Yes... yes, thank you, Vittorio," he was flattered.

They had returned to where Esposito had fallen and, as they greatly feared given the severity of the wounds, they had found him dead. D'Aiazzo had closed his eyes. Side by side the two men had then inspected the area scattered with fallen patriots, looking for, but hoping not to find Mariapia's body. Happily, they hadn't found it.

Vittorio had become more and more disconsolate during the patrol. In his heart he had supposed that it was becausem of the nerve-wracking sight of the countless unknown corpses that covered the area of the clash. That was true in part, but not only that; his sadness had also been triggered by a repressed but still deep disquiet: the subconscious distress for his companions who had died a bloody death a few hours before in front of the tobacconist shop and from the impression left in his subconscious by the dreadful sight of the slaughtered tobacconist, castrated and slumped onto his own dung. And on the other hand, Vittorio's anguish had been made worse by the memory, which touched his own conscience, of the two faceless Germans he had killed on September 9 with his own ordinance Beretta when without taking aim, he had fired into their group out of an instinct of anger, and had not first considered that he had individual human beings children of God before him, not an impersonal array of uniforms.

And now, suddenly, that last scene had reappeared very clearly in his mind. With a slight sensation of nausea at the mouth of his stomach, Vittorio had wished fervently that he had not killed those two poor wretches, and had instead become the grim murderer merely to vendicate the poor boy. Now, though, those two strangers were dead and he could not bring them back to earth.

In that twilight of September 27, the Deputy Commissioner had stood on the ground of the fresh clash, his feet widespread, arms folded, and had let his gaze run mechnically in a semicircle over the panorama of the witnesses of freedom fallen in battle; and, in his sense of guilt, he had realized that if the figure of the individual human being always prevailed in the hearts of leaders rather than that of anonymous totality, perhaps there would be no more wars.

He had said to the brigadier: "You know what? Whether it's annihilation in battle by marauders like the Nazis, or a single massacre like the tobacconist suffered, basically the difference lies in only two things, the size of the slaughter grounds and the number of dead. That at the head of an entity, whether gigantic or small, there are unscrupulous leaders of nations or corrupt neighborhood camorra bosses, the substance is always the same, that because of them History since Cain is an entire series of poor Abels being killed. War is bloody shit, always, and personal aggression on another human being is shit too, always, and anyone who gives the order to kill, no matter whether it's to plunder entire populations or to rob a single person, is shit."

Vittorio had lapsed into vulgarity, despite the good education he had received, because of the overly gloomy mood which overwhelmed him at that moment; and pointing to the dead bodies scattered sprawled in front of the castle he had added: "Like countless others in this war, these poor people too have been killed personally by Hitler and Mussolini: with an invisible weapon, their decisions made at a table. Yes, Marino, it is just as if they had been killed, one by one, by those two greatest murderers."

Bordin was a man of little culture, boorish by social origin and, furthermore, his long-standing experience in Public Security which until shortly before had been a pro-fascist militia where brutal methods had often been used, had led him to approve of the use of violence against suspects, as we know, a feeling that his young superior's influence was beginning to direct towards the path of moderation and pity. But apart from all that, the brigadier was an intelligent person, so he had remarked to his new friend: "Excuse me, Vittorio, just now you spoke of the victims like Abel and, if I'm not mistaken, you compared them to Peppino Scognamiglio in a certain way: excuse me, okay? but to me he doesn't seem to have been an Abel, if anything he was a Cain of the same cloth as his own boss. Actually, to use your own words, shit like him. So perhaps it was not by chance, but by the will of fate that he died in the john in his own stench lying on his shit."

"Hmm... well, yes: I can't say you're wrong about that camorrista. To tell the truth in was thinking in general and the case of the tobacconist is not a good example, I should not have mentioned him but other victims, such as the poor devils killed for theft. And furthermore, I don't believe in fate, I think that God created us free." Then he had set off to the castle, Marino behind him, so that they could both lie down and, finally, get some rest. Meanwhile, they had given their voices a rest.

Vittorio's crisis of conscience would not have prevented him from continuing to fight for freedom until the liberation of Naples, in the days that followed.

A lieutenant colonel had assumed command of the fortress and, once the defeated had been disarmed, had given orders to let them go. With their dead and wounded on their shoulders, the surviving Germans had already left Castel Sant'Elmo at nightfall. Their release would have entailed the obvious consequence that they would join other Germans and resume fighting, but the Italian commander had judged it impossible to keep them captive and under guard; on the other hand, he had not wanted to shoot them out of respect for the Geneva Convention, since they were uniformed fighters who had handed themselves over as prisoners under a white flag: very different from the criminal massacres of Italian soldiers perpetrated in Kefalonia and Corfu by the Wehrmacht on the same days, the 27th and 28th of that month[107], a massacre of which Naples was as yet unaware.

The lieutenant colonel did not know that the Germans now had the immediate objective of evacuating Naples and feared that they wanted to take back the fortress as soon as possible. He had therefore asked the patriots who had returned from the battle to volunteer for the defense from the battlements. Nevertheless he had let those who preferred to fight elsewhere to leave or simply go home if they were civilians.

---

[107] It is quite well known that, after many days of combat between the Italian units and the former Nazi allies to whom they had not wanted to surrender after the armistice of September 8, they had indeed surrendered and that, nevertheless, many of the prisoners had been massacred by the Germans. The others had been deported on ships which, with great misfortune, had in part been torpedoed by British submarines and the rest had blown up on sea mines, with further serious Italian losses.

Contrary to the fears of the senior officer, those who remained garrisoned at the castle would not have fired a single shot more. That would not be the case for many of the others.

At dawn, under the command of a lieutenant named Enzo Stimolo, a company made up predominantly of soldiers had left Castel Sant'Elmo to fight where the enemies were still under arms. The officer's primary objective had been to meet and engage in combat with those Nazi-Fascists who had withdrawn the night before, after the assault on the patriots on their side. In addition to Stimolo's large unit, small autonomous groups and some individuals had left the fortress that same morning in search of outdoor clashes. Vittorio and Marino were among them and, completely independently of them, Mariapia, who had been unharmed in the combats of the previous day and was still full of hatred for the Germans. She had hoped to find uncle Gennaro among the survivors the previous evening and, after the capitulation of the castle, had gone looking for him first of all in the place they had fought side by side in the first moments. Without ever meeting or seeing Vittorio and Marino, she had discovered her relative's body after the two policemen had already gone, so she did not know who, mercifully, had closed his eyes. She had not wept, even though her heart had leapt in her breast when she saw the corpse. She had recited a prayer for the deceased, then had gone in search of her brother inside the fortress, aware that the armory had been the target of his platoon. Hoping to find him at least alive, she had gone up into the corridor where the fighting had taken place. Giuseppe was there asleep on the floor with his men, while other soldiers, sent by the lieutenant colonel commander, had replaced them in the surveillance of the secret weapons. Very relieved to have found her brother unharmed, the young woman had not roused him and had gone to sleep next to him. It was Giuseppe who had woken her. He had learned of the death of his uncle Gennaro. Despite her brother's disapproval, Mariapia had left Castel Sant'Elmo at dawn with her Garand on her shoulder, looking for more Germans to slaughter.

Chapter 15

In the night between September 27 and 28, many citizens in the various areas of Naples had crept out of their homes to join their countrymen who had already rebelled, not just replacing the patriots who had been killed, but swelling the ranks of the combatants and making the insurgence enormously popular. Some of the new rebels had come with the rifles and pistols they had in the house, which they had never handed over to the authorities despite the orders firstly from the fascist regime and then of the German commander. Many, with or without firearms, had switchblades or kitchen knives in their pockets or belts. Some had prepared Molotov cocktails with rags and gasoline, formidable in their simplicity.

On September 28 the audacity of the Neapolitan people was fully manifested in a storm of devastating actions. At dawn the gunfights had already resumed, many more and much more intense than the previous day. Among the many episodes, one of the most impressive had been the assault at Maschio Angioino, garrisoned by a large number of Germans, by an equally large unit composed of men of the Guardia di Finanza and civilians of various social backgrounds, led personally by commander Antonio Taraia. At the same time Lieutenant Stimolo's company had gone in search of the Nazi-Fascists that had sheltered inside the Littorio Sports Field at the Vomero the night before. They had rounded up a number citizens of both sexes In that area and had concentrated them in the sporting arena, which was fenced, to use them as hostages. When Enzo Stimolo's strong partisan unit had arrived in the area its action had been powerful: the patriots had besieged the area of the Sports Field and ordered the Nazi-Fascists to surrender and to not shed the blood of the hostages unnecessarily. At first the enemy had reacted by firing at the lieutenant's forces, but the German officer in command had soon seen reason, considering that the patriots were more numerous, and had decided to play for time by asking for a temporary truce and promising not to hurt the kidnapped civilians. The stand-off had lasted throughout the night between the 28th and the 29th and nothing had happened.

Meanwhile, in another area in the dark of night, an improvised company of insurgents, with Mariapia among them, had besieged the German Supreme Command in Corso Vittorio Emanuele II. Lieutenant Stimolo had heard about it at dawn on the 29th via his field radio. Of his own initiative he had gone to the headquarters of the German Command and, under a white flag, had contacted Colonel Walter Scholl, asking him to order the release of the Italian hostages imprisoned in the Littorio Sports Field. Given the very tense situation, the German commander had agreed, obtaining in return that the rebels surrounding his Command abandon the siege and, moreover, that the Nazi-Fascists at the sports field be allowed safe passage and be granted a partisan escort until they were outside Naples and from there could move away safe and sound. That had been the first time during the war that the Germans had negotiated a surrender with insurgents.

So, in the second half of the morning of September 29, following the German Command's order by radio, the men under siege at the Littorio Field had surrendered, had freed the hostages and had come out unarmed. The freedom fighters had let the Germans go without roughing them up, but for the first hundred yards the former hostages and residents of the neighborhood whose relatives had been kidnapped had instead kicked the Fascists in the butt.

Mariapia had continued to fight in one of the disorganized rebel squads that had formed when they had, ceased the siege of the German Command headquarters. Her group had peeled off from the larger one and had headed to Porta Capuana, where the young commander worked as a baker. There were fourteen of them, Mariapia and another woman and twelve men including a fourteen-year-old. When they arrived at their destination, they had set up an improvised checkpoint, stacking furniture that had been thrown onto the road two days beforehand onto a German truck that was passing by, without hitting it, and was now lying on the road. Under cover of this barricade, and taking advantage of surprise, the fourteen patriots had fired on a squad of German sappers who were arriving on foot to lay mines in the neighborhood. They had prevailed without suffering any losses and had taken four prisoners, including the sergeant commander, after killing six, two of whom had been killed by Mariapia alone with her Garand. They had died much more painfully than the others, because the young fury had aimed at the lower abdomen and belly, shouting each time: "There, take it inside!" By shooting she had wanted to make the enemy suffer exactly where she had. When the battle came to an end she had inspected the dead Germans and those that had been captured, once again not finding the ones who had raped her.

The prisoners had not remained alive for long because the baker, having learned from a woman that another German squad had killed her thirteen-year-old son the day before and looking at the uniform and not the single human being, had given the order to shoot them on the spot exactly as Mariapia had done. The young avenger had requested and been given permission to line up with the riflemen and had fired half the magazine into the belly of a trembling, sobbing blond nineteen-year-old.

The young woman would continue to fight with her thirteen companions the following day, during which five of the squad would die, one by one, including the other woman, while the young fourteen-year-old would be injured by a barrage of MG into his back to remain quadriplegic for the rest of his life. As if some mysterious force had constantly protected her, she did not get a scratch.

Although leading exponents of the democratic parties sat in the Neapolitan section of the National Liberation Front and that there were, moreover, several officers of higher rank, no real strategic plan had been formulated. They had only addressed groups of insurgents with objectives judged particularly important, such as the Maschio Angioino and, when pushed by the Americans, Castel Sant'Elmo. A real coordination of the units had not been implemented during the conflict until the afternoon of September 29: the initiative had been left largely to the leaders of the bands of insurgent civilians and the platoons and squads of the Guardia di Finanza, the Carabinieri and the Public Security who had joined with them, while individual policemen like Vittorio and Marino had fought in isolation joining, on occasion, one group or another. During that afternoon, however, some senior officers and some influential men of the neighborhood had tried to plan the uprising as far as was as possible, coordinating the operations at least within the individual districts and managing, in some cases, to connect groups of neighboring quarters. Among those military commanders was Major Francesco Amicarelli who had organized a small company in the area of Piazza Mazzini, composed of about fifty bourgeois and military including Vittorio D'Aiazzo and Marino Bordin.

The combats had recommenced in the area of Via Monteoliveto on the same day and were much more intense than on the morning of the 27th: in the din and rumble of gunfire and explosions, Concetta and Antonio Scognamiglio had spent the day sheltering under the double bed, fearing more for their daughter than for themselves, because she was going around Naples and who knows if she had been injured or, worse, was dead. More than one bullet had come through the windows of the house and had stuck into the walls inside.

Of course, not all partisan actions had been victorious. Thus, despite managing to do damage to the enemy, Major Amicarelli had had no luck: at a certain moment his small company, engaged in combat against a unit of German infantrymen in Piazza Mazzini, had been attacked in force by German tanks that had arrived as reinforcement for the infantry, including the Panther of the unlucky Nazi Marshal Konrad Müller. The patriots had turned back leaving on the pavement twelve dead and eleven seriously wounded while six, less seriously injured, had been picked up and taken away by their unharmed comrades. As for those close to death on the ground in the square, they had been finished off by enemy tank drivers who had crushed them under the tracks; but not those of the racist Müller's tank, because by then his Panther had been destroyed by one of the patriots, Marino Bordin, who was now close to death.

Just before being almost sawn in half by a volley of the MG on the bow of another armored vehicle, he had managed to throw a molotov against the damn tank which had caught fire and, in just a seconds, had exploded killing the entire crew. Brigadier Bordin would learn only later, as he entered the paradise of heroes, that he had annihilated precisely the Panther which had blown up his armored car in Via Cesare Battisti, and also that the beastly Bavarian marshal had pronounced in his dialect: "I will kill you all, you fucking Italian asshole sewer rats!" just a moment before the tricolor incendiary bottle of the brave Italian hit him.

In the same hours, in different areas, many other patriots had been killed. In particular, a very fatal shelling that had targeted the Ponticelli district, inhabited by working class people, had massacred the majority of them. After that, soldiers of the German infantry had arrived in force and in the houses left standing had slaughtered anyone they had found still alive, including women, old people and children: in this case too it had been soldiers of the Wehrmacht, not the Waffen SS.

On the morning of September 30, 1943, the German units had begun the evacuation of Naples while powerful Anglo-American forces had now arrived very close from the direction of Nocera Inferiore; but the Nazi battles against the Neapolitan insurgents had not completely ceased. Indeed bitter clashes had taken place in the area of Porta Capuana, while from the hills of Capodimonte still occupied by the Germans, cannon blasts had been launched on Naples for almost the entire day. It had caused massacres in the areas of Piazza Mazzini and Piazza Dante and in the neighboring Via Port'Alba, near the homonymous ancient gate. In cowardly retaliation, before fleeing, the Germans had also burned and destroyed the Historical Archive of Naples near Nola, which had until then been the main source of information on the history of southern Italy since the Middle Ages.

That same morning of September 30, Professor Antonino Tarsia In Curia, a teacher in the Sannazaro high school, who had already been one of the main characters of the liberation of Naples in previous days, had appointed himself head of the rioters assuming full civil and military powers and, then and there, had created a Single Revolutionary Front. At first, on his own initiative, he had assigned himself the direction of the Vomero district, then he had moved to the Prefecturer headquarters to perform prefectorial functions, escorted by carabinieri he collected along the way just by proclaiming that he was the new prefect.

He had become a coagulating factor in the final phase of the insurrection, giving clear instructions to all public entities dependent on the prefectural figure, even the Chief Commissioner. He had also acted as a replacement for the mayor and the entire city council, issuing many municipal orders in writing the very same day, even concerning the opening hours of the shops. Despite the last fires of warfare, the climate of peace was obvious in the air now, if all the insurgents obeyed the *new prefect* who was also the *mayor* and *general in chief* Antonino Tarsia In Curia: a splendid example of brilliant Neapolitan improvisation.

At sunset of that final day of revolt Vittorio had returned to Castel Sant'Elmo, having left the surviving companions of Major Amicarelli's unit, but promising to return to recover Bordin's body as soon as possible. Not forgetting his duties as a policeman, he wanted to start the investigation into the case of the tobacconist again. He intended to speak with Giuseppe immediately about his cousin's murder and with his soldiers as well and, hopefully, with Mariapia, if he found her with her brother.

In the last three days Lieutenant Scognamiglio had remained on guard at the armory with his men, even though he had really wanted to go out and fight, but the order from the OSS had been imperative, not just conquer, but defend and deliver the secret weapons to the Americans.

It was dark by the time the Deputy Commissioner went inside Castel Sant'Elmo. Explaining his reason for being there, he had asked and, thanks to his uniform, had found out where the armory was. He had gone up to that corridor and when he met Giuseppe's team there, had asked for him: not only did Vittorio not know that man, but he could not identify him by sight, since the lieutenant was in civilian clothes like the rest of the group. Scognamiglio had introduced himself. D'Aiazzo had quickly told him about his cousin Peppino's murder and everything else that had happened; then he had asked the officer where he could find him in coming days, since he would summon him to Police Headquarters as a witness as soon as possible.

"I'll be going to live with my parents as soon as I can. The address is..."

"I know the address, through Mariapia. Will you be staying with them permanently?"

"No, only for a few days, then I'm intending to start fighting the Germans again."

Vittorio had asked the other eight soldiers if anyone was from Naples or its surroundings. There was no-one from the area, they had all been serving in city barracks or on ships at anchor and, caught unexpectedly by Badoglio's announcement of the armistice on the radio the evening of September 8 and unable to return to their villages, they had hidden in the city. Vittorio had made a note of their names and domiciles in his address book: as civilians six lived in center-north regions occupied by the Germans, the other two were from the south, one from Palermo and the other from a village near Potenza. He had told them that, like the lieutenant, they would be summoned to Police Headquarters to testify very soon and had ordered them not to leave the city before that. He had added: "This is a Police order." Then he had asked for their temporary address in Naples. All they could do was provide the address of the Sannazaro high school. Five of them had promised the policeman they would go back there and stay until they received the summons, while the rest had assured him that they would remain in daily contact with the others. Vittorio had ordered: "Tell me now, one by one, even if you will have to repeat it to me at Police Headquarters in a few days with a written report, when and where you last met the tobacconist Peppino Scognamiglio."

Each had replied that he had seen that man, for the first and only time, as he arrived in his courtyard, standing at the top of the steps that led to the cellar telling them to go down there. No one had seen him since.

Giuseppe Scognamiglio had intervened: "I also saw him for the last time as I went down to the cellar, and the others were already down there apart from an American captain, a certain Jones, who came down with me."

"I know who he is. Where is he now?"

"Killed in combat, and his body is with the others downstairs. We've put them in the cool of the basements in the meantime."

"Hmm... I'd like to know something about the movements of that American last night, at your cousin's place."

"You can't be thinking murdered my cous..."

"... I don't think anything, it's is normal procedure to inquire about everyone's movements." In reality, Vittorio had not ruled out the possibility, albeit remote, that the OSS had ordered their agent Jones to eliminate the camorrista who had acted as intermediary, so that he would never talk about it with anyone, and disguising the murder as a heinous underworld crime: the cynicism of the Italian secret services was well known at Police Headquarters and the policeman didn't think the Allies would be any more compassionate.

"Commissioner, there is not much to say: when all our men had gone down to the cellar, Jones gave my cousin some packages containing gold lingots. I was next to him and saw this. Then while my cousin..."

"... I know it was the third and final instalment of the compensation for the camorra."

"Exactly, but I was saying that while my cousin went into his house with the packages to check them, we two officers had joined our men in the cellar. Neither I, nor Jones, nor anyone, at least as far as I know, went out until we were leaving, around 6.00 am; and there was no sign of Peppino when we went out."

"According to what Mariapia told me, she had gone to the cellar too and stayed there. Do you all confirm that?"

"Yes," Giuseppe had replied, "Yes sir" came from the others.

"Lieutenant, your sister told me that she too had seen her cousin for the last time when she had gone downstairs. Meaning, none of you survivors saw Peppino again when you were leaving; but one or more of your men who were killed may have seen him as they went out, and they might have told someone amongst you before they were killed. Do you know whether that happened?"

Silence.

"No? Nothing?"

"It would seem not," Giuseppe had replied, but had asked his men nevertheless: "So, do any of you know anything about it?"

Chorus of no.

"One more thing, Lieutenant: do you know where your sister is now?"

"No, and I hope to God she is alright. She left us at dawn the day before yesterday saying that she was going out to fight and I tried to keep her here, of course, but to no avail. Let's pray that she is alive and well, Commissioner."

Chapter 16

On October 1 at 9.30 am the Anglo-Americans, led by an American squadron of M4 Sherman tanks, had entered Naples scowling like proud winners. But since the Neapolitans had welcomed them as liberators amid enthusiastic ovations, their attitude had softened; and furthermore, there were descendants of Neapolitans who had emigrated to the United States among the Americans and some of them had relatives in the city: strangers to them, but relatives just the same.

Mariapia, with her trusty Garand on her shoulder, had joined the cheering crowd on each side that was watching the passage of a motorized unit of American infantrymen. Unexpectedly, a resolute corporal of the Military Police had approached and disarmed her, almost tearing her rifle from her, admonishing her sharply. He then passed the Garand to a fellow soldier in one of the jeeps in the column. During the course of the day all the armed patriots surprised by the Anglo-Americans would be forced to hand over the weapons, of whatever origin, to the new occupants, exceot for the uniformed members of the three police forces, including the Deputy Commissioner, let alone lieutenant, Vittorio D'Aiazzo.

Around noon of that same day, a platoon of American military specialists had collected the chemical and bacteriological weapons stored in Castel Sant'Elmo which had been seized and defended by Jones' and Scognamiglio's stormtroopers. They would be transported carefully out of Naples on two especially sprung trucks to the warehouses of the US Army's biological and chemical company to which those men belonged. Four soldiers has also taken delivery of the remains of Joseph Jones and before entering the basement where the captain's corpse lay, had put on gas masks against the stench that was now emanating from the corpses awaiting burial. The dead man had been closed in a bag, taken outside and placed among the containers of weapons on one of the two trucks, to be buried the following day with military honors in an improvised Allied war cemetery.

Giuseppe and his eight soldiers had not received any thanks from the snooty lieutenant who commanded the platoon, a

Californian over six foot two tall with carrot-colored hair, nor would they receive any praise in the future, and even less would they be decorated by anyone whatsoever for the dangerous operation they had carried out.

The entire city had been invaded by the former enemies. They had become "the liberators" for everyone even though Naples had freed itself and even though, above all, the American weapons parachuted to the insurgents there had been relatively few, not many more than the ones they had stolen from the Germans and fascists. The citizens who had lined the streets at their entry had then started exalting the new invaders individually, and loudly, in all parts of Naples and, here and there, celebrating them with improvised songs and sounds of putipù, tambourines, trumpets and bell-collars. Fireworks had shot into the sky at nightfall, as if it were the festival of Piedigrotta.

Not all Neapolitans, however, had celebrated. First and foremost, not the ones who deep down had been and were still followers of fascism, and who had closed themselves in their homes hoping for the best, because they had not been able to get away from Naples in time. The lukewarm had suddenly gone from being fascists to anti-fascists when the Allies had arrived, and many of them had gone out into the streets to shout praise for the "liberators". Very differently, the bereaved families had not celebrated: in the days after calm had returned to the city, five hundred and sixtytwo dead would be buried, according to the lists of the Poggioreale Cemetery, among whom only a few dozen had died of natural causes; the others had been unarmed civilians slaughtered by the Germans, or people who died when the houses hit by cannons had collapsed, or they were patriots killed in combat, among those 1589 insurgents who had fought during the 72 hours of the uprising. Beyond the official figures, a much higher number of Neapolitans had been killed by German hand if we take into account those declared missing and never found, because they had been shattered to bits by cannonades or burned to death by enemy flamethrowers. Nor had there been celebrations by the relatives of the more than 300 injured people herded at best into the devastated hospitals, 75 of whom would remain permanently disabled,

On the same first day of October, Air Field Marshal Albert Kesserling, commander general of the German troops in Italy, had sent a report to the Führer in which he had stressed, almost as if it had been a victory, that the retreat from Naples had ended positively, with minimal losses of men and assets, and that the troops had been solidly deployed along a new, well defensible front north of the city. He had been careful not to reveal to Hitler that, thanks to what would go down in history as the Four Days of Naples, the mass deportation plan ordered by Colonel Walter Scholl had been compromised and it had been impossible for the Germans to organize a resistance to the enemy inside and outside the borders of Naples with anti-tank and anti-personnel mines and with cannons and machine guns. The field marshal had also concealed the fact that the Italians had avoided, as the German dictator had instead ordered, that the city be razed to the ground in the end turning it, in the very words of the diarrhoeic and long-winded Hitler, into "mud and ash."

It should be noted that the balance sheet would soon prove to be even more positive, when you think about its socio-political and moral effect as a spur to the subsequent resistance in Italy and an example to the rest of Nazi-occupied Europe.

And yet, despite the merits of many Neapolitan citizens, the Allies, although flattered by the festive welcome, had behaved much more like occupiers than as heralds of freedom. On the other hand, hunger had led the Neapolitan commoners to submit voluntarily, almost like slaves. So, in a Naples that had essentially descended into becoming a famished colony, *scugnizzi*, [108] some of whom had fought the Germans risking their lives, were seen ending up as mortified shoeshines – *"sciuscià"* – of the occupying soldiers, receiving a buck or two in return for food or a few cigarettes, and others acting as pimps for older sisters wanting to sell themselves to the invaders: the scandalous spectacle of girls reduced to prostitutes of the new conquerors – the *segnorine* – to get some food for themselves and their family became common too. Yet not a few of those young women had recently taken up their rifles or thrown Molotov cocktails at the Nazis. Worse still, some young boys and even children, had allowed themselves, for a fee, to be sexually molested by degenerate *goumiers*, Franco-African soldiers of the *Corps expeditionnaire français* under the orders of French General Alphonse Juin. Among these, indifferently attracted by males and females, there had also been

---

[108] (t/n – street-children, ragamuffins)

cases of brutal carnal violence, sometimes resulting in bloodshed and even in mutilation; in particular, the *goumiers* considered all Italian women *qabba*, meaning whores, each one of whom was a *haggiala*, that is a *widow-prostitute* in their particular Arabic-French jargon, a definition deriving from the custom of poor Arab widows to prostitute themselves to support their children and themselves[109].

From October 1943 in the Naples occupied by the Allies, delinquency had prospered enormously and, above all, the organized camorra groups had been greatly enhanced. Among many other things, they had schemed with U.S. military warehousemen and had obtained the food, cigarettes, chocolate of the US Army at a low price as well as vials of that precious penicillin which had been available to wounded Anglo-Americans for just a few months. But it was certainly not available to the civilian population of Naples and, in particular, not to those many women who had been sexually infected first by the Germans and then by the new occupants: in Naples only the very rich had benefited from antibiotics, on the black market.

---

[109] These North African and Senegalese soldiers had already carried out some atrocities in Sicily and, as is well known thanks also to Moravia's novel and De Sica's film "La Ciociara", in May of the following year, after the battle of Monte Cassino they would behave in an enormously worse way against many Italians of both sexes and of all ages in Ciociaria. They had received *license to rape and loot* by their very own General Juin himself! He would never be tried as a war criminal, as he had been ranked among the victors, as if victory had erased that reprehensible authorization to his men. The Nuremberg and Tokyo courts would later hand out a minimum of justice towards Japanese-German war criminals, but for the crimes of the victors, nothing; and the crimes of the Allies had been perpetrated not only by *Goumiers*, but by many other members of various armies; think, for example, of the massacre of unarmed Polish officers in the Katyń forest, carried out by the Soviets, followed by the extermination of civilians in the same place and in other places, for a total of 21 857 unarmed Polish being massacred.

Chapter 17

Early on the morning of October 2, 1943, Vittorio D'Aiazzo and two officers had gone to Piazza Mazzini in a small jeep. In the meantime, the survivors of Major Amicarelli's company and some local people had recomposed the bodies of the people who had died in the clash with the panzers as far as was possible considering the damage done to them. The corpses had been lined up along one side of the square and, in the many cases of absolute slaughter, hessian sacks and shovels had been used to collect the scant compressed organic matter to which those patriots' bodies had been reduced after the Nazi panzer tracks had passed over them again and again.

Marino Bordin's body appeared among the few who had remained almost intact, apart from a wide purple line that crossed the entire person of the former brigadier waist high: the enemies must not have thought it necessary to flatten that body when they had seen it immobile and alsmot sawn in half by the rapid fire of a machine gun. Vittorio and the two agents had collected his remains, the Deputy Commissioner in the middle holding his forearms and hands on each side, so as not to risk separating them, the officers holding the body one under the armpits and the other under the popliteal. They had laid it gently on the floor of the truck, between the two side benches. Vittorio had sat on one of them with one of the policemen on the opposite side, and the other officer at the wheel. They left and took the dead man's body into the parade ground at Police Headquarters, where several other bodies of colleagues which had been recovered in Naples and in the area around Castel Sant'Elmo had already been composed. Among them was the body of D'Aiazzo's direct superior Remigio Bollati in his uniform of lieutenant colonel, and there were the remains of Marshal Aroldo Bennato and the other two policemen killed in Via Cesare Battisti on the first day of fighting.

Apart from the most recent deaths, the corpses were now giving off the nauseating sweetish stench of decay. With no distinction of rank, the remains of the fallen had been lined up next to each other along one side of the rectangular square, waiting to be closed in coffins as soon as possible with a military and religious funeral ceremony to follow. As the Chief Commissioner Carmelo Pelluso had ordered, it would take place at 7.30 am the following morning,. Then the coffins would be delivered to the families, while the dead without relatives in the area would be buried in the municipal cemetery where the officers fallen in service already rested, all arranged and paid for by Public Security. Bordin would also be among these, as Police Headquarters did not know where the widow and orphans of the former brigadier had been evacuated.

About ten days after the burial, and not having heard from her husband for some time, Marino's wife had returned to the city to enquire about him at Police Headquarters. Only then had she learned of the uprising and that the city had been liberated. And when an emotional Vittorio would tell her of the tragic, glorious death of her husband, she had decided that her husband would remain buried there. The Deputy Commissioner would also give her two receipts from Lotto for respectively 100 and 250 lire, which he had played on Naples and on all the wheels at his own expense on behalf of the widow, both with the same ambo of 30 and 31, which had luckily come out. Vittorio had remembered the words of his brigadier: "Since I've done 30, I can do 31." He had said to the woman: "Mrs. Bordin, your husband had these winning lotto receipts in his pocket, I checked the results and I can guarantee you that they are winners: as his heir, go and cash in the winnings."

In the late morning of October 3, even though it was Sunday, Vittorio had received the reports on the autopsies from Dr. Palombella for the two corpses of Rosa Demaggi and Peppino Scognamiglio. In a separate envelope there was a note, addressed to him personally, on which the anatomopathologist had written: "You were right, Commissioner D'Aiazzo: Dr. Giordano Bruno Amicale had joined the patriots. I heard that he died fighting bravely outside the Maschio Angioino. If you are a believer like me, say an Eternal Rest for him, even though he was a die-hard anticlerical atheist because of a long family tradition: it is no coincidence that my poor colleague boasted that his father had called him Giordano Bruno. But God certainly has compassion on anyone who has sacrificed himself for others. Cordially yours, G. P."

The report on Demaggi essentially confirmed what Dr. Palombella had already said to Vittorio, accidental death caused by alcohol and drug abuse with loss of balance and hitting her skull against the edge of a piece of furniture. Thus the case could be archived after the Chief Commissioner's visa, without sending a report to the Court. As for the tobacconist, death had come after his throat had been cut around 5.30 in the morning "fifteen minutes either way", while the castration had taken place post mortem, " a quarter to a half hour after his death", "a wide and not sharp blade, almost certainly a bayonet" had been used to kill and emasculate. Appalle's knives and razors had nothing to do with it and therefore, as the doctor wrote, they remained "at the disposal of their owner at the morgue, upon presentation of a withdrawal authorization form, signed by an official of the Police Headquarters." The anatomopathologist had also noted that the victim had been a robust person but when he was alive had suffered an impairment to the left hand caused by an ancient trauma that had paralyzed the index and middle fingers in a half-bent position, which could have made it more difficult for him to defend himself from the murderer's attack. Thus the assassin could also have acted alone and was not necessaily a very strong person. The dissection had also found that the victim had suffered from "chronic purulent colitis."

In the afternoon of the same day, Vittorio had a motorcyclist officer sent written orders to the bicycle repairman and his wife at their home address, to Giuseppe's eight men at the Sannazaro high school, and to Giuseppe himself and Mariapia at their parents' home. They were obliged to come to Police Headquarters the next morning to testify regarding the murder of Peppino Scognamiglio. With an interrogation plan in mind, D'Aiazzo had not summoned everyone for the same time: the repairman and his wife were to present themselves at 9:00, Giuseppe's soldiers at 9:15 and the Scognamiglio siblings at 9:30.

Chapter 18

At 8:50 am on Monday October 4, the Appalle spouses had arrived at the front door of Police Headquarters.

"*Too early, let's wait!*" the man had ordered after checking the time on his old onion-like watch with a steel case but a gold chain and medal of San Gennaro which was also gold, gifts of his baptismal godfather, a Perse brand watch, as he boasted, just like the stationmasters of the Ferrovie dello Stato used.

She had replied, stubborn: "*No, Gennari', trasìmo[110], it's the same, the same!*"

They had started to squabble about going inside yes and going inside no, in increasingly raised voices.

After a couple of minutes of this exchange the sentry on guard at the door, annoyed, had approached them and had rebuked them sharply in his marked Emilian accent: "What's going on, ve'? Are we at the market, ve'?"

"Uh!" she had said.

"Ah!" he had uttered.

"What do you want here?" added the defender of order in an even more severe tone.

Appalle had tossed off an explanation: "We have an appointment."

"Who with? What's the reason? Be clear, ve'," he had investigated.

"Eh... uh... *Cuncetti', cómme...* uh, no, it's that, excellency, *'mo* I don't remember anymore *cómme he's called chillo there.*"

"*Gennari'*, it's written on the *fuóglio* " his wife had suggested, speaking almost in Italian so that the *foreigner* policeman also understood.

"Ah, yes, it's *'o* true... so... *te' qua*[111]: *'o* Deputy Commissioner Dr. Vittorio D'Aiazzo, to be exact, is expecting us... on the second floor like it's written here... and only at 9:00 o'clock so we, if you will allow, would wait."

"... but what do you want to wait for? There's not even five minutes left, ve'."

---

[110] Let's go in.
[111] Here his name.

"See I had *raggióne* from *'o* start eh?" Mrs. Appalle had triumphed, always in quasi-Italian so that the guard could appreciate her victory over her husband.

After giving the documents to another agent who was sitting behind the reception table, on the ground floor, a corporal with functions of usher had taken them up the staircase leading to the upper levels and, on the second floor, they had been introduced into the office of the Deputy Commissioner.

Vittorio had had ten chairs brought into his room earlier and with the two permanently destined for guests or the witnesses, depending on the case, he had had them placed in a semi-circle in front of his desk.

He'd had the Appalle couple sit on the middle chairs, in front of his armchair then, before dismissing the corporal, he had asked him: "Listen here: are you able to type?"

"No sir, I can only write by hand."

"You can go then." Unwillingly, but resigned to having to type using just his index fingers whatever he considered useful to record of the conversation with the Appalle couple and the others who had been summoned, he had got up and gone to the table which the deceased Bordin had used. He had taken the heavy Olivetti M1 model 1911 typewriter that was sitting on it, carried it to his desk, had returned to the dead man's table and had taken a half ream of paper and two carbon papers from the only drawer. Sitting down again, and before saying a word to the spouses, he had written two lines by hand on Police Headquarters letterhead, and had signed them: it was the authorization to pick up the knives and razors at the morgue. He had handed the sheet of paper to the husband who had taken it and put it in his pocket without reading it, while Vittorio explained to him what it was. Finally the young official had asked the woman: "Donna Appalle, tell me everything you and your husband did between the evening of last Saturday the 25th and the morning of Monday 27th."

"Uh, I... huh?"

"You don't know?! It's only a few days ago, after all."

The husband had stepped in: "No, sorry, Commissioner, my wife is a very simple woman. *'na fèmmena 'e càsa* and *se scunfònne*[112]. So sorry, but maybe I can talk first and that way, maybe, you then ask *illa herself if it is 'o true.*"

____

[112] She is a houewife and gets confused.

"Alright."

"Commissioner, that Saturday evening, at 7:30 pm exaactly, I closed *'a putèca* as *'o* usual and I went up into the house to my wife to have dinner. Then, after washing the dishes so as not to have *'e* stink *'n* house until *a' matina* that bothers you, we..."

"... that's fine, but get to the point, Appalle."

"Sorry, I was just about to say *the point* and that is that we went to bed and, with shutters closed for the blackout we listened *'nu* little *'e* radio: we do it practically always, but we soon turn off the light and goodnight. We rested until dawn *cómme dùie prète, pecché*[113], thank *'o* Heaven, we do not have insomnia, so much so that *'na vòta*[114], last year, we had only woken up when they were already bombing Naples. Anyway, the next morning, meaning Sunday, we got up as always *c'o primmo* sun, we had that little *primma colétion*[115] crap with *dùie* crusts *'e* black bread all bran and rubbish and also with *'a* broth of that surrogate that passes itself off as *'o café* but that's pure *fetenzia*, and then we went, you understand, to the first Sunday Mass in our parish and, after the blessing *d'o prèvete parrucchiàno*[116] Don Aristide Carignotti, we went straight home. Being Sunday and with the *putèca* closed, I was *'nu poco stufato* all*'o juórno* like on all feastdays, although I helped my wife clean the floors and prepare lunch and then dinner and I listened to *'a* radio, but well, I got fed up. Then we had dinner, it will have been 7:30 pm, 7:35 at the most, and then like the night before and all the previous ones, *'nu poco 'e* radio and sleep until dawn. At the first ray of that very bad luck Monday 27 that seemed like *'nu* Friday the 17th" – he had touched his testicles –[117] "I got up and went to work, and the rest, if you don't mind, Commissioner, I already told you in the morning that we met each other."

Vittorio had asked the woman: "So far do you confirm your husband's statement?"

"Eeh?" was all she had said, not understanding the meaning of *confirm your husband's statement*.

"*Cuncetti'*," her spouse had rescued her, "the commissioner just wants to know if what I told him is *'o true*".

---

[113] Like two stones because

[114] One time.

[115] breakfast.

[116] parish priest.

[117] (t/n – In Italy, Friday 17th and not 13th is considered unlucky)

"Ah, that? Yes that is *'o true*; but if you have already told him, why does he want to know from me as well?!"

Vittorio had ignored the woman's clumsiness and had asked both of them: "In the night between Sunday and Monday, especially between 5 and 6 in the morning, did you hear something or see someone in the courtyard of your laboratory? Words, noises, movement? Individuals who were moving around and looking around circumspectly?"

The craftsman had blurted: "Circum...?"

"Circumspect: the word refers to people who try not to be seen, who act like thieves, stealthily."

"Ah, stealthily! *Aggio capi'*. Commissioner, we did not hear anything, because we slept very well: you too, *Cuncetti'* isn't that *'o* right?"

"Yes, *Gennari'*, like you said."

"As for seeing the courtyard, certainly not, because our apartment is in the middle, meaning between two other apartments and we can only see Via Monteoliveto. Isn't that right, *Cuncetti'*?"

"Of course it's *'o vero 'O vero* it is!"

"Eh, you see. Commissioner, I am very sorry, but since we know nothing else, perhaps we could now take advantage of *chista istessa matina* to pick up our things at the morgue and then I would go *chista istessa matina* to open and to *faticua'*, with your permission you understand, considering that I have work to do because I haven't dared to open in these days of gunfire and explosions after that famous *matenàta iellata* [118] that you know, and yesterday was Sunday and I respect", he had hyphenated emphatically, "do-ve-ro-sa-men-te![119] the municipal rules and also the Church's precept of resting on feastdays; but Saturday night our neighbors on the landing had assured me that *'a pace* had returned in Naples, so with your permission, of course, I would go directly to the morgue."

The ambiguous meaning had made Vittorio smile, and serious again had said to the man: "Appalle Gennaro, you cannot leave yet, because now you have to repeat everything you told me on the morning of Monday, September 27, when you discovered the corpse: I'll put it in writing, you'll sign it and then ... we'll see."

---

[118] (t/n – unlucky morning)

[119] (t/n du-ti-fully)

"Eeh... if you say so..." Gennarino had resigned himself, intimidated by that bureaucratic *Appalle Gennaro* which had reminded him of when he was in the military.

His official deposition had been the same as the unofficial one of September 27, but it had lasted much longer because D'Aiazzo, bad typist that he was, had typed each sentence with exasperating slowness, often interrupting the repairman so he could accurately report his words on paper.

Finally he had removed the typescript in triplicate from the machine and said to Appalle: "Read and sign, here at the bottom, all three sheets."

The other had signed with shaky elementary handwriting and without reading it; then he had pleaded: "... and now we can finally leave, can't we, Your Excellency?"

"No sir, and I had already told you that I am not Excellency, but just Doctor and Deputy Commissioner. No, you can't go, but now you and your wife go out please and wait in the hallway, where there are some chairs. You will be sent away when the time comes, because I may have to ask you something else first."

"... and excuse me", the woman had allowed herself naively, "*pecché nun ce le dimannàte 'mo?*" [120]

"*Pecché primma aggio a sentì àta*[121] *gènte*", he had replied kindly.

The woman had not investigated further, she trusted that doctor and Deputy Commissioner now, who also knew Neapolitan.

There was a knock on the door.

"Come in," Vittorio had said mechanically.

It was the corporal acting as usher: "Sorry, Mr. Commissioner: those other eight would be here."

"Send them in," he had ordered, "and let these two go and sit on the chairs in the hallway."

The soldiers had entered passing in front of the corporal and the Appalle pair.

After indicating the chairs to the man and woman, the graduate moved towards the staircase to go back down, and the couple sat there waiting. She had sat down immediately, but he had started walking restlessly back and forth, in front of his wife.

---

[120] (t/n – and why can't you say it now?)

[121] Because first I have to hear other people.

The sentry on the floor had stared at him for a while, and a minute later had said: "Couldn't you sit down a little, you're making my head spin?!"

"Very sorry, excellency," the bike repairman had stopped. But instead of sitting down he stood still on the spot.

"... so sit down then, will you?" the sentry had shot back, even more annoyed at seeing him standing there like a statue than by his previous up and down.

"I'll do that, excellency," Appalle had resigned himself, and as soon as he sat down had lit a Tuscan cigar, fouling the air in the corridor.

D'Aiazzo had asked the eight soldiers to sit in front of him in a senicircle. The two who had been slightly injured in the clash with the German grenadiers were wearing bandages. One of them, a bersagliere, around a forearm because of a graze, the other, a corporal truck driver, on his the head for a nick on the forehead.

The Deputy Commissioner had again asked for their personal details, one by one, and had typed them, comparing them with the ones he had marked in his diary on the evening of September 30, To get a better idea, he had asked each of them for their level of education: almost all had not gone beyond compulsory schooling, but a seaman in the Navy originally from Camogli, called Annibale Bacci, had said that he had obtained the diploma of master mariner in a merchant navy school in Genoa and had added that, having been conscripted at the beginning of 1939, and not expecting they would go to war, he had not applied for the course to become reserve midshipman so as to avoid the frequent call-ups into service which officers were expected to do; he had added: "Seeing that war broke out, it would have been better if I'd applied."

Before hearing the testimonies of the eight men, the Deputy Commissioner had warned them: "What I'm going to ask you is official this time and, as you can see, it is being recorded. Remember that what you are about to tell me will have to be repeated in Court later, so it's best that you get your ideas clear right now. In other words, it's not about answering me with things like *I didn't notice* or *I don't remember*: in Court you will speak under oath and, furthermore, the jury will read what you tell me now, so in your own interest it must coincide." He had got them worried to perfection: they had been silent for several seconds, and then he had added: "Yes, you were right to think about it, so now you will respond correctly too. One by one, tell me first of all whether, from the moment you arrived at Peppino Scognamiglio's place, about 5:00 am on Monday 27 September, until you left on the truck at 6:00, you saw anywhere, I mean in the courtyard or on the street, the middle-aged man and woman who are sitting out there, or even just one of the two... you noticed them as you came in to me, didn't you?"

Everyone had agreed that they had.

"They're husband and wife. He has a cycle repair workshop in the same low building as the tobacconist. Answer one at a time and we'll start with the person sitting furthest to the right. Then gradually the next person to the left will answer me."

One after the other they had said that they had met the couple only shortly beforehand, in the corridor.

"From when you had arrived in the courtyard to when you left, who did you encounter, if anyone, other than the tobacconist and the others in your group including Lieutenant Scognamiglio's sister?"

The bersagliere, a certain Remo Colonna, *romano de Roma* as his pronounced accent revealed, had replied: "Not encountered sir, but when we went back to the street to leave, I saw a civilian from behind who was walking away; as I would find out later on the truck, it was the man who had driven it there; one of us got behind the wheel instead of him, this man here..."

"... corporal truck driver Ambrogio Manzotti, at your disposal," the nominated man had introduced himself in a robust Milanese accent: "I didn't see anyone else either, apart from the civilian driver, but I also spoke with him before he left, to ask him to explain some things about the vehicle, because it was a model that I had never driven and a little different from the CL that I was driving while on duty."

In short: from the moment of arrival in the courtyard to departure, none of the eight soldiers had seen anyone extraneous to their group except that driver.

The Deputy Commissioner had typed the answers, then said: "The question I am about to ask you now is very important. I want to know if anyone from your group, including your two officers and the lieutenant's sister, went out of the cellar and into the yard between the time you got off the truck and the time you went back to the truck."

The truckdriver had spoken again: "The American captain and I went up, it must have been a few minutes to six, to open the gate on the driveway. When the truck arrived shortly after, he went downstairs again to give orders to the others to come up, while I was talking to the driver. That civilian left then and all my companions got into the truck."

"Alright, thank you, but I didn't mean to talk about service reasons, I wanted to know if someone, after five and before six, had gone up to the courtyard on their own."

A certain Rosario Patanò, a foot soldier with the Engineers, originally from San Cataldo near Caltanissetta, had told him: "After we'd each taken our own weapon and ammunition, we sat down on the ground in small groups in various places, separated by walls, and I personally was not in sight of the door but in an internal area, so I saw nothing."

"Those who were near the door could have seen," Vittorio had remarked towards them all.

"Maybe yes and maybe no," Patanò had considered, "because there wasn't much light down there, just the light of candles, one here and one there, and there was smoke too."

Finally Vittorio had been given a positive statement: "Yes sir, I saw one of us go out," the seaman Annibale Bacci had spoken, having wanted to think about it before opening his mouth, considering that he was about to indicate a friend: "It was the first-class soldier Salvatore Cuoco, who later fell in combat outside the armory of Castel Sant'Elmo."

"Are you sure of his identity?"

"Yes, Mr. Commissioner, I knew him well because he was embarked with me on the destroyer Mameli and had the bunk next to mine; what's more, when we came on shore leave here in Naples, being Neapolitan he had wanted to invite me to his home."

"When precisely did this sailor go back up into the yard?"

"I didn't look at the time."

"Roughly."

"Well, we'd been down there for quite a while: let's say over three quarters of an hour? A quarter to six?"

"Did he have a bayonet with him?"

"Yes sir, he had his own, at that point we all had them in our belt, because the captain and the lieutenant had already distributed the weapons."

"You told me that he was Neapolitan: as far as you know, could he, by pure hypothesis, have met the dead tobacconist before?"

"Yes sir."

"Ah! so he had... but this is very important! Did he tell you that?"

"Yes sir."

"What was the relationship between him and that Peppino?"

"Personally none, I know that before the tobacconist directed us to the cellar that night Salvatore had never seen him before, but I had realized that he detested him."

"Oh really? Tell me about that."

"Salvatore had told me that several years earlier that Peppino, who didn't have the shop yet though and worked for the camorra, had used violence to send his sister Margherita into prostitution, and that's why he detested him. The delinquent had taken advantage of the fact that their father had died three years earlier, hit by a tram, when she was eighteen years old and Salvatore was a child of just four: there was a great difference in age between the two because of some physical problems due to the first birth, as my friend had learned from his mother when he was older; and as a result of those problems, his parents had not expected to have a child again, but he had arrived instead. Apart from that, the point is that there were no children in the house old enough to defend Margherita, there was only Salvatore who had just turned seven when she had come of age[122] and the camorra boss had noticed her. Obeying his orders, Peppino had forced the girl to follow him, a command that was accompanied by vandalization of their poor accommodation and death threats not only for her, but for her mother and little brother as well if she disobeyed him.

Terrified, the two women had submitted and the daughter had gone with Peppino. He had deflowered her the same day and had also taught her various dirty things that I won't name out of decency, threatening her with a knife; then she had been locked in the trunk of a car, bound and gagged, taken to the province and forced into prostitution there. Even though it seems that she had resigned herself, over the years she had always been watched and sometimes threatened, like all her poor companions, real slaves: not by Peppino, however, who worked in Naples, but by his partners in crime. The young woman wasn't able to see her mother again for a very long time. As for Salvatore, five years after his sister's rape, when he was twelve years old, he had gone to work at

---

[122] At that time the major age was twenty-one, not eighteen.

sea as ship's boy on a merchant ship, always wandering around the world without any news of Margherita: his mother had not wanted to make him suffer and had told him that in the meantime the young woman had married and lived in Australia.

In 1939 Salvatore had been called up to serve in the navy and, after a course as a engineer had been embarked on our Mameli, and had remained in service on board permanently, like me, because the war had begun. His mother, who knew how to write well enough, had sent him a postcard at the beginning of January of '41 with the news of his sister's death. It was addressed to the military port authority in La Spezia where our destroyer was based, which she had learned from her son during his first leave. Unfortunately the Mameli, had been commanded elsewhere in the meantime. Salvatore had received that postcard, but months later, after going through two ports, as it appeared from the stamps. In the end it had been redirected to the right one, Taranto, where we had made a long stop for repairs. His mother asked him to go to Margherita's funeral if possible or, at least, if he had not been in time, to visit her tomb. Just imagine, it's war and news always arriving after an eternity! He had kept the postcard and looked at it occasionally, rather than reading it again: there was a view of the port of Naples still intact, before the bombings.

In the night between September 6 and 7 we docked here at anchor offshore because of the damage to the port facilities. Salvatore and I had gone ashore on the launch during the first round of shore leave, thirty six hours from 9:00 am on the 7th to 9:00 pm on September 8th. He had gone straight to his mother who lives in a basso on Corso Umberto I, and took me with him to meet her and invite me to lunch. They had made me sit in the kitchen, then mamma and son had gone to talk by themselves in the other room. When Salvatore had came back to me he looked shocked, but he didn't say anything. They had gone out together, telling me that they were going to the cemetery to Margherita's tomb and that, if I wanted, I could wait for them there or return at 12:00 for lunch. I replied that I wanted to visit Naples which I didn't know and that, if it was alright with them, I would just return for dinner. Of course, I had brought something to eat that evening as we always did at the time. After dinner the mother had cleaned up and gone to sleep, and Salvatore and I played several games of chess on the kitchen table. I could see that his head was elsewhere, he always lost, and at a certain point he burst into tears. I asked him if he felt sick and that's when he got it off his chest and told me about his sister and that delinquent. I slept on a couch in the kitchen until late in the morning. After lunch, Salvatore and I went out and walked around Naples, and I bought some vegetables and fruit to give to his mother for dinner in the evening. We returned just before 7.:00 pm. There was no nows yet about the armistice with the Anglo-Americans, because the it would be announced on the radio only around 7:00 pm, meaning not long before our permit expired.

Towards the end of dinner my friend turned on the radio in the kitchen, and we heard the voice of the Marshal of Italy Badoglio announcing the cessation of hostilities. We rushed to the quay where the tender to take us back to the ship was supposed to wait for us, but I don't know if it was or not, because we didn't get there. In fact along the way, a man in plainclothes had seen us in uniform, and told us that he was a Major of the Military District and showed us a card as proof. He stopped us and warned us about the Germans saying that they had already moved to occupy the strategic points of Naples and do more damage to the port and had starte shooting the Italian soldiers they met on the street. Long story short, the officer took us to his own home and gave us civilian clothes and hospitality for a couple of days He burned our uniforms in the kitchen stove. On the morning of the 10th he took us to the Sannazaro high school, where the first rebels were getting organized and where they would teach us to fight the Germans, using a particular technique of what they called urban combat..

The following week, one evening, before we went to sleep, Salvatore went back to the matter of his sister again, and told me that she had died from the consequences of a syphilis she had contracted prostituting herself: she had died at home because those scoundrels had taken her back there in the spring of 1940[123], because she had become unusable and was almost paralytic; and they had had the cheek to tell her that she should thank them because they could have got her off their hands simply by killing her and burying her somewhere, like a bitch."

"One of those scumbags was Peppino?"

[123] We must bear in mind that penicillin was not yet available in Italy in 1940, which would have cured syphilis and other venereal diseases. The Anglo-Americans themselves would have antibiotics for their wounded soldiers only in mid-1943.

"No, Commissioner, other people. But Salvatore had learned from his mother not only that Peppino had started everything, but that some years befote he had become a prosperous tobacconist and, to top it all off, had a shop near them in Via Monteoliveto, so his mother had met him in the street several times. That's all I know. Do you want to tell me if it was Salvatore who killed that delinquent?"

"I don't know, I'll ask you some questions just to understand things. Can we say with certainty then that it was a quarter to six when Salvatore Cuoco went up into the courtyard?"

"Well, maybe five minutes later: it was just before we left."

"He hadn't been upstairs long, then."

"A few minutes at most."

Victor had asked the others: "Do any of you remember if someone else had gone out too?"

Without hestitation, a gunner named Aroldo Gerbino, his inflection revealing that he was Piedmontese, had replied: "I was sitting near the door, but as had been said before there was the smoke of the candles and the very little light and, above all, I didn't really think about looking at the door right then, neh? I was there thinking that we were about to go into action and I was feeling sleepy too and had my eyes closed, maybe because of the time or for the tension I don't know ..."

"... and so?"

"And so, I hadn't seen anyone go outside, I mean not even that sailor there, neh?"

All the others had stated that they were inside and could not see the doorway. This meant that, excluding Bacci and Gerbino, those near the door had died in combat. Perhaps Mariapia and her brother had seen? Vittorio promised himself he would ask them about that a little later.

He had told the eight to go out and wait in the hallway.

"Can we smoke?" the Sicilian engineer had asked him.

There were sounds of approval from the group and the Piedmontese Aroldo Gerbino had exclaimed hopefully: "*Eh magàra, boia fàoss*[124]!"

"That's fine, but only if it doesn't bother the lady out there. Tell the sentry to come here a moment."

---

[124] "Eh, maybe, false hangman!" *Faoss* is pronounced fàus.

They had gone out leaving the door open and a moment later the policeman had entered: "Command, Mr. Commissioner."

"If it doesn't bother Mrs. Appalle, let those boys smoke, but get an ashtray, because I don't want them getting ash on the floor."

"Actually, Mr. Commissioner, the Appalle are already smoking themselves, he's got a Tuscan and so has she."

"Oh, her too?!"

"Yes sir, and I had already given them the ashtray and I had also opened a window because the corridor was so full of smoke you could no longer breathe."

Chapter 20

Mariapia and Giuseppe had arrived in the meantime and, after their documents had been checked and left at the entrance, the sentry usher had taken them to D'Aiazzo's office.

Vittorio had them sit on the middle chairs opposite his armchair and after a few words of circumstance he had said: "On the morning of your cousin's murder I saw that the basement he owned is not made up of a single room, but has internal concrete walls like in anti-aircraft shelters that more or less converge on each other like a spiral and meet in a central area. Could you two see the exit or or were you inside the cellar, that night?"

Giuseppe had replied: "We had moved towards the central part of the basement immediately."

"So you entered the cellar together? But you told me ..."

"... no, we didn't go in together, just that Mariapia was standing near the door when I went down with Jones, and seeing that I was going further in she followed me."

"Yes," she had confirmed.

The brother had continued, "Jones and I got the weapons and distributed them immediately and we explained how to use them. Then I, Mariapia, and some others sat on the ground in the middle of the basement, waiting for the time to go into action, but Jones had gone back near the door. The rest of the men were spread around in various other areas of the cellar. What's more, both Jones and I moved around several times, up and down, to check that no one fell into a deep sleep, and also to reassure those who were showing signs of anxiety."

"I understand; and the times when you were near the door, you didn't see anyone go upstairs?"

"No one."

"Another question: did you by any chance see the cycle repairman alone or with a woman in the tobacconist's courtyard or nearby, before you went down to the cellar or when you went back up at six?"

"No, he had replied, and Mariapia had asked him: "By woman you meant his wife, who is out there with him?"

"Exactly."

"My brother didn't know her, he saw her for the first time here a little while ago, but I did because she is a customer at the tobacconist shop. No, during that time I didn't either of them, but the previous evening I'd run into him, just before Giuseppe arrived at shop, let's say about 7:15 pm: he had come in with his ration cards and his wife's to buy two packets of Tuscan cigars. Then I saw him again the following morning, when he told you that he had found Peppino dead."

Vittorio had slowly typed questions and answers, then asked: "I will formally repeat a question you have already unofficially answered: When did you see your cousin alive for the last time?"

She had said: "When I was about to go down to the basement, while Peppino was approaching the American officer and my brother. I didn't see him alive after that, only dead in the lavatory the next morning when I glanced inside, just before you, Vittorio, had your men stand in front of me so I couldn't see anything again."

"It wasn't a public spectacle, Mariapia."

Giuseppe had said, "I hadn't seen him since Captain Jones gave him the gold. If you want to know if he was alive or dead when we left, I have no answer. I know Peppino wasn't in the courtyard and I had no reason to look for him. I remember though, just now, that on the way out I had noticed in passing that some light was filtering between the slats of the lavatory and I had assumed that he was inside, doing what he had to do."

Instead he was already dead, Vittorio had said mentally to himself, knowing that the autopsy stated that the victim had been killed between 5:00 and 5:45 at the latest, whereas the patriots had left at 6.:00. He had turned to Mariapia: "What can you tell me, about that light in the lavatory?"

He had received a sharp, unexpected response: "I don't give a damn."

Why did she say that? he thought amazed. A moment later he had heard even more peculiar words.

The young woman who had gone pale and was starting to sweat, had squealed at him, stumbling into a slip that could not have been more Freudian: "At that moment all I cared about was going to assault ... aah! to a...attack Nazis! I attacked a lot of them and filled their bellies with bullets and made them squeal like slaughtered pigs!" Although the poor young woman had eliminated enemies for four days in a row, in an impulsive attempt to cancel the trauma of the sexual violence she had undergone, the suffering in her soul had not been alleviated even a little. At times, just as now, she violently relived the flashback of the rapes.

Not knowing anything about it, Vittorio had felt a strong sense of repulsion for Mariapia, imagining that she was a sadistic person. He had not been able to stop himself and had said to her in a very severe tone: "They were enemies, it's true, they had oppressed us, it is true, but it's war! Someone else had sent them to fight us: the culprit is the person who had declared war! How can you be so happy about having... attacked them?!"

The young woman had yelled furiously at him: "Hitler sent me those two beasts to take me by force and screw me?!"

Her brother had pulled her to him and kissed her on the hair.

She had laid her face on his chest.

Victor had remained silent, embarrassed.

At his silence Giuseppe had refuted: "The majority of Hitler's soldiers are guilty, Commissioner. While most of us Italians went to war out of duty and unwillingly, there were very few German soldiers who had not enthusiastically obeyed their führer; and the OSS is very much aware that Mariapia's is not an isolated case: for the Nazi soldiers, and many German soldiers are Nazis, not only the SS, it is frequent practice to rape the women in the occupied countries, both to make them pregnant and increase the number of newborns of the so-called Aryan race, and because those abuses fit into the distorted philosophy of their idolized Hitler, which states that all non-Aryan peoples are breeds of slaves and the Germanic race can do as it pleases."

His sister had meanwhile lifted her face and with those words was staring the Deputy Commissioner defiantly in the eye.

Vittorio had tried to reciprocate her hostile look with a benevolent one, but had not been able to bear those two stinging wasps looking into his pupils for long.

To better explain things, Giuseppe had added: "Mariapia had that nervous reaction because her spirit is totally defeated, and unfortunately it's not the first time that her nerves have frayed. She has had serious reactions just like that at home in the past two days; and dad and mom make things worse because they don't know what happened to her, nor does my sister want them to know, so, believing it's because of the battles she has participated in, they reproach her for them which exacerbates it even more."

"I'm sorry, Mariapia, I didn't know," Vittorio had said to her.

She had not answered.

After a few seconds of general silence, the Deputy Commissioner had spoken to Giuseppe again: "You, Lieutenant, when did you know about those sexual abuses?"

"What do you care, you idiot?" she had said angrily.

"Calm down, Mariapia," her brother had tried to sedate her, "remember that we are in the Police Headquarters during an official interview."

Vittorio had wanted to be indulgent: "I'll pretend I didn't hear the insult. Answer my question, Lieutenant."

"My sister had told me about it that night, before our group arrived and only after the cousin had fallen asleep, because she didn't want him to hear. It was almost four in the morning and Peppino, at that point, was finally sleeping, we could hear him snoring: he had stayed awake until half an hour before, running to the lavatory for hours."

Vittorio had completed: "Later, while your group was in the cellar, your cousin had a further attack of diarrhoea and ran back to the toilet again. He was killed there between 5:15 and 5:45, according to the autopsy, meaning at least a quarter of an hour before you all got on the truck; so when you were leaving and had seen the light of the candle filtering between the planks of the little room, he was already dead."

It had seemed as if Mariapia had suddenly found her tranquillity again, but it had been just another manifestation of her shock; she had intervened in a quiet voice: "Yes, he suffered from systematic dysentery, he had to go to the toilet many times every day. They had diagnosed him with *chronic colitis*, according to what he told me once: I don't know why he had confided in me, that he considered a zero, and I don't think he'd wanted to justify his coming and going in the courtyard, maybe he was drunk that time, in fact I remember the stench of Arzente[125] on his breath; he

---

[125] This is how Italian brandy was defined during fascism, which rejected foreign terms and had replaced them with Italian words, sometimes coined specifically. The name Arzente, an archaic synonym of ardent, had been created by Gabriele D'Annunzio to replace cognac.

had told me of his illness after returning from the lavatory for the umpteenth time, it was a Wednesday, I remember it because only two days later they raped me."

"Try not to think about it, it's not good for you," Giuseppe had urged her gently.

Still apparently serene, she had contradicted him: "No, it helps me, it's a release, and I want Vittorio to understand very well because he had a bad opinion of me. I was talking about that Friday when..."

"... no, Mariapia, it doesn't help!" her brother had tried to block her, this time abruptly.

Instinct had suggested to Vittorio that he should not join in the encouragement, but to humor Mariapia: "That Friday when ...?"

With her voice and facial expression still outwardly calm, looking up to the ceiling as can happen recalling to mind something that happened, she had resumed: "I was saying that Friday when they raped me, the day before the uprising. It was almost closing time and a motorbike stopped outside the door of the tobacconist shop which was wide open because it was hot, and two Germans came in and one of them, as soon as he saw me, grabbed me as if I were goods on display to the public, he put me on the floor face down, stripped me below the waist and deflowered me; then it was the other's turn. After that they stole things and then went away calmly with their arms full, leaving me on the ground confused, bleeding and half-naked, on my belly."

"Mariapia, that's enough now please," her brother had almost yelled at her, turning purple.

"Yes, Mariapia," Vittorio had agreed, "there's no need for the details, it's very clear how much you have suffered. I was to ask you something else, though: Peppino wasn't there?"

"Oh yes he was! Yes, he certainly was!"

"So he saw it all happening."

"Hm..." was all she had muttered, her jaw clenched.

"Peppino was present and hadn't tried to help you?"

"Hmm..." she had mumbled longer.

"I see. He didn't act like a lion that wretch, although I can understand that a man alone against two armed soldiers..."

"... yeees?!" she had snapped to her feet from the chair like a rampant hissing dragon, losing control again in a single moment, "so do you also understand why he had his way inside me too?!"

"Mariapia!" Giuseppe had sprung up too, standing straight without moving with his mouth half open, to then sit down again a couple of seconds later, as if drained.

What had risen, instead, was the policeman's attention, and a lot. He had asked himself: *The brother knew nothing about it, this third rape, or did he? Did he know this and, a little while ago, had repeatedly urged his sister to keep quiet not so much because he feared for her health, but with the dread that the cousin's violence, a possible motive for murder, would come out? and he has exploded with anger now because instead she has talked? Or on the contrary he didn't know anything about it until a moment ago, he was only worried about Mariapia's sanity and now, having learned of his cousin's filthy behavior, he jumped to his feet aghast?*

Apparently Mariapia had not told her brother, and in fact, when she sat down again at his side, she had squeezed his face in her hands and, looking compassionately into his eyes as if he himself were the one offended, had said to him in a hoarse voice: "Yes, as soon as those two left, Peppino closed the front door with the inside hook and threw himself on me, still on the ground half-stunned, and he raped me too."

Giuseppe was deathly pale and had not made a sound nor had he pulled his face from his sister's hands.

Vittorio sat there silent, very attentive.

With the two men in silence, the poor young woman had continued, looking alternately at the Deputy Commissioner and her brother: "In the end he pulled me up onto my feet by force and ordered me to wash and get dressed. While I was doing that he threatened me, telling me that he and his friends would kill dad and mama and me as well if I told anyone about his abuse and that, in any case, it was in my own interest not to talk about what the Germans had done either." Here Mariapia had let go of Giuseppe's face and turned only to the Deputy Commissioner: "He told me, I remember his precise words by heart, that it was best to *stàrme zitta pecché 'na fémmena che nun è spósa de l'òmmo che l'ha chiava' è 'na zòccola pe' tutt'o munno e resta signurìna e nun se 'mmarèta cchiù*[126]. He made me swear to God and our Lady of Pompeii to be silent: as if he was devoted to Our Lady! Then he sent me home. I didn't tell mama and dad not only because of the death threats but, perhaps, even more because of what Peppino's said about the bad female who never marries. I had the illogical fear that my parents could let something slip: I was ashamed as if it had been my own fault and I felt the anger later, not in those moments, no: shame, just shame and the desire to hide what had happened."

Her brother had said: "What are you wanting to achieve by continuing to talk about these things? Punish yourself when you have done nothing wrong?"

Vittorio had disapproved of that: "No, Lieutenant, your sister must continue now. Go ahead, Mariapia."

"Yes, Vittorio. The next morning I was strongly tempted not to go to work, then I realized that my parents would ask me why and, with an effort, I went. As soon as I entered the store, which the cousin himself had opened that morning perhaps thinking that I wouldn't come to work, he asked me if I had kept quiet and, even though I told him yes, he repeated the threats to me, then he made me swear again on God and Mary Most Holy to be silent forever. At that moment I must have still been confused, I just remember that essentially I continued to feel ashamed and I told him that he needn't worry, because a girl doesn't go around saying certain things because, if she does, no one will marry her and all the men will treat her like a prostitute, just as he had explained to me the night before, and that I would therefore certainly follow his advice to keep quiet forever. I would only realized later that I had not really felt that way. But he had believed me and, all cheerful, he gave me a lousy pat on the cheek."

Vittorio had remembered that, going on what Giuseppe had told him, it was only towards 4:00 am, after Peppino had fallen asleep, that Mariapia had told her brother about the rapes by the two Germans, because she had not wanted their cousin to hear. The Deputy Commissioner had therefore wondered: *Why would she care, assuming that she only intended to tell Giuseppe about being raped by the two Germans, seeing that Peppino had witnessed it?*

---

[126] It was best to keep my mouth shut because a woman who is not the wife of the man who has fucked her is a whore for the whole world and will always be signorina and never get married.

Hadn't she intended, rather, to tell her brother about the relative's rape as well, and that was why she had waited for her cousin to go to sleep?

Hoping that the young woman still had her guard down as had been clear until just a while ago, Vittorio had asked her this basic question: "Mariapia, when exactly did your brother find out about Peppino's abuse?"

Giuseppe had looked at his sister, a quick glance but the policeman had understood that he wanted to warn her.

She no longer had her guard down and had replied decisively: "What do you mean, when?! Just now, no?"

Silence had fallen in the room, during which Vittorio had reflected: *On the other hand, if the brother had known about the relative's rape since that night, he could have slit his throat and castrated him, that pig, to avenge her. Would he have acted without telling her anything while she was down in the basement, unaware? and he wouldn't have told her later either, so she would have realized it only a moment ago? and having suddenly understood that she had put him in trouble by opening her mouth, would she have tried to cover him by denying that she had told him beforehand? Or maybe they could both be guilty? But, in both cases, would she have been so clumsy with me, if she had known that Giuseppe was the murderer or if she had actually had a part in the murder? Attacks of hysteria yes, but going that far? Apart from the fact that there is not the slightest evidence at the momennt that one or both are the murderers: no one saw at least one of them leave the basement during the half hour in which the crime was perpetrated.*

The Deputy Commissioner therefore, going on mere assumptions and with other hypotheses also possible, such as a camorra killing, had not wanted to make accusations against the two young people. He had instead started to summarize the criminal event with them hoping that, perhaps, they themselves would absentmindedly arrive at an inconsistency, if not an admission of guilt: "Listen. Certain things can now be considered sufficiently certain. First of all, the time interval and the way in which the murder and castration took place. According to the coroner, your cousin was killed between 5:00 and 5:45 in the morning of last Monday 27th with a blunt bayonet, while he was in the lavatory in the courtyard attending to his bodily needs. When he went into the hut he had not locked the door: just as I checked after the discovery of the corpse, the door, which opens outwards, does have a lock but the keyhole is only on the outside while, from the inside, you have to close it with a sliding hook that, for sure, had not been done, because it wasn't twisted as it would have been if someone had pulled the door to force their way inside. I imagine that Peppino had not closed it because of his urgency, just as he had not locked the house as he went out: he must raced there with diarrhea ready to escape, due to his chronic colitis. That morning I also noticed a candle in the toilet, just the end which had gone out really, in a candlestick on the floor to the left of the door as you go in. Since there was no electric light in the latrine, the candle was used so you could see when you were there at night. I believe, though, that Peppino had lit it only after the first attack of diarrhoea, meaning that at first he had defecated in the dark: his dung was spread over the floor, it had not ended up in the specific hole above an underground sewage connection, and this makes me think that at the start it was pitch dark in there and that your cousin had not been able to see where he was directing his feces. After the first, urgent discharge, Peppino must finally have lit the candle and it wouldn't be extinguished after that. It would have burned down slowly until the flame went out and became the small piece that I would find later; but in the meantime, precisely because of the flame, during the period of time between five fifteen and a quarter to six the murderer must have realized that Peppino was in the toilet and must have gone inside with no problem because it hadn't been hooked from the inside, and he must have cut his throat. Second thing..."

"... his throat and also his revolting crap," Mariapia had added impulsively.

"We'll talk about the mutilation later. I was saying that, secondly, the basement door had been found open as well because Peppino, who was dead by now, hadn't been able to lock it after you left with your group. As I verified, the lock does not have a half click, to lock: and since there also no handle attached to the door or a recessed groove in the wood, you have to turn the key as you pull the door towards you with the key itself, which is a large long thing in an old shape, that we found in the kitchen hanging from a nail on a wall. Tell me, Lieutenant: who was the last person to come out of the basement? One of you two officers?"

"Yes, myself. Starting from the middle of the room and heading towards the exit, I had checked that no weapons or ammunition had been left behind because of an oversight. One by one I extinguished the candles as I headed to the door and, finally, I went out pulling the door behind me because it was only partly closed."

"That's right because it was not a springlock. It goes without saying, since you had not discovered that Peppino was dead, that you had simply gone to the truck without looking for him to tell him to close the basement; but I seem to remember that you've already told me that you had not looked for him."

"Exactly, and on the other hand there wouldn't have been any reason to do so, it was obvious that he would close it later: it was his home."

"Yes, apart from the fact he could not have done so because he was dead when you left, but ... you could not have known this."

"Yes, of course, but I don't understand why you keep repeating it to me."

"Hmm... you're right, sorry, I'm a bit tired. A third thing, and you have not heard this yet: the autopsy report states that the castration took place between a quarter of an hour and a half hour after death and one could therefore wonder if the killer had returned later to cut off the dead man's sex because he was not sufficiently satisfied by the murder ..."

"... and that's why he would have left the candle burning, earlier," Mariapia had suggested.

"Hmm... no, I suppose the candle was alight simply because the killer had left quickly, so as not to risk someone seeing him at the scene of the crime. If anything, if the murderer and the castrator are a single individual, he would then have thought about it again and returned a second time to add castration to the murder, thus giving greater weight to his revenge: because, if murderer and castrator are one and the same, it's about revenge and not the theft of the gold. For me, however, it is not the same person, but two: the only coincidence, both had been attracted by the light of the candle filtering between the planks and both had not extinguished it after their crime, in their haste to escape. But now I want to ask you something: not when the went up to go to the truck, but previously, had you two seen a certain Salvatore Cuoco go up into the yard, alone, with a bayonet on his belt?"

Giuseppe had spoken first: "He was a sailor who would die by my side during the assault at the armory: a hero."

"I didn't ask that, Lieutenant: answer the question."

"Sorry. Actually yes, I've just remembered now that I had seen him go up, it was while I was talking to Jones not far from the door."

"Didn't that seem like something anomalous to you?"

"No, Salvatore may have needed to urinate or wanted to drink at the pump in the yard."

"And you, Mariapia, did you see him?"

"I don't even know who that sailor was, they were all in civilian clothes, not in uniform. Anyway, I hadn't seen anyone go up ahead of time, and unlike Giuseppe I had always remained in the central area."

"Lieutenant, I would like you to tell me exactly when Cuoco went to the courtyard and when he came back down. Even though I already have an answer, I would like confirmation of it."

"Well, let's say he went out about ten minutes before we left and he came back a few minutes later."

"He went out that one time or another as well?"

"Once, at least as far as I know."

"So it remains confirmed that he had gone upstairs when Peppino was already dead. In my opinion it was Cuoco who castrated his body and, since no one had seen him go up previously, it may have been another person who had killed. This, however, does not mean that the sailor had not gone up for the precise purpose of killing: he could not have known that Peppino was already deceased. He must have meditated for a long time before he moved, but once he had decided and had gone up into the courtyard, he must have headed to the latrine, attracted by the light of the candle that filtered from the hut, went inside and, at that point, he must have seen your dead cousin with his throat cut: who knows what a disappointment that was! All the same, he nurtured so much hatred towards that camorrista that, since the manly attributes of the corpse were in sight because his breeches had been pulled down, he must have cut them off on impulse and then placed them next to him, as a warning to all camorristi, perhaps. Then he must have quickly gone out and back down into the basement, leaving the candle lit because of his haste."

"Why so much hatred for Peppino?" Mariapia had asked.

"Because your cousin, on the orders of his cosca boss, had initiated his sister into prostitution, a fact that had led her to fall ill and die; and if Cuoco had no longer been able to take his life, at least he had avenged her as far as was still possible for him."

"How do you know about the sister?"

"From another sailor's testimony, one of the eight who are out there in the corridor. Cuoco had told him about her and Peppino, a few days before the castration."

"Excuse me if I ask you again, Vittorio," had continued Mariapia who had not only found complete calm, at least apparently, but seemed increasingly interested in the investigation: "In your opinion, did the sailor take the gold?"

"No, he didn't and, in my opinion, neither did the murderer."

"Oh, but then... who did?"

"... the camorra boss's courier! Who is not the killer, though. As we know, Peppino should have delivered the gold to that man after your departure, but the delinquent had found him dead and also castrated in the toilet. Goodness knows what he thought! At first he must have thought it was murder for theft, but he must still have rummaged through the corpse and happily found the gold in some pocket and had taken it immediately so he could get away quickly, given the situation. But tell me, Lieutenant: when you were leaving, did one of your group close the gate, the gate on the road?"

"Yes, Commissioner, I did it myself as I was the last to leave: I pulled it behind me and triggered the lock."

"So the courier had found it closed. I imagine that your cousin would have opened it for him himself, most probably to give him the packets of gold quickly without even letting him in. The man was still able to get inside, though, because those people are experts at picking locks and, furthermore, the gate has only half a turn so it's easy to open it without forcing it. Then, on the way out, he pulled the gate behind him too, which is why we found it closed and had to access the courtyard through the laboratory of that Gennarino, and then reopen it from the inside with the handle."

"Which I had done for everyone," Mariapia had finished, now clearly very tranquil.

Her brother, also apparently calm again, had shown that he was in agreement with Vittorio: "I think too, actually I'm convinced that the camorra took the gold, and in fact it's true that Peppino would have personally delivered it to the boss's right-hand man, precisely that morning around six thirty. I know because I had taken part in the agreements alongside Captain Jones, where Peppino was also present and had introduced us to his boss; and keep in mind, Commissioner, that if the gold had been stolen instead by a stranger, when the cosca boss learned from his courier that the gold had disappeared, he would have immediately thought that I was the thief and murderer, because I was aware of everything; and therefore, when I got home I would have been kidnapped and tortured to make me talk and, perhaps, those delinquents would have tortured my family to better induce me to confess, but since this has not happened, I'm quite sure the camorra is in possession of all the gold and that you, Commissioner, are right."

"Yes. The question remains as to who killed your cousin and why he did it."

Vittorio had pressed a button on the wall behind him, to summon the sentry in the corridor. There was a row of numbers on his table corresponding to the different offices on the floor, which lit up accompanied by the sound of a buzzer, showing the room from which the call came. The number of Vittorio's office was two, certainly not because of the occupant's modest rank, but because the room was next to the room of the now deceased deputy Chief Commissioner, who had number one.

When number two lit up, the sentry had quickly gone to knock on the door of the young superior and, at his "Come in!" he had entered.

D'Aiazzo had ordered him: "Tell the Appalle spouses that they no longer need to stay and that they can go."

"Yes sir."

"Then send those other eight back in here."

"Yes sir," and the guard had gone out closing the door behind him.

"You two, on the other hand, must have the patience to wait a few more minutes," Vittorio had said to the brother and sister.

Shortly afterwards, despite the closed door, the loud sharp voice of Mrs. Appalle was heard going down the corridor, towards the staircase: "*Gennari', pecché chillo strunzo nun ci ha premmésso*[127] *d'ascì app...*"

"*...Cuncetti', shut up: later, later, not mo'! Ooh!*" he had said back to her alarmed.

" *Io vulevo solo dicere: 'ascì apprimma*[128], *ma mai che tu me fai parla' sàno sàno*[129]. *Uuuh.!*"

"*Uuuuuh!*" the worried consort had said back to her, even longer.

An indulgent smile had escaped Vittorio.

____

[127] (t/n – Gennari' why didn't that piece of shit give permission to let us go as soon...)

[128] I just wanted to say to let us go earlier, but you never let me say things.

[129] completely.

Chapter 21

The meeting was coming to the end and the Deputy Commissioner did not invite the eight soldiers to sit down. He had stood up, Mariapia and Giuseppe had automatically stood up after him, and the young official had said to everyone: "It is my task to determine, in consultation with the coroner, whether a violent death that has been assigned to me was caused by accident, murder or suicide. There is no doubt that it was murder for Peppino Scognamiglio. I will pass on to the examining magistrate everything I have gathered on the case, and he will decide whether or not to open a trial against someone. I have no proof to give him, because none of you saw anyone go up into the courtyard in the half hour in which the victim, according to the autopsy report, had been killed: the sailor Cuoco had gone out only when Peppino Scognamiglio was already dead. Perhaps someone among your deceased comrades saw another person in the group go to the courtyard before the victim's death, but if that was the case, they could no longer testify to it.

My report will be based on the anatomopathologist's report and on your depositions this morning, which are determining as far as the castration of the murdered man is concerned, but not for his murder. If a trial is opened, you will be called to testify as will that Gennarino Appalle even though, in this case, his wife will probably call me *strunzo* again as she did just now as she was leaving" – everyone smiled – "but, jokes aside, if you can, stay where we can reach you, if possible, although I think you will be fighting again: expelling the Germans is certainly a duty in this our fifth war of independence[130] that, in fact, we started here in Naples. It seems that it will continue officially at the behest of his Majesty; in fact we've learned from the carabinieri that on September 28, with the approval of the Allies, a brigade-level unit has been formed in San Pietro Vernotico, in the province of Lecce, called 1st Italian Motorized Grouping, and its purpose is to fight the Germans as soon as the Anglo-Americans tell them to start. Who knows,

---

[130] In Italy the First World War had also been called the Fourth War of Independence, as it had led to the liberation of Trentino and Trieste from the Austrians. Now it was a matter of driving out the Austro-German Nazis by recapturing the occupied Italian territory.

maybe you'll want to join that Group to swell its ranks[131]; but wherever you are, as soldiers or civilians, please write to me if you can letting me know where you are: you just have to send it to Naples Police Headquarters, Deputy Commissioner Vittorio D'Aiazzo. In the event of a trial, the Court will send a summons to your civil domicile, and will arrive if it's in the areas which are not occupied by the Germans; but if there is no way to find you the jury will understand the reason and will limit itself to reading my report with your depositions made today. Thank you all and I wish you good luck." He had smiled at Mariapia: "You, though, will stay quietly at home. And anyway, they don't want female soldiers and the Naples uprising is over."

She had nodded in agreement.

The same day, shortly after lunch in the Police Headquarters canteen, Vittorio D'Aiazzo had started to write his report on the case of the tobacconist for the Public Prosecutor's Office. He intended to make the observation in the first place that, in his opinion, if Mariapia had wanted to kill Peppino she would have had a much better opportunity before that fateful September 27, taking him by surprise in the shop, stabbing him in the back or hitting him violently on the head with a blunt object once or twice, and making his death look like the consequence of an aggression by strangers; or she could have, more certainly even if less courageously, poisoned his food or wine or the Arzente: no-one would have thought of her, as it was well-known that Peppino was linked to the camorra, but of some lowlife of the same gang or a rival gang. Of course, only if Mariapia kept quiet with everyone and forever about being raped by her relative.

Vittorio also intended to write that, still in his opinion based on the interrogation of the young woman, she must not have thought that her brother had carried out the murder, but that it was the camorra, given Peppino's acquaintances, assuming that the motive had been the gold at first and, after learning from Vittorio that that hadn't been the reason for the murder, some other unknown underworld reason. Nevertheless, the Deputy

---

[131] At first it was only 5000 soldiers. The Italian Motorized Grouping consisted of an artillery regiment, an infantry regiment and a battalion of engineers, and in reality was mixed because it included soldiers of various specialties from different units that had been based in the South. On April 18 of the following year, replenished with men and means in the meantime, the Grouping would be transformed into the Italian Liberation Corps.

Commissioner contemplated and intended to point out to the magistrate the diverse possibility that, on that tragic night, Mariapia had told her brother about the parental rape too and not just the abuse by the two Germans, and that, in any case, she had not suspected Giuseppe as being the author of their cousin's murder until that morning, suddenly, during the interrogation, and at that point she had said she had not told him to cover him.

Seeing it from yet another angle though, the young official did not exclude the hypothesis, which he would therefore also present to the judicial authority, that fearing Peppino's revenge Mariapia had not told her brother about their cousin's sexual abuse the night before the uprising, nor to anyone else later on, until the trauma which was dormant in her subconscious took absolute prevalence over her; and then the poor girl would explode while in Vittorio's office, and start ranting uncontainably about the cousin's rape. In that case, the brother who was unaware of it, would not have been suspected of having killed his cousin.

Thus, these were the hypotheses, and not the certainties, that D'Aiazzo intended to express in his report to the Public Prosecutor's Office, without coming to any conclusion with making any accusations. On the other hand, in his heart he did not want either of the two siblings to end up in prison: he thought highly of them both and was very sorry for her, the innocent victim of three brutes. In those youthful years not yet illuminated by a long and knowledgeable professional experience, Vittorio had not dismissed as unacceptable a questionable idea that had come to him at university reading certain ethical-legal writings of Thomas Aquinas for the Philosophy of Law exam. In these writings the saint had considered the physical elimination of the tyrant absolvable before God[132], because every despot denies that freedom which is an indispensible gift of God to human beings and differentiates them from brutes.

The young man had imagined himself in that time by analogy and continued to suppose that, when requesting justice from the law was psychologically impeded, entailing very serious risks not only for one's own life but for that of innocent third persons – as the parents of Giuseppe and Mariapia indeed were –, killing the dangerous criminal could elevate itself, or almost, to the right to self-defence, just as killing a tyrant was. In other words

---

[132] In "De regimine principum".

that, in this case, even though the law of the State prevents it and sanctions it always and in any case, private murder could become a sort of quasi-social justice, without which no justice on earth would have been possible. In the hypothesis that Giuseppe had killed that intimidating scoundrel, in Vittorio's opinion he would not have done, after all, anything dissimilar to what was carried out during the Four Days when in the name of justice Giuseppe had killed followers of that diabolically supreme camorra boss that was Adolf Hitler, who had denied freedom to the highest degree. Morally, D'Aiazzo compared every neighborhood or street tyrant to a political despot just as Peppino had been in the area of Via Monteoliveto and Corso Umberto I, that Peppino who had believed not only that he could violate Mariapia with impunity and use her as a thing, just as the two Nazi soldiers had done, but had then threatened her and, indirectly, her parents with death threats, most likely not in vain given his perverted life and his criminal acquaintances, in reality taking from the young woman the possibility of resorting to the law of the State to get justice.

Years later, with the experience of many other crimes, Vittorio would change his mind and consider all murders inadmissible, although some with mitigating factors. For now, however, he was still of that mind. The fact remained, that in spite of the ethical-legal reasoning of Aquinian inspiration and because Vittorio had a liking for the two siblings, he was already aware in that October 1943 that as a policeman he was not permitted to stand as judge and absolve the pair by omitting the fact of the abuse Mariapia had suffered from Peppino when writing his report to the Prosecutor's Office. He was aware that it was his duty to report everything that he had garnered in the conversation with the Scognamiglio siblings.

Despite this, he intended to point out that he had not been able to ascertain in any way that the young woman had had the courage to tell her brother about the parental rape and that, indeed, he personally considered it unlikely, because she been seriously threatened with death by her cousin if she revealed it to anyone. In addition, Vittorio intended to make it very clear that Giuseppe and Mariapia had been heroic fighters during the struggle for the liberation of Naples.

As for the sailor Salvatore Cuoco, of whom the Deputy Commissioner would write in the second part of his report to the

Prosecutor's Office, he intended to recount to the magistrate everything he had learned about him from the petty officer Bacci, adding his supposition that Cuoco had been responsible for Peppino's castration but not his assassination, since he had been seen going upstairs to the courtyard at the earliest at ten to six, that death had takrn place before then, and that there was no testimony that he had already left the cellar a first time.

Chapter 22

Giuseppe Scognamiglio had donned the uniform of the Royal Army very quickly. Having learned of the establishment of the 1st Italian Motorized Grouping from D'Aiazzo, he had already left Naples on the same day of the interview and, at the end of a problematic journey, had presented himself to the Command of the brigade at San Pietro Vernotico in Puglia. As a paratrooper unit has not been reestablished[133], he had been readmitted to service in an infantry battalion of the 67th Regiment. Promoted to captain, he had been assigned to the I office – Information – at the Regimental Command. However, a few days after October 13, the day on which, as expected, the Kingdom of Italy had become co-aggressor[134] against the Nazi-Fascists, he had been transferred with a U.S. DC3 aircraft, along with other officers, to an OSS base in Campania, to be trained for guerrilla warfare in the areas occupied by the enemy.

At a notary's office his father Antonio, as Peppino Scognamiglio's closest relative, had commenced the procedure for inheritance of what had been his cousin's assets in his favor. An accountant in the professional's office had drawn up the inventory of the goods with an evaluation of their worth. The amount would be subject to the taxes foreseen by law together with the average market value of the property and the substantial amount of 225,000 lire, which the camorrista had deposited over the years on a Post Office savings book. Once he had paid the notary's fee and the

---

[133] The Folgore would be reconstituted, at brigade level, only years after the war, on January 1, 1963, although a small infantry unit under this name had operated in the Liberation War alongside the Anglo-Americans; moreover, individual Italian paratroopers, including veterans of El Alamein – the Folgore had reached Africa with 5912 soldiers of which only 306 had survived – would have participated in launches in airborne missions during the war of the Kingdom of the South against the Germans, especially in central and northern Italy, to the rescue of the partisans and in exploration and sabotage operations , either autonomously, or alongside British or American paratroopers.

[134] General Eisenhower and the other Anglo-American commanders had not accepted the Kingdom of Italy as an ally and had admitted only the so-called *co-belligerence*, which would have served no purpose to lighten the peace treaty after the end of the war, despite the acts of valour of the military of the Kingdom of the South and the Italian partisans.

inheritance taxes to the State and the real estate registration tax thanks to the money in the passbook, Antonio had come into full ownership of the remaining assets. He and his wife and daughter had left the rented mezzanine and had set up house in the back of the shop, as they waited to commence commercial activity. Since it concerned monopoly goods (salt and tobacco), he had to complete the paperwork at the Autonomous Administration of State Monopolies, and this too had to be done by a notary. While waiting for the last formalities to be completed, and since Mariapia was unemployed, the family's fixed income had been reduced to Concetta's wages at the Lotto office; but fortunatel monthly remittances of 50% of Giuseppe's officer's salary had started to arrive by Army Post to boost the family economy.

Dr. Roldano Pinzillo, investigating magistrate for the case of the murder of the deceased Giuseppe Scognamiglio known as Peppino, had read the copy of Dr. Palombella's autopsy report and the report from Deputy Commissioner D'Aiazzo. Then he had placed the dossier at the bottom of a pile of papers that had been accumulating in that chaotic period with a shortage of personnel, because a considerable part of the registrars and employees of the Neapolitan Court had been called to arms. The magistrates' cupboards were overflowing with files and more files and their desks were covered with them. It should be added that, in the very early days of the Allied occupation, no magistrate and no registrar knew exactly who to obey, whether the President of the Tribunal or certain Anglo-American *law consultant* officers who, creating confusion, had moved in beside the registrars to purge the fascist hierarchy in Naples and its surroundings. Few of those people, however, had been arrested, as most had fled with the Germans or hidden in the countryside. In short, as far as possible, nothing was happening in Court while waiting for life to return to some kind of normality again.

At the beginning of November of that same 1943, with the Allies having agreed with the co-aggressor Kingdom of Italy that it would be up to the Italians, in due course, to settle accounts with fascist leaders and their lackeys, and seeing that the *consultants* were essentially superfluous, operational order and the pecking order had been re-established in the Court of Naples. All the same, because of the previous cases, long over-due, much time had gone by before, finally, at the beginning of June 1944, Dr. Pinzillo picked up the documents of the Scognamiglio case, studied them thoroughly, and decided that Giuseppe and Mariapia were suspected of both murder and contempt of corpse and that they were to be put on trial.

That judge was a hard man and had formulated the accusation of premeditation. So, since the death penalty was still in force in Italy, if the magistrate President of the[135] Court recognized the accused as being fully culpable, they would be shot. Not so if he identified the so-called *reasons of honor* as the motive for the assassination. According to article 587 of the penal code then in force – it would be abolished several years later, in Republican Italy – the person guilty of *honor killing* had to undergo a sentence from a maximum of seven to a minimum of three years in prison. In the particular case of Mariapia and Giuseppe, in the unfortunate hypothesis that the jurers had considered one or the other or both of them guilty of murder, the defending lawyer could invoke, for the brother, the second part of Article 587 which referred to killing the illegitimate lover of a family member of the murderer[136]. For the sister, he could put emphasis on the sexual assault as the cause of momentary madness; for both, the lawyer could have stressed their high moral figure, recalling the valiant military contribution they had provided to the liberation of Naples, a fact that, as we know, had been highlighted by Vittorio in his report to the Prosecutor's Office. As for the accusation of contempt of corpse, the defense was totally optimistic: he would certainly have cast the blame for castration on the deceased sailor Cuoco now deprived of speech

Since bail had not been instituted at that time, and nor had house arrest, the accused awaiting trial was imprisoned to prevent

---

[135] The Court was composed of the magistrate and 10 jurors drawn by lot from among the members of the electoral roll at the beginning of each session. Only later, in the Italian Republic, the Court of Assizes would be composed, as it still is today, of six lay judges, called popular, and two togated magistrates, the president and the judge a làtere.

[136] Criminal Code, art. 587: "Whosoever causes the death of his spouse, daughter, or sister ... in the act in which he discovers the illegitimate carnal relationship and in the state of anger determined by the offense brought to his or his family's honor, he is punished with imprisonment from three to seven years. The same penalty is given to those who, in the said circumstances, cause the death of a person who is in an illegitimate carnal relationship with his spouse, daughter or sister [...]".

his possible escape. An arrest warrant had therefore been issued by the prosecuting attorney Pinzillo against the Scognamiglio siblings.

The carabinieri had gone to the previous family home in Via Monteoliveto to arrest them and obviously had not found them. After making inquiries in the area they had arrived a little further on across the road, at the tobacconist shop which, in the meantime, had reopened for business. They had found Mariapia at the sales counter. Tbey had identified and handcuffed her among her father's remostrations. Her mother was at work in the Lotto office, having preferred not to resign despite the inheritance.

The young woman had been incarcerated in the women's prison of Pozzuoli.

Her officer brother, though, had not been found even after Judge Pinzillo, passing through the Military District of Naples, had learned much later that he was in force at the 67th regiment of the Motorized Grouping: no more than that since Scognamiglio's job was classified *top secret*. On the other hand, the captain had now been parachuted with an American of equal rank, into a *top secret* area of the Italian Social Republic to organize boycotts and guerrilla warfare against the Nazi-Fascists.

The President of the Chamber of the Court of Assizes of first instance in charge of directing the trial, considering that the accused were the children of the universal heir to the victim's assets, had ordered the latter to be frozen as a cautionary measure. Therefore, in addition to the fact of the temporary interruption of the business activity, had come the risk that the Scognamiglio spouses would be forbidden to live in the back of the shop and could end up in the street in those times of serious shortage of housing, because of the persistent bombings of Naples.

Vittorio D'Aiazzo had been informed of the measure by Antonio Scognamiglio himself, who had hastened to his office begging him to intervene. The young official had telephoned the Court directly to the president of the chamber and the latter, benignly, had appointed father Scognamiglio as judicial guardian of the premises of the tobacconist shop, with "right and duty of residence in the back"; but it was not, however, possible to reopen and run the shop. Antonio had thanked Heaven and all saints that his wife had not left her job and that the remittances of 50% of his son's salary continued to arrive as well.

The criminal proceedings had begun with the accused Giuseppe Scognamiglio in default of appearance and the accused Mariapia Scognamiglio present in the courtroom in the defendants' box.

Gennarino Appalle and Deputy Commissioner Vittorio D'Aiazzo had been summoned and presented themselves, Appalle because he had discovered the corpse, D'Aiazzo because he had carried out the initial investigations at the scene of the crime and had taken the statements of the Scognamiglio siblings, the artisan and wife and the eight soldiers at Police Headquarters. The latter had been justified absentees as they were engaged in combat, seven of them having gone north through Italy with the Anglo-Americans, warrant officer Bacci serving on his own ship employed in escort services for the Allies' transport ships. The depositions they had made at Police Headquarters had therefore simply been read in the courtroom by the registrar, with the president then asking for D'Aiazzo's verbal confirmation.

The proceedings had lasted only two days.

Mariapia had declared that she was innocent of both murder and castration and, although she had not been asked, she had added that it was the same thing for her brother. On the other hand, the public prosecutor had not been able to prove that Giuseppe had known of the rape perpetrated by Peppino before the man had been killed, but only that he had been informed that night of the sexual assault by the two Germans. Mariapia had admitted that she had been subjected to assault by her cousin, but denied having told her brother about it, adding that he had found out about it only during the interview in Police Headquarters; and she had specified emphatically: "I kept quiet because I was afraid that my cousin and his camorra cronies would take revenge on our parents and me, as he had threatened and, what's more, that they would hurt my brother too if he asked Peppino the reason for what had happened: I mean ask with words, not with violence, because Giuseppe is a soldier, not a murderer."

With regard to the castration the defense lawyer, as he had intended, had accused the late sailor Cuoco, making reference to warrant officer Annibale Bacci's statements recorded in Vittorio D'Aiazzo's report to the Prosecutor's Office. As for the murder, in the absence of any eyewitness the lawyer had put into play the possibility, perhaps not very likely but possible, that the castrator

Salvatore Cuoco had firstly cut the victim's throat and, only later, had returned to the lavatory to castrate the corpse because he was not fully satisfied. He had asked for the acquittal of both Scognamiglio siblings from the charge of murder and also contempt of corpse, in both cases *for not having committed the act.*

Even before the jurors were closed in the jury room, and in the event of a guilty verdict for one or both defendants, the president of the chamber on his part had found that he was leaning towards a light sentence because it was a crime of honor, with concession of all the mitigating factors,

In the afternoon of the second day the ten jurors had already withdrawn to decide. According to the legislation of the time, they alone, without the intervention of the President of the Chamber, were arbiters of innocence or guilt, while the Judge was then responsible for establishing the penalty if the verdict was guilty and if found innocent, to pardon either *for not having committed the act,* or *for insufficient evidence,* or possibly, but this was not the case, *because the fact does not exist* or *because the fact does not constitute a crime.* The college of the ten jurors of the Scognamiglio trial was composed of four bourgeois, including three professionals and a bank manager, who certainly did not like the camorra, and six commoners all of whom, according to the law, eere in possession of at least a diploma of compulsory schooling. Two of them were shopkeepers harassed by camorristi, while all six were quite easily moved to tears in the face of sexual assault, and multiple moreover, of a virgin. Not one of the ten jurors had felt they could issue a judgment of guilt towards a poor girl who was the victim of a camorrista brute or against her brother, his Majesty's officer, both heroic fighters during the Four Days of Naples. So, after just half an hour in the jury room, they had returned to the courtroom with the verdict of innocent, both in relation to the charge of contempt of corpse, and that of murder.

The president, however, had fully acquitted the defendants only from the charge of contempt of corpse, while for the murder he had acquitted them *for lack of evidence.* For his part, the prosecutor, who in the final indictment had asked for a conviction for premeditated murder and acquittal with dubitative formula from the charge of contempt of corpse, had appealed against the first charge, allowing the second to become *res judicata.* Mariapia remained in prison pending the second-degree trial.

Vittorio, feeling in his heart that the young woman was innocent, had not agreed with the sentence given her: in his opionion, she should have been acquitted with full formula. As for her brother, even though he suspected that he was guilty, the acquittal with a dubitative formula had seemed fair to him considering that there was no proof but only leads.

Dad Scognamiglio, thanks to the decision that provisionally absolved his children, had received authorization to return to full ownership of his assets and had reopened the tobacconist shop. The prudent Concetta had continued, however, pending the appeal process, to work at the Lotto kiosk and receive her nice monthly salary. Meanwhile, the remittances of 50% of the officer son's pay, which had become superfluous, had been set aside for him on a bank savings book which his father had opened. Unfortunately that money, together with the rest of the salaries that Giuseppe would receive at the end of the conflict when he returned to his unit, would have a modest purchasing power in the post-war period, due to the gigantic inflation the war had brought.

In the meantime, in the Tuscan-Emilian mountains, Captain Giuseppe Scognamiglio had formed a partisan band of so-called Badogliani supporters, combatants of moderate liberal-monarchist inspiration, and had continued to fight clandestinely with his men against Nazi-Fascism until April 29, 1945, the day the Treaty of German Surrender in Italy was signed. Operating clandestinely in enemy zone and never able to hear from his family, he had not learned of the trial.

On May 2, 1945, having disbanded his group of badogliani partisans, or rather what remained of it after many clashes and many fallen, Giuseppe had been reunited with what remained of the 67th regiment, of which his battalion was part, a unit that had meanwhile traveled up the Peninsula fighting alongside the Anglo-Americans on various fronts, starting with the epic San Pietro Vernotico and Monte Curvale-Monte Marrone. Scognamiglio's battalion was now in Bologna, part of the Legnano division, and had established its headquarters in a barracks that until recently had hosted a fascist unit. Giuseppe, who still knew nothing of the trial and the appeal that was about to take place, had submitted an application to the secretariat of his battalion to be admitted to effective permanent service, with the hope, after having fought throughout the war with valor, of pursuing a military career up to the rank of general, even if he came from the reserve, on a par with those who had followed the courses of the Academy and the School of Weapon Application and had attended the War School. The application had been sent to the regiment's office from the battalion's secretariat office by hierarchical means, and from there to the higher addresses and other competent offices, including the Neapolitan Military District.

The latter, having registered the previous request of the Court of Naples to know where Giuseppe was in service, had bureaucratically reported his current location to the Court. The lieutenant colonel commanding Scognamiglio's battalion had received notification from a certain Dr. Romualdo Brandacci, prosecutor of the Court of Assizes of Appeal in the section responsible for the Scognamiglio trial of second degree, that the officer was wanted by that Court on charges of premeditated murder. The report had been accompanied by the formal request to put him under guarded arrest, pending his transfer to the prisons of Poggioreale by soldiers of the Benemerita. As a precautionary measure, while awaiting the outcome of the appeal process, the Army had demoted the captain to simple soldier and put him on temporary leave. He had been locked up in a cell in the barracks after being dressed, as best as possible, in civilian clothes. He had not remained in the cell long, because the following day he had been handcuffed and picked up by a couple of carabinieri to be taken to Naples. He had sat in handcuffs in the middle of the two soldiers, as the law required, for the entire journey by train: a long trip because it was hindered by the damage to the railway lines during the war. On several occasions, the patriot Scognamiglio had had to endure insults and totally fantastical accusations from various passengers, such as "Blackmarketer!" Among other humiliations, somewhere near Florence, an elderly hysterical woman, blocked just in time by the carabinieri, had thrown herself at him with claw-like fingers shouting senselessly: "Give me that fascist bastard who hanged my nephew!" Later, a young woman who got on the train in Rome with her child who looked about four or five years old, had pointed to the handcuffed Giuseppe saying to the little boy: "See what happens to thieves?"

The President of the Chamber of the Court of Appeal, unlike the President of the Court of First Instance, had not frozen the assets which dad Scognamiglio had inherited. But since

Antonio had feared it would happen, based on previous experience, he had put aside all the cash he had been able to save in the previous months, into a bearer's bank book which he had opened.

The Court had met on Monday, June 4 1945, this time with both siblings in the box.

Appalle and D'Aiazzo had been reconvened and, this time, also the driver Corporal Manzotti and the sailor Warrant Officer Bacci, who had now been discharged. The other six soldiers had died in combat.

According to the law, the appellate jurors all had a degree or a diploma. They were less inclined than the Neapolitan people to give in to sentiment, but were not insensitive to the heroism of officers like Giuseppe; and as for the sexual assaults on Mariapia, if that didn't arouse heart-breaking pity in them as it did in the simple people, it did arouse civil indignation, that yes.

After a trial which was not as short as the first, four days of debate, on the evening of the fourth day the jury had withdrawn to their chamber. They had formulated the judgment of innocence for both defendants after hours of discussion. However, just as the President of the Court of Assizes of First Instance had done, the Court of Appeal had also acquitted them *for lack of evidence* and *for not having committed the crime*. Since there were no procedural defects or errors of any other kind that justified an appeal to the Supreme Court of Cassation, the prosecutor had accepted the acquittal sentence which had therefore become final.

Mariapia and Giuseppe Scognamiglio had been released from their respective prisons on June 8, a Friday. Already the following Monday he had submitted an application to the Military District of Naples for reinstatement to his rank and, in addition, a new application to be admitted to service in a permanent role.

He had indeed been reinstated in the Royal Army as captain, but only in the reserve, while his request to become a career officer had been quashed: an acquittal for mere lack of evidence did not leave the person really clean in public opinion. The Army was perhaps not entirely wrong in wanting that not even the slightest suspicion of a stain weigh on its officers in effective permanent service. The error, if anything, was in the very formula of absolution *for lack of evidence* that in fact, decades later in the Italian Republic, would be abolished, clearing itself from that moment with full formula even in the case of guilt not absolutely proven[137].

As with the judgment of first instance, Vittorio had not agreed with the sentence regarding Mariapia, while his instinct had continued to tell him that Giuseppe was guilty. Even if he had not discovered any fact that proved this idea, the policeman perceived that Mariapia had already told her brother about the relative's rape on the night of the crime. He believed that Giuseppe, even though he was burning with anger, had not killed his cousin instantly so as not to compromise the mission and that once in the cellar, still with anger in his heart, having distributed the weapons and explained their use to the unit, he had taken advantage of a moment when no one had noticed, not even Mariapia, to go back to the courtyard with his bayonet in his belt in search of Peppino. When he had not found him in the house but at the lavatory, he had silently cut his throat in there, and had then returned downstairs quickly without extinguishing the candle.

In any case, it seemed right to Vittorio that Scognamiglio not only had not ended up being shot for premeditated murder, but had not even had to serve three to seven years in prison for *crime of honor* according to Article 587. He had considered the acquittal adequate because of lack of evidence since strong mitigating factors had been recognized to the officer and, even more, thinking he was now vindicated thanks to the many courageous acts he had performed with serious risk to his own life. On the other hand, as he had in the past, D'Aiazzo continued to consider that his idea of Giuseppe's guilt remained an unproven suspicion and that, if the man had been innocent, aquittal with dubitative formula would have been just as unfair as Mariapia's. In any case, he had resigned himself to never knowing the truth: he could not know that it would not be so forever.

------

[137] The formula *for lack of evidence* would be repealed with the reform of the Penal Code, because it was considered contrary to the presumption of innocence provided for in Article 27(3) of the Constitution.

Chapter 23

In the early months of 1944, Vittorio d'Aiazzo's parents had returned to the city. First the mother, at the end of February: since the bombings on Naples had now ceased, her unlicensed son had gone to the farmhouse where she had been evacuated in a rental car with driver and had taken her home. His father, who had followed his king to Salerno, where the sovereign had transferred throne and capital, the following day April 22, 1944 when the second Badoglio Government had been established, through the hierarchy he had contacted the new Minister of the Interior, Salvatore Aldisio, who was in charge of the Carabinieri.[138] When he met him days later, he had asked for and been granted permission to resume service in Naples. He had turned up at the family home late one evening, unexpected. Vittorio's rebellious brother, Emanuele, had also returned to Naples, but only in December 1948: not of his own initiative, but repatriated with an expulsion order after serving a sentence for crimes against property in the Canton of Ticino committed in January 1940 on Swiss territory,. He had immigrated there, illegally, passing through the mountains guided by *spalloni* smugglers[139]. In Italy the conviction in absentia of the Military Court of Naples was still hanging over him for avoiding conscription, and after the outbreak of war it had become a death sentence by being shot in the back, for desertion. At the time, in fact, due to the disorder during the war, the news of his imprisonment in the Canton prisons which the Swiss authorities had sent, had not arrived at the Martial Court.

When he was returning to Italy and had showed the exulsion order at the border, two carabinieri had taken Emanuele into custody and was transferred in handcuffs to his last known domicile, Naples, or rather to the Neapolitan prison of Poggioreale. He had been allowed to advise his family through the prison administration. His father had not wanted to see him, but on the

---

[138] It was not yet an Armed Force with autonomous arrangement in the Ministry of Defense, as it is today, but a Force belonging to Army, even if it was governed by the Department of the Interior and not by the Department of War as far as its functions as a civil police were concerned.

[139] (t/n - mountain smugglers on the Italian-Swiss border, from the post second world-war period to the '70s

contrary his mother and brother had gone to see him and had obtained and paid for legal assistance. Emanuele's lawyer had demanded a review of the trial to which the accused was entitled since the military code of war no longer in effect and had been replaced by that of peace. Moreover, since the country had become a Republic in the meantime with approval of the Constitutional Charter, according to which Italy rejected war as an instrument of offense, unlike had been the case for Fascism.

In any case, since there was legal continuity of the Italian State for the principles of Public Law, not precluding the fact that the previous regime had been dictatorial, Emanuele, though he escaped the death penalty which moreover had been suppressed also in civil law, had not dodged the sentence of imprisonment for draft evasion: two years and nine months to be served in the military fortress of Peschiera, which would be followed by military service in a detention battalion. During the routine medical examination when he arrived at the stronghold, Emanuele had been found to be suffering from a heart murmur. But since the sentence concerned not having presented himself at the time for the draft medical – to crown it all off, he would have been excused back then because he was cardiopathic – it had to be served in its entirety. At least, though, at the end of the period of imprisonment Emanuele had been exonerated and had returned to Naples as a free citizen. Because of his father's hostility, he had not even tried asking to live with the family. Every now and then he called by their home, but only to get money from his mother at times when he knew his brother was in the Police Headquarters and his now retired father was out for his daily walk. He had scraped together a living committing new petty crimes against property: fortunately for him, without being found, at least for the moment, by neither the Police, nor by the Benemerita.

Since Emanuele's conduct had not changed, and fearing that sooner or later his brother could hinder his career, Vittorio had applied for a transfer in the spring of 1953, asking to be sent to Rome. He had nurtured high hopes that this would be granted, because his skills had greatly improved over the years with several professional successes, and his references had always been excellent; in fact his superiors had contented him, and he was transferred to the *Vice squad* at Police Headquarters in the Capital. He had, moreover, been promoted to commissioner.

Chapter 24

It was 10:15 am on June 12, 1953 and at 10:24 the direct train to Roma Termini would leave from Naples Central Station. The train was still being formed on track four and, preceded by a long whistle, a local train arrived on track three, which was separated from platform four by a covered platform. It was composed of two old fascist diesels, which provided the service up and down the region along the waterfront, stopping at every station.

Vittorio D'Aiazzo was standing up straight under the shelter, with his suitcase on the ground to his right, waiting for the direct train to Rome to be fully formed and for the conductor to allow access. He was wearing his uniform, so that it wouldn't have to be ironed on arrival after being packed in a suitcase. It bore the rank of captain to which a commissioner was entitled, with three stars on each epaulette sewn on by his mother under the supervision of the meticulous retired colonel Amilcare D'Aiazzo.

The local train had been standing on track three for about twenty seconds, when Vittorio noticed a passenger he knew get off the last carriage, not far from him, and quickly unload two large suitcases from inside the carriage which he had left at the step a moment before: "Captain Scognamiglio!" the commissioner had called to him in a loud voice.

The other, recognizing him in turn, had quickly clarified: "Just surveyor." He had come towards him, one large suitcase in each hand, and had stopped a couple of paces away and put down his luggage. Then the pair had shaken hands and Giuseppe had explained: "I am still captain, but only in the reserve unfortunately."

"Would you have liked to go into active duty?"

"Yes, Commissioner, of course, but they didn't want me; and did you know? the commander of my regiment nominated me for the silver medal for military valor, but it was never awarded to me. Obviously, all because of the acquittals in those two trials which were only only dubitative."

"Hmm..." Vittorio had sighed.

"No, let me be clear, I have nothing against you: you did your duty and I, as an officer, understand that; and it's water under the bridge now. I've been a salesman for two small factories for some time, one makes tiles and the other wall paints: up and down along the coast of our region on those trains": he had smiled indicating the local train behind him with his left thumb. Then, pointing to the two suitcases on the ground, he had added: "My samples are in here, very heavy, I can tell you." Since the temperature was already like summer, his forehead was wet with beads of perspiration.

"Mariapia?" Vittorio had changed the subject.

"She runs our tobacconist shop."

"By herself?"

"No, with Erminia, my wife: we've been married for three years, we have a little girl and another baby is on the way, hopefully a boy. I do this work because the income from the shop would not be enough to give us a good living, the store had been closed for too long because of the first trial and several customers didn't return. We would be able to live with just the tobacconist shop, yes, but we couldn't save for the future. But apart from that in '46, with the money deposited in a bank book and a small mortgage, we were able to buy Gennarino Appalle's place when he retired, and being a surveyor, I turned it into three small rooms which I designed myself, and doing most of the work myself. It's a nice apartment, you know? You should see it."

Vittorio had appreciated the creator's pride that shone on Giuseppe's face: "I am happy for all of you," he had joined in the man's satisfaction.

"I know, I had realized that you... can I say were fond of us?"

"Yes."

"You know, Commissioner? The apartment has an entry on Via Monteoliveto as well since then, through the glass door of the former workshop, and there is a brass plate fixed to it, modestly, saying *Surveyor Giuseppe Scognamiglio, Sales Representative*. During the day the entry hall also acts as my study; but at night and when I'm not there, I also close a second door in solid wood that I added myself behind the glass one, against the bad guys." He smiled radiantly as he described his imaginative work: "I also built a wall with a window instead of the shutter that gives onto the courtyard of what was the workshop, which gives light to the corner room, which is the one where my wife and I sleep, next to the one where Mariapia sleeps; and for air and light in the third room, the one I made in the middle and is the little girl's, I opened a small window in the outer wall." Here the smile had faded: "Of course I also knocked down the latrine in the courtyard which not only wasn't hygienic but ... it held that terrible bad memory."

"Like the tobacconist shop did too," the commissioner had remarked without thinking.

"Oh yes, unfortunately," the surveyor turned sad momentarily: "Commissioner, like in confession?" He evidently wanted to confide in someone deserving of trust, which he felt was Vittorio having heard his sister speak so highly of him, what's more.

"Yes," the commissioner had agreed, with a nod of his head too.

"I believe that that trauma had entered Mariapia's soul, indeed even merged with it: she is unable to detach herself from it and get rid of it definitively. Sometimes, when she is in the shop and there are no customers, she suddenly gets angry and yells words full of insults and threats at nothing, and the next time she starts all over again. The first time in the early days I tried to distract her, but I've left her her alone for quite a while because I've realized that they are emotions that are unavoidable and that those outbursts of anger, if nothing else, give her some temporary equilibrium. Anyway, Commissioner... that's enough! Let's leave aside the afflictions and return to the good things. The apartment is fairly large, four rooms plus kitchen and bathroom which I put right next to the kitchen, because of the water. A dining room was there before, and I got not only the bathroom but also a short corridor that connects it to the kitchen and my sister's room, so you don't have to go through the bathroom. There's plenty of room in the apartment."

"Do your parents live there too?"

"Eh... no, Commissioner, not any more unfortunately. Our mother died of diabetes in '47, her blood sugar was over 900, just think. After the war she had started eating too many candies from the tobacconist shop and also *baba al rum, sfogliatelle* and other sweets from a nearby pastry shop: she didn't even know that she was sick, and her blood sugar was only measured in the hospital where we took her urgently by ambulance because she had lost consciousness: *She fell into a hyperglycemic coma*, the doctor told us. She died not long after she was hospitalized, without regaining consciousness. Dad did not last much longer, he died in '48, he had a skin cancer which was already at an advanced stage: *Too much sun at sea*, the doctors said, *for too many years*."

"I'm very sorry, Giuseppe: my condolences, even if they are late."

"Thank you, Commissioner."

"... and your grandmother?"

"She was the first to die, just a few days after uncle Gennaro's funeral, with a broken heart."

"Poor woman... but pain aside, congratulations on your marriage and for the little girl and also for the little one you're expecting. What did you call her, the little girl?"

"Concetta, like my mother; and if the second one is a boy, Antonio like his grandfather."

"But your sister hasn't married."

Without wanting to hurt, Vittorio had touched another very sore point for the Scognamiglio family.

It took just a moment and Mariapia's brother had erupted like a Vesuvius, instinctively in the Neapolitan that was used at home: *e chi vulite che s'a pigliasse? Grazie a certi giornalisti mareditti che 'a nnummenàrono e 'a fellarono, 'o sùio triplice stupro è canosciuto in tutta Napuli e nell'Italia intera; e certa gènte 'e 'mmerda dice che chilla che nun vule fàcerlo se mòve e se sbatte e nun fa 'a schifezza cascasse 'o mùnno intero! Que' fetenti crérono sia 'na putt... hmm[140]*": he had covered his mouth with his two hands on top of each other pushing hard. After a couple of seconds of silence, taking a long breath he had continued in a less heated tone: "It's that I can't stand the idea that Mariapia suffers: during the trials, revealing name and surname they put her in the newspapers and even on the front page of a few rags!"

"We need a law that prohibits the publication of the names of victims of abuse."

---

[140] ... and who do you think would want her? Thanks to certain damned journalists who named her and sliced her up, her triple rape is known all around Naples and throughout Italy; and some fucking people say that someone who doesn't want to do it does something about it and doesn't let the whole world fall apart because of that rubbish! Those assholes believe she's a whor... hmm.

"Yes sir! It would have been helpful when dealing with malicious people[141]; but on the other hand it would not have prevented... Commissioner, still like in confession: there is an invisible enemy in Mariapia's heart, a bad ghost that makes all men flee. Even if she sometimes talks of making a family, they're only words, in reality she fears men very much, she no longer trusts anyone apart from me who is her brother and... yes, and apart from you who she values very much; but for everyone else... I think she even despises the male figure; and in my opinion, it was precisely the absolute loss of trust in men that was the most serious harm that Mariapia suffered, truly diabolical, a girl who dreamed of Prince Charming, a wedding in the parish before God and a beautiful clean family with little boys and girls and all the other lovely things that a girl who is all heart has the right to aspire to."

Vittorio had been moved; and yet something deep down inside him, which came from his now lengthy experience as an investigator, had instinctively pushed him to provoke Giuseppe: "It would have been better for Mariapia if she had a... uhm... no, it doesn't matter."

"Say it," the surveyor's curiosity had been aroused, just as the policeman in Vittorio, now well rooted in him, had spontaneously hoped for.

"... well all right, I wanted to say that, in all conscience, I couldn't blame your sister, if she was the one who actually killed that scoundrel."

"That scoundrel... Peppino?! Ah, no! You shouldn't have said that, Commissioner! I swear to you on the memory of our parents and on all the Saints in Paradise: my sister only killed Nazis!" He had turned pale.

"Giuseppe, if it wasn't Mariapia, then..." *...it was you*, had almost come to his lips.

Giuseppe had replied: "Commissioner, there's the whistle that your train is leaving: get in or it will leave without you. I'll hand the suitcase to you, you jump up."

"All aboard!" the conductor had said after the whistle.

Vittorio had stepped into the car, while the former partisan picked up his suitcase, handed it to him and then closed the door.

---

[141] Quite appropriately, for some years the names of the victims of rape have no longer been made known, within the scope of the privacy law.

Then leaning out the window the commissioner had said in friendly tone: "They can no longer put you on trial. Tell me for my own satisfaction: if it wasn't Mariapia, did you cut Peppino's throat?"

Scognamiglio had remained silent, as the train began to move and gained speed; but when the carriage behind the policeman's car was about to go past him, Giuseppe had shouted at Vittorio, responding to him apparently not as a comeback, as if the verb he had used had arrived distorted: "I swear to you that I have never castrated anyone; and whoever can and wants to believe it... then believe it!"

***

NOVELS AND TALES WITH CHARACTERS OF VITTORIO D'AIAZZO AND RANIERI VELLI (ACCORDING TO THE CHRONOLOGICAL ORDER OF EVENTS)

- L'IRA DEI VILIPESI, romanzo: italiano – LA FURIA DE LOS INSULTADOS (traducción de Mariano Bas): español - **THE RAGE OF THE REVILED Historical fiction (translation by Barbara Maher): English -** *In this first novel the character of Ranieri Velli does not appear -*

- IL MOSTRO A TRE BRACCIA e I SATANASSI DI TORINO, due racconti lunghi in unico volume: italiano – EL MONSTRUO DE TRES BRAZOS y LOS SATANISTAS DE TURÍN (traducción de Mariano Bas): español

- LA TRAGEDIA DEI TRASTULLI, romanzo: italiano - LA TRAGEDIA DE LOS TRASTULLI Novela (traducción de Mariano Bas): español

- IL METRO DELL'AMORE TOSSICO e IL FU D'AIAZZO, un romanzo e un racconto in unico volume: italiano – EL METRO DEL AMOR TÓXICO y EL DIFUNTO D'AIAZZO (traducción de Mariano Bas): español – O METRO DO AMOR TOSSICO e O DEFUNTO D'AIAZZO (traducción de Aderito Francisco Huo): portugués

- VITTORIO IL BARBUTO, romanzo breve: italiano – VITTORIO EL BARBUDO (traducción de Mariano Bas: español - VITTORIO O BARBUDO (traducción de Aderito Francisco Huo): portugués

- IL CANE, romanzo: italiano

- IL TERRORE PRIVATO, IL TERRORE POLITICO, romanzo: italiano – EL TERROR PRIVADO Y EL TERROR POLÍTICO *(traducción de Mariano Bas):* español - **PERSONAL TERROR, POLITICAL TERROR A novel (translation by Barbara Maher): English**

Guido Pagliarino

Over the years, the author has published several essays, novels and books of poetry. Many of these works received first prizes; for his work published since 1996, he was awarded the "Cultural Award of the Presidency of the Council of Ministers" in 1997. If you wish to read a detailed biobibliography and find references to reviews of works by Guido Pagliarino, see the following page of the author's website: http://www.pagliarino.com/biografia.htm (Italian only).